D...

Ian Botham is one c̶ ... game has known. His autobiography, published by HarperCollins in 1994, has sold more than 250,000 copies. He is now a press and television commentator on the game.

Dennis Coath is known as the face and voice of sport in the ITV Midlands region. As well as being a TV presenter, he is the author of several works of non-fiction.

IAN BOTHAM
AND DENNIS COATH

DEEP COVER

HarperCollins*Publishers*

HarperCollins*Publishers*
77–85 Fulham Palace Road,
Hammersmith, London W6 8JB

This paperback edition 1996
1 3 5 7 9 8 6 4 2

Copyright © Mannez Promotions Ltd 1996

ISBN 0 00 649827 2

This novel is entirely a work of fiction. The names, characters and
incidents portrayed in the story are the product of the authors'
imagination. Any resemblance to actual persons, living or dead,
events or localities is entirely incidental.

Set in Meridien by
Rowland Phototypesetting Ltd,
Bury St Edmunds, Suffolk

Printed and bound in Great Britain by
Caledonian International Book Manufacturing Ltd, Glasgow

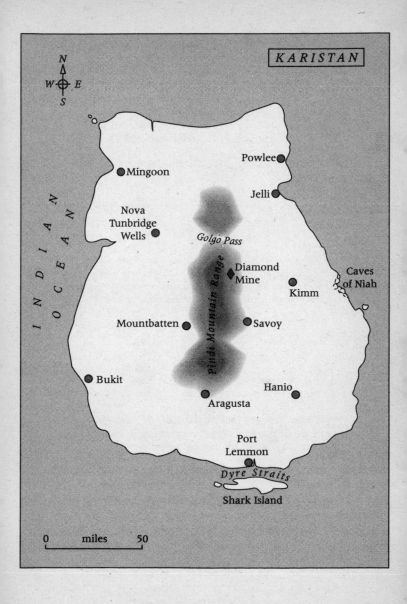

ENGLAND TOUR OF KARISTAN

TOUR ITINERARY

	TEAM	VENUE
1.	President's XI	*Nova Tunbridge Wells*
2.	Port Lemmon XI	*Port Lemmon*
3.	Western Province	*Yanis*
4.	Mingoon University	*Mingoon*
5.	FIRST TEST	*Mingoon*
6.	Powlee XI	*Powlee*
7.	SECOND TEST	*Kimm*
8.	Eastern Province	*Kimm*
9.	Karistan A XI	*Hanio*
10.	Gilbert and Sullivan XI	*Hanio*
11.	THIRD TEST	*Aragusta*

ONE

James Henry Fotheringhay was off the mark before anyone had time to count the number of vowels in his name. The first delivery was stroked to the boundary with languid ease. A delicate leg-glance sent the next ball in pursuit of four more irresistible runs. A square cut off the third delivery was stopped within yards of the rope but the batsmen crossed twice without undue effort.

It was vintage Fothers. Elegant artistry. Sophisticated violence. Timing, technique and arrogance in equal measure.

When the inevitable bouncer came, he met its challenge without flinching and hooked it contemptuously for another boundary. The fifth ball was studiously ignored and it went harmlessly down the leg side to the wicket-keeper. A sly single was then taken off the demoralised bowler so that Fothers could retain the strike. Inspiring cricket.

Fifteen runs off the first over. He was on form. The supporters turned Lord's into a bubbling cauldron of delight. Cheers, whistles and sustained applause greeted their hero. J. H. Fotheringhay, Captain of England and national icon, was leading his county from the front. Hamcestershire started the Benson and Hedges Final as the underdogs against a strong Yorkshire team. When they lost two early wickets, Hams were struggling. Fothers then came to the crease. Within minutes, he had transformed the situation.

Tall, slim and wiry, he had a patrician air which cowed most men but infuriated others. He also had a wholesomeness which endeared him to potential mothers-in-law. Here was a man in whose hands their nubile daughters (and the future of English cricket) were completely safe. Whether sweeping a girl off her feet or a ball off his pads, he would always play honourably to the rules.

'Fo – thers! Fo – thers!'

It was not the crude chant of a football crowd but a joyous hymn of praise to a superior being. A demi-god in white flannels had just scored yet another heavenly half century. Hams were no longer strung.

'Fo – thers! Fo – thers!'

He acknowledged the thunderous applause with an imperious wave of his bat then took his stance once more. Fifty runs were nowhere near enough for him or for his county. They were just a staging post on the road to glory. The next delivery was lifted in a graceful arc over the bowler's head and bounced twice before securing another boundary. With a deft late-cut, he collected a single and surrendered the strike. The scoring rate immediately dipped.

It picked up again when Fothers faced the new bowler. He scored sixteen runs without leaving his crease but reserved his Shot of the Day for the final ball of the over. It was a vicious bouncer, which sped towards the batsman's face with the velocity of a bullet. Fothers pirouetted like a ballet dancer, hitting the ball in the middle of the bat and sending it high into the stand for one of the most sensational sixes ever seen at Lord's.

The supporters exploded with glee and rose from their seats to acclaim their Messiah once again.

'Fo – thers! Fo – thers!'

It was a perfect stroke and they loved it. Fothers loved it himself. So much so, that he played it again and again, hooking the ball with identical precision to the same part of the ground and setting off the same elation among the Hamcestershire faithful.

After ten successive sixes, Fothers let the video recording

run on until the face of Kevin Sowerbutts filled the screen. He used the remote control to kill the picture.

'Fantastic six!' said Derek March.

Fothers nodded. 'Best way to deal with a bouncer.'

'You were in sublime form that day.'

'The runs just seemed to flow, Uncle Derek.'

'You were on course for a certain century,' sighed the other. 'Such a pity they brought on Butty! He took out your middle stump with the first ball you faced.'

'Complete fluke.'

'It was the turning-point of the game.'

'Unfortunately.'

'You were the star of the show yet it was Butty who inscribed the name of Yorkshire on the cup. I still think that you should have been chosen as Man of the Match.'

'Water under the bridge.'

'I mean, I know that Butty finished with 7 for 33 and got a half-century off only twelve deliveries but he has none of your class. That first six of his may have gone out of the ground but yours was still the superior stroke.'

'Thanks, Uncle Derek.'

'Mind you,' admitted the other, 'Butty's second six was amazing. I've never seen such a . . .'

'He's a slogger,' interrupted Fothers. 'No more, no less.'

'Sloggers win games. Butty certainly won that one.'

'Don't remind me.'

'I can still see him tearing in to bowl to you like a white tornado with a Yorkshire accent. Your middle wicket must have cartwheeled thirty yards.'

'I didn't notice!'

'You have to hand it to Butty. A big occasion always seems to light his fire. In that Benson and Hedges Final . . .'

'Forget the match,' said Fothers through gritted teeth. 'Forget my dismissal. Forget my middle wicket. Forget that horrendous mistake over the choice of Man of the Match.

11

And most of all,' he added grimly, 'forget Kevin Sowerbutts.'

'We will, James.'

Derek March poured himself another glass of whisky and dropped two ice cubes into it. He was a chunky man of medium height with a rubicund face. Father Time had scythed away every hair on his head but left him with bushy eyebrows and a walrus moustache. His boyish enthusiasm for the game of cricket kept other signs of age at bay. Approaching sixty, he looked as if he was waving a cheerful farewell to forty.

'Shall we get on with it?' he suggested.

'I'm ready,' said Fothers.

'Let's start with the batsmen.'

'They pick themselves, Uncle Derek.'

'That's my feeling. The bowlers will be our problem.'

'Anyway, let's start at the top.'

They were in Fothers' luxury flat in Knightsbridge. He and his uncle had met to pre-select the English team for the winter tour of Karistan. Derek March was the reigning supremo, chairman of the selectors and team manager. The sixteen names which he submitted to the board of selectors on the following day would cause a certain amount of dispute but he was confident that his wishes would prevail. They usually did. Especially when buttressed by the captain of England. Uncle and nephew invariably sang the same tune.

'So much for the batsmen,' said Derek, drawing a line under the names on his list. 'Now for the bowlers.'

'Olly,' insisted the other.

'I've already put him down. John Cromwell. Master of the new ball. He's done wonders for Hams this season. Scored a few runs as well. Olly Cromwell is a must.'

'Who else have you pencilled in?'

'Ben Jenkins.'

'He's *Welsh*!' said Fothers with disdain.

'Strong as an ox and built like King Kong.'

'The Celts are an inferior breed.'

'Tell that to Ben as he comes in to bowl and you'll put an extra zip into him. He *has* to come, James. His bowling analysis for last season was phenomenal. I vote for Big Ben. Apart from anything else, it will get the Glamorgan chairman off my back. He accuses me of being anti-Welsh.'

'We're pro-English, that's all.'

'Will you give Big Ben the nod?'

Fothers shrugged. 'Reluctantly.'

'You'll need a work-horse out in Karistan.'

'Ben Jenkins is a pit pony.'

'He could turn out to be a second Butty.'

'God forbid!'

'Big Ben is developing into a useful batsman,' said Derek, sipping his whisky. 'Give him another season or two and we could be looking at a formidable all-rounder. Kevin Sowerbutts the Second.'

'A Welsh version of Butty. That's all we need!'

'The difference is that Ben will behave himself.'

'How do you know, Uncle Derek?'

'He's religious.'

'A religious Butty – that's even worse!' Fothers gave an involuntary shudder, then he remembered something. 'By the way, how are we going to explain the fact that we've omitted Butty himself? Even among those who should know better, he has a huge following. Butty the Beast was not only the outstanding bowler of the season, he was second to me in the batting averages. Far too close for comfort.'

'The board of selectors will not even consider Butty.'

'But they'll have to, surely?'

'Not after tonight,' said Derek complacently.

'Tonight?'

'Arrangements are in hand.'

*   *   *

They had reached the cigar and brandy stage. The food had been so rich and the wine so plentiful that they were ready to laugh at almost anything. Even the oldest and corniest jokes provoked wild mirth. Over fifty cricket correspondents and sportswriters were attending the Annual Awards Dinner with their wives, mistresses or partners of intermediate station. Plunging necklines and black ties filled the room at the Park Lane hotel.

As yet another feeble anecdote created more undeserved uproar, the speaker took the opportunity to glance at his notes. He was given a jolting reminder of why they were there. He held up both hands to quell the general hilarity.

'Ladies and gentlemen,' he announced, grandly, 'this, as you know, is an Awards Dinner. And our guest of honour this evening is none other than Kevin Sowerbutts.'

'Good old Butty!' yelled a drunken voice.

Everyone pounded their tables appreciatively.

'Kevin Sowerbutts,' resumed the speaker, 'or Butty – as he is affectionately known – is a cricketing legend. The only problem they have in his native Yorkshire is to decide whether Butty is the greatest batsman ever to come out of the county or the greatest bowler.'

'Both!' came the shout from a dozen throats.

The tables took more punishment from flailing palms.

'Some of you may have heard the story of the cricket correspondent who went to heaven . . .' They'd all heard it a hundred times but brandy had kindly obliterated the memory. 'St Peter showed the newcomer around. The first person they saw was a man in a Yorkshire county cap, reclining on a cloud as a thousand angels worshipped him. "That's Butty," said St Peter. "They think he's God."'

Baying laughter went on for a full minute.

'The next person they saw,' continued the speaker, 'was a dignified old gent with a long white beard. He, too, had a Yorkshire county cap on and a cricket bat under his arm. "Who's that?" asked the newcomer. "That's God," explained St Peter. "He thinks he's Butty."'

The laughter was even more hysterical this time and one of the tables collapsed under the relentless battering. All eyes turned to Kevin Sowerbutts, who replied with his famous toothy grin. In his dinner jacket, he looked like a bouncer from a sleazy Bradford nightclub. Butty listened politely to the litany of familiar gags about him, his craggy face giving no hint that he was terminally bored. He asked himself the same weary question over and over again.

'When will this stupid bastard *stop*?'

Eventually, he got his answer and his award. It was a bronze statue of Kevin Sowerbutts (Yorks. and England), swinging his bat with awesome power. When he stood up to receive it, he reminded himself that he had to stay on his best behaviour. Guests could get thoroughly ratted because the cameras were not on them. But the moment Butty stepped up to the microphone, the photographers came to life. They shot him indiscriminately from all angles.

A sozzled Butty had sprawled across the sports pages far too often. He resolved to clean up his act this time. When the England team selectors opened their morning papers next day, they would see a sober and responsible Butty. That was the image of him they would take into their crucial meeting about the tour party to Karistan.

He beamed at the happy pandemonium all around him. Statue in one hand, he used the other to scratch his head. As the tumult subsided, he shrugged his shoulders.

'I don't know what to say,' he began in the blunt Northern accent so beloved by his fans. 'And if I said it, I wouldn't mean it.' A gentle titter. 'And if I meant it, you wouldn't believe me.' Throaty chuckles through a haze of cigar smoke. 'And if you believed me, you'd probably sue for slander.' The first few belly laughs. 'So I'd wish I'd never bloody well said it in the first place!'

Butty floated on a sea of good will. They loved him. He

could have recited the Turkish national anthem and got away with it. As it was, he limited himself to one joke about Fothers, two about umpires and three against himself, ending on such a note of grinning self-deprecation that nobody could take offence.

When Butty sat down again, the noise was deafening. Those who criticised him most severely in their columns now raised the loudest cheers. Kevin Sowerbutts had been the quintessential Butty with one huge difference. He had, for the first time ever, shown a surprising dignity. The hell-raiser had been to charm school. It worked.

Afterwards, he was besieged. Stoned scribes wanted him to sign their menus, listen to their life stories or relive a magic moment in his career. Lustful ladies competed to touch his arm, catch his eye or wave their cleavages beneath his nose. Butty was a model of self-control. Those who waited in the slips to catch one of his notorious gaffes were disappointed. He never gave them a whisper of a chance.

It was an hour before he was able to sneak out of the rear exit and dive into the waiting taxi. He belched with relief.

'Where to, sir?' asked the driver.

'Soho!' growled Butty. 'I want some action.'

The policemen had never seen a Volvo Estate parked on a traffic island at two o'clock in the morning before. It was tucked neatly behind the bushes with its headlights still on. They got out of their patrol car to investigate. One of the policemen shone a flashlight through the windscreen. What they saw made them gape in astonishment.

Butty was lying half-naked behind the driving wheel. Asleep on his shoulder, wearing nothing but a pair of cricket pads and a Yorkshire county cap, was a curvaceous blonde with a nostalgic smile on her face.

A press photographer stepped out from behind the bushes.

'Stand aside, please,' he said, easing the two uniformed constables apart. 'This won't take a moment.'

Taking telltale pictures of the happy couple through the windscreen, he used up a roll of high-speed film. With a nod of thanks to the policemen, he stepped back and gestured towards the slumbering saviour of English cricket.

'He's all yours.'

The waning headlights suddenly dipped another foot.

'I know how he feels.'

TWO

The crash of a falling idol resounded throughout the morning. Butty was left coughing in a cloud of dust. Poor coverage of two bodies in a Volvo Estate got rich coverage in the media. A trouserless Butty dominated the headlines. The latest crisis at Westminster, the new twist in the Bosnian saga and the setback in the peace process in Northern Ireland were all relegated to subsidiary status. Not even the end of civilisation as we know it could have displaced Kevin Sowerbutts from centre stage. Butty's night made the journalists' day.

He took refuge in his hotel room and barricaded the door against the slavering hordes. They launched the first wave of attack with their mobile phones. He snatched up the receiver and bellowed into it.

'Who is this?'

'Horace Cochran. *Times*,' said a cultured voice.

'Piss off, Cocky!'

'Any chance of an interview, old boy?'

'Only with my arse.'

Butty slammed the phone down. Instantly, it rang again. He grabbed it and turned up the switch on his volume control.

'Get off my back, Cocky!'

'Simon Scouse. *Guardian*,' said a Liverpudlian exile. 'We're behind you all the way, Butty.'

'Bollocks!'

'We are. We're championing your freedom of expression.'

'Fart off, Simon!'

Once again, the telephone rang as soon as it was replaced. Butty yanked it angrily to his throbbing ear.

'Which toss-pot is it this time?'

'Conrad Wingright. *Daily Telegraph*,' came the smooth reply. 'Have you considered the repercussions, Butty?'

'What reper-bleedin'-cussions?'

'How will this sorry episode affect your career?'

'Get lost!'

'You were caught with a naked female draped across you, old chap. Not cricket. Do you really think that you're a suitable role model for the adolescent male?'

'Bugger off!'

'May I quote you on that?'

When the phone went down for the third time, Butty disconnected the lead and silenced any future callers. Ignoring the banging on his door, he slumped in a chair and switched on the television, only to see his own baleful countenance staring through the windscreen of a Volvo Estate. His head pounded even harder. Whether it was from guilt or alcohol he didn't know but it felt as if fifteen red-hot cricket balls were simultaneously bouncing around inside his skull.

He changed channels to a Bugs Bunny cartoon but even the sight of a reliable favourite could not hold him. Turning the set off, he leaned forward with his head in his hands. The fifteen cricket balls merged into one sphere of molten lead which was substantially larger than the space in which it was encased. His cranium was splitting apart.

Butty forced an eye open to check his wristwatch.

'Jesus Christ!' he moaned. 'Two o'clock?'

Was it only twelve hours since he and his sportive companion had been discovered opening the innings in a Volvo Estate? Years of humiliation seemed to have passed. A generation of media cannibals had eaten him alive. How long would they stay camped outside his room?

He sat up with a start. There was an eerie silence. The

siege army had been firing questions through the door like flights of arrows. Had they packed their quivers and gone? Or were they simply tunnelling under the floorboards so that they could surface in his bathroom?

One word explained everything. The voice was soft.

'Kevin.'

His blood curdled. It was Barbara.

'Kevin,' she repeated.

The very last person he wanted to see at that moment was his fiancée. Had she come all the way down from Yorkshire?

'Kevin!' she snarled. 'Open this flaming door!'

'Er, yes,' he mumbled obediently. 'Coming, love.'

Butty cleared away the furniture he'd stacked against the door and slid back the bolts. Bracing himself, he opened the door and manufactured a penitent smile.

'Barbara! Great to see you!'

'Well, it's not great to see you, you two-timing rat!'

'Where did they all go?' he said, looking at the empty corridor. 'There were hundreds of 'em out here.'

'I asked them to leave.'

'And they *agreed*?'

'At a price,' she said crisply. 'A press conference. I tell them exactly what happened between us in here. Not that there'll be all that much to tell.'

Barbara pushed him back into the room and followed, closing the door behind her as she did so. Alone in a hotel with his fiancée, Butty automatically reached out to stroke her buttocks. He was given a sharp jab in the stomach.

'What was that for?' he gasped.

'Starters.'

'Barbara . . .'

'Shut up!'

'Babsie . . .'

'Sit down.'

'I *missed* you.'

20

'Lying swine!' she said, shoving him down on the sofa. 'Don't upset me any more than I already am. I warn you, Kev. I'm not in the mood.'

Barbara Ollerenshaw was a short, shapely Northern lass in her early twenties with a waterfall of red hair down her back and a face which Butty described as 'gob-smackingly gorgeous'. She would not have won the Miss Scarborough title now. Butty was looking into the face of a Gorgon.

'Who is she?' demanded Barbara.

'She?'

'Yes.'

'Who d'you mean, love?'

'Her, of course!' hissed Barbara, pulling a glossy photograph from her bag and tossing it into his lap. 'That vixen in the Volvo Estate.'

One glance at the photo made him shudder all over.

'Where did you get this from?' he asked.

'A well-wisher.'

'It's not the way it looks, Barbara.'

'Every picture tells a story.'

'I was set up.'

'That's what you said last time. Now – who is she?'

'Don't know her name.'

'Oh, I see. One more anonymous poke, was she?'

'No!'

'Where did you meet her?' she pressed, looming menacingly over him. 'Tell me, Kevin. Where?'

'Nightclub in Soho.'

'Pick her up, did you?'

'No. She was serving behind the cigarette counter.'

'The girl with the filter-tipped nipples.'

'It wasn't like that, Barbara.'

'Then what was it like?'

He shrugged hopelessly. 'No idea. That's the truth, love. All I can remember is having a pint or two then – zonk! Out like a bleeding light. Next thing I know, two coppers

21

are banging on the windscreen of the car and I'm tangled up with this bimbo.'

'In her cricket pads.'

'And county cap.'

'How many did you score, Kevin?'

'None!'

'Just sat there discussing the price of tobacco, did you?' She leaned in close. 'How many times, Kev? Once, twice or was it a hat trick? I've seen the photo. It's obvious the pair of you shagged yourselves into exhaustion.'

'I never touched her, Barbara.'

'Taken a vow of chastity, had she?'

'There was something in the beer.'

'There always is.'

'Whole thing's a stupid mistake. I'd like to put it behind me and start afresh.'

'I bet you would, Kevin Sowerbutts,' she said, eyes blazing and hands on hips. 'You want to pretend it never happened. But I can't do that, I'm afraid, because I'm being laughed at by the entire population of the British Bloody Isles. "That's Barbara Ollerenshaw," they're saying. "Poor woman! Engaged to a man with a vagabond cock. Silly fool!" Not any more, though!'

'What do you mean?'

'That you can have your sodding ring back.'

'But we're engaged to be married.'

'*I* was – you never were!'

'Barbara!'

'Here!' she yelled, pulling off the ring and hurling it at him. 'Trade it for a packet of fags next time she walks past in those cricket pads!'

'You haven't let me *explain*,' he wailed.

'That photo is all the explanation I need. When you went off to that Awards Dinner, you swore blind to me that you'd behave yourself. Vital to project the right image, you said.'

'It was, Barbara. And that's what I did. I was marketing Kevin "Squeaky Clean" Sowerbutts. Creating a sort of Feel Good factor.'

'Not according to that photo,' she observed acidly. 'All that shows is a Good Feel factor.'

She turned expertly on her heel and stalked off.

'Wait!' he begged.

'Goodbye, Kevin.'

'I want you. Come back!'

'You're out LBW.'

'LBW?'

'Leg-over Before Wedding.'

One thing about Barbara. She knew how to slam a door.

The meeting that afternoon was a relatively straightforward affair. Derek March wisely scheduled it for three o'clock at Lord's. He worked on the principle that, if his colleagues arrived after an excellent lunch, at least two of them would drop off to sleep during the discussion and a third would be too inebriated to do anything more than burble his assent. Selecting the team to tour Karistan should be a painless process. The only potential fly in the ointment was the Colonel.

'Where *is* Karistan?' he asked.

'Thousands of miles away,' said Derek patiently.

'Is it? Thought it was in the Isle of Wight.'

'That's Carisbrooke.'

'Are you quite sure?'

'Yes, Colonel.'

'Why did they change a perfectly good name?'

'They didn't. Karistan and Carisbrooke are different places in quite different countries.'

'Thank heaven for that!' grunted the Colonel. 'Spent my honeymoon on the Isle of Wight. Hate to think it had been

23

taken over by our dusky allies. What? Very good, Derek. Do carry on. Won't hold you up. Bad form.'

Colonel Arthur Totter clicked his dentures back into place and sat upright in his chair. He was a tall, angular man with an air of ravished nobility about him. Silver hair was exquisitely groomed along with his military moustache. Even at his advanced age, he had a ramrod straightness of bearing. Derek March knew that he could rely on the Grand Old Man of the selection committee. Since the Colonel was also Chairman of Hamcestershire County Cricket Club, he would not obstruct anything that Derek or Fothers proposed. Hams hung together.

The Colonel's problem was an intermittent memory.

'Damn shame I'm not going to Carisbrooke!' he sighed.

'Karistan,' corrected Derek. 'Tan, tan. Karis – *tan*. And you *are* coming with us on tour, Colonel.'

'Am I?'

'It was decided at our last meeting.'

'Blow me down! So it was. Glad I checked.'

'No problem.'

'Will the lady wife be accompanying me on safari?'

'She died five years ago,' said Derek gently.

'Just as well. She never liked Carisbrooke. Even on our honeymoon, she was restive. Women are, you know. Seem to lack concentration. Splendid mother, though, the lady wife. Sad that we never had any children.'

They let him meander through his reminiscences for a few minutes before winding up the business of the afternoon.

'Is everything settled, then?' asked Derek. 'James?'

'I'm very happy with the selection,' said Fothers on cue. 'It's only a short tour and Karistan is not yet a major cricketing nation but that's no excuse for sending a weak team out there. England needs it best sixteen players and that's what we've chosen.'

'Sowerbutts in, then, is he?' asked the Colonel.

'Not this time.'

'But he was Player of the Year.'

'Bad advertisement for the game,' said Derek, moving his copy of the *Times* in front of the Colonel. 'He's blotted his copybook disgracefully, as you can see.'

'By Jove!' exclaimed the old man, jabbing his finger at the front page photo. 'Is that Sowerbutts?'

'No,' explained Fothers. 'That's an unnamed young lady. Kevin Sowerbutts is next to her. Need we say more?'

'Lucky blighter!' murmured the Colonel.

Derek was brisk. 'He's not an appropriate candidate for selection. Butty is too brash, too rebellious. Wherever he goes, he attracts damaging publicity. We don't want to export any of that to Karistan. We'll be there to build bridges. It would be madness to take a saboteur like Sowerbutts with us. Are we all agreed on that?'

Grunts of approval came from around the table and the one selector who was still sleeping off his luncheon broke wind by way of affirmation. Derek used his gavel to bring the meeting formally to an end.

'That's it, chaps. Thank you very much.'

'Good luck in Karistan!' said the Colonel.

'You're in the tour party, Colonel.'

'Am I? Bless my soul! So I am, Derek. Must look out my sun hat. Anything to escape an English winter. Karistan, eh? What sort of a welcome will we get?'

'A cordial one,' assured Fothers.

'You've been to the country?'

'Yes, Colonel. I was at Oxford with the Karistan captain. Zaki Meero. First-rate fellow in every respect. He invited me out there for a holiday. I was most impressed.'

'Can't say that I am,' grumbled the Colonel. 'Friendship between rival captains? Dangerous tactic.'

'We're only friends *off* the field.'

'Keep it that way. Cricket is a game of enemies.'

'We realise that.'

'Good, good,' said the old man, shaking hands with everyone in turn. 'Must be off. Got to inform the lady wife about my travel plans. Likes to keep abreast. Sorry I can't take her to Carisbrooke with the team. But she's used to disappointment. I trained her well. Goodbye!'

Colonel Arthur Totter tottered off into happy oblivion.

The rest of the committee drifted away at their own pace, confident that they'd done their duty and maintained the essential traditions of the game. Fothers was left alone with his uncle. They glowed with satisfaction.

'You're a genius, Uncle Derek!' he congratulated.

'All it takes is a little organisation.'

'How did you set it all up?'

'That's a closely guarded secret,' said Derek, preening himself. 'I knew Butty's weaknesses and exploited them.'

'The tour will be a positive joy without him. While we're acting as ambassadors for English cricket, Butty will be twiddling his thumbs in Huddersfield. Pleasing thought, that,' said Fothers, savouring the other's fall from grace. 'Kevin Sowerbutts will not be involved in any sport this winter.'

'Unless it's car racing in the nude!'

'Perhaps he can get Volvo to sponsor him.'

'Yes,' said Derek, smirking. 'They could send Butty on a sponsored bonk. Getting Laid Is Great In A Volvo Estate. Avoid The Clap With A County Cap. We may have done Butty a favour. A whole new career is opening up before him.

'As long as it keeps him away from Karistan.'

They shared a laugh and sauntered towards the Long Room.

THREE

The three of them had been on tenterhooks all afternoon. Their cricketing careers were being enhanced or encumbered in the meeting over at Lord's and they shuttled between hope and despair. Harry Smart sounded a note of optimism.

'The old farts have *got* to pick us,' he decided.

'They'll certainly select you,' said Tom Horgan with envy. 'You're the best wicket-keeper in England. Your passage to Karistan is already booked, Snatcher.'

'So is yours, Tombo,' argued Peter Brooksby. 'You and Snatcher got a head start on the rest of us poor sods. Both of you play for Hamcester. Fothers and the March Hare have had much more chance to see you in action. You're definites.'

'My money's on you, Peebee,' said Snatcher.

'What if none of us are selected?' said Tombo, gloomily.

Snatcher grinned. 'We get pissed out of our tiny minds. And if we *are* in the team – we get even more pissed!'

The three friends were at an exclusive snooker club. Snatcher and Peebee were playing a desultory game on the green baize with Tombo acting as scorer. But all three of them were keeping one eye on the television set above the bar. Sooner or later, their fate would be decided by the selection committee.

Snatcher Smart potted a red and got a good position on the black. His confidence soared. He was a tallish man with a wicket-keeper's stoop and lithe movements. A fitness fanatic, Snatcher was famed for his impossible catches behind the wicket. Many a disbelieving batsman had turned around at the crease to be greeted by his gap-toothed grin of triumph.

Peebee Brooksby was a more solid individual of medium height. A medium-pace bowler, his tally of wickets had kept Essex near the top of the county table in recent seasons but he never enjoyed his success. He was a martyr to self-criticism and his chubby face was always a mask of anxiety. When he bowled a man out, Peebee always chided himself for not producing that delivery earlier in the match.

Tombo Horgan was a big, brawny man with a broken nose and fierce eyes. There were faster bowlers but few who could maintain his accuracy. A somnolent character, he only came properly to life on a cricket pitch. In full flight, he was an inspiring sight for all but the batsman facing him.

When Snatcher finished his break, Tombo moved across to the scoreboard on the wall. The newsreader's voice stopped him dead.

'And now, with the Sports News, here's . . .'

The three of them abandoned all pretence of indifference and darted across to the bar. Sixteen names came up on the screen. The three most important ones were spotted instantly.

'We're in!' yelled Snatcher.

'All three of us!' said Tombo excitedly.

Even the worried Peebee smiled. 'Karistan – here we come!'

They held hands impulsively and danced round in a circle. It was only when the euphoria wore off that they realised what they had seen up on the screen. Obsessed with their own success, they had not at first taken in someone else's failure. They swung back to the television but it was now offering them a weather report.

'Did you see what *I* saw?' asked Peebee.

'Yes,' said Snatcher with disgust. 'No Butty.'

'They can't leave him out,' insisted Tombo. 'Butty

28

destroyed us in the Benson and Hedges Final. He can win a game on his own.'

'Not in Karistan,' noted Peebee. 'He's out.'

'Yes,' added Snatcher, 'and I'd hate to be within a hundred yards of him when he finds out. Butty is not the kind of man to take this philosophically. He'll go ape.'

Butty hurled the ashtray through the television screen with vicious force. The glass shattered and the set exploded. Sixteen names had just flashed up before him and Kevin Sowerbutts was not among them. Dropped from the touring team. It was a cruel act of betrayal. As the full horror of exclusion began to sink in, a new surge of violence took hold of him.

Grabbing the television, he pulled it away from its moorings and flung it through the window. After plummeting through space, it landed in the car park seven floors below. Hotel security was alerted and two uniformed men rushed out to take stock of the outrage. Butty plugged the telephone back in and rang Reception.

'Room 791,' he said calmly. 'My television set fell through the window. I'll pay for the damage. Just don't send anyone up to bother me. That clear?'

'Yes, sir,' said a terrified female voice.

'I want to be left alone.'

Butty slammed the receiver down and paced the room in search of something else to destroy. The television had borne the brunt of his rage. He only wished that he could have pitched Fothers and Derek March out of the window after it. They were the villains of the piece. He was convinced of that. The England captain and his Wicked Uncle had deliberately stopped him from going to Karistan.

When a fresh burst of fury came, he was about to vent it on a bedside lamp but another object caught his attention. It was lying on the carpet with a forlorn sparkle.

Butty knelt down to pick up the engagement ring and place it on the palm of his hand. Burning anger was extinguished by a deep sadness. He had lost Barbara. After a year of bliss, she'd dumped him. What made it worse was the fact that he was an innocent victim. For once.

No walk down the aisle. No trip to Karistan. He sat cross-legged on the floor and brooded on a malign destiny. When the knock came on the door, he did not at first hear it. Tentative knuckles rapped on the timber again. Butty came out of his reverie like a wounded lion at bay.

'Go away!' he roared.

'Kevin?'

'I'm not here!'

'It's me, Kevin.'

'Fuck off, me!'

'But I've got something for you.'

Butty recognised the light American voice and he was immediately soothed. His visitor was Des Toyovsky. The one person whom Butty could bear to see at that precise moment. Des was a good friend. More important, he was a complete outsider. He would not sit in judgement.

Butty strolled across to the door.

'Have the rest of them gone?' he asked warily.

'Yes, Kevin. I'm on my own.'

'You'd better be.'

He opened the door to confront the massive frame of Des Toyovsky, a gentle giant with the build of a Dallas Cowboys nose-tackle but the temperament of a gazelle. He wore a loose-fitting suit and carried a battered briefcase. The huge face broke into a warm smile.

'They bet me I'd never get in here,' he said.

'Then you've cleaned up, Des. Come on in.'

The lumbering American followed him into the room and shut the door. He was jolted by the sight of the broken window.

'What happened, Kevin?'

'The television set did a high-dive.'

'Of its own accord?'

'I didn't like the programme they were showing.'

'Hell!' said Des. 'You can't just sling a TV through a plate glass window. Somebody might have got hurt.'

'Yeah,' agreed Butty. 'Unfortunately, the bastards weren't standing down in the car park.'

'The bastards?'

'Fothers and the March Hare.'

'Talk English. These nicknames still confuse me.'

'Nicknames *are* bleeding English,' said Butty cheerily. 'That's how we talk over here. Fothers is James Henry Tight-Arse Fotheringhay. And his Uncle Derek is the Mad March Hare. You'll catch on eventually.'

'Hope so.'

Butty waved him to a chair and sat opposite him. Unlike all the other journalists who'd cornered him, Des Toyovsky had bided his time. He was not interested in a sensational headline for a tabloid newspaper. Instead of coming to pester Butty, he was there to offer sympathy and succour.

'Tough luck, Kevin!'

'It was on the cards.'

'Not the way I read them,' said Des. 'I still don't know much about cricket but I can pick out a star when I see one. And you're just about the brightest they got.'

'Thanks.'

'They're insane to leave you out.'

'Insanely jealous, maybe.'

'It must go deeper than that.'

'It does. Much deeper.'

'Why?'

'Stick around and you'll find out.' Butty shook his head to try to clear it. 'You said you had something for me.'

'I do. Information.'

'About what?'

'Last night.'

'Spare me!' groaned Butty.

'But it might be helpful.'

'I'm trying to wipe the whole of last night out of my mind. It was one big black mistake. The media have been hounding me all bleeding day about it.'

'*I* haven't, Kevin.'

'No, you're the one exception. Every other hack wanted to chase the story until they scented blood.'

'What I scented was a frame-up.'

'You did?' said Butty, rallying at once. 'You mean that when the news broke you knew it couldn't possibly be true?'

'No,' admitted Des. 'I believed every word of it at first. Kevin Sowerbutts with a naked bimbo lying all over him. I had no difficulty accepting that.'

'Thanks a bunch!'

'What I couldn't buy is that you'd be dumb enough to pose for a press photographer. Or that you'd park a car on a traffic island and leave the headlights on to attract attention.' Des spread his palms in a gesture of incredulity. 'That's the next best thing to selling tickets for the event.'

'Never thought of it that way.'

'I did. Where did that snapper come from?'

'Snapper?'

'Photographer. The cops say he just stepped out of the bushes. *How*? You know any photographic agencies got their head office on a goddam traffic island?'

'What are you saying, Des?'

'He was tipped off.'

'The bastard!'

'Someone arranged for him to be there.'

'Who?'

'I'll tell you when I find out. First off, I gotta find the guy with the camera. That's the information I brought you, Kevin. Count on me. I'm on your case.'

'That's fantastic, Des!'

32

'I figure somebody ought to give you an even break.'

'Yeah. Barbara certainly didn't.'

'That lovely fiancée of yours?'

'Lovely *ex*-fiancée.'

'She ditched you?'

'Cut off both my balls. With her teeth.'

'Didn't she give you the benefit of the doubt?'

'Not this time, Des. I'm a repeat offender.' He held up the engagement ring. 'Barbara threw this back at me. Cost me a bomb. Most expensive thing I ever bought a woman.'

'Hang on to it,' advised his friend. 'Who knows? Before too long, Barbara may come crawling back to beg for a second chance.'

'I've got no more balls left to bite off.'

'A second shot at being the future Mrs Sowerbutts.'

'Unlikely. Great idea – but unlikely.'

'Wait and see.'

The telephone rang. Butty lifted the receiver.

'I'm not taking any calls.'

'This is the hotel manager,' said a querulous voice.

'Then go off and manage your frigging hotel.'

'You've caused damage to our property, sir.'

'I said I'll pay. Shove it on the bill.'

'What's going on up there?'

'I'm being held hostage by Arab terrorists. If you don't stop bothering me, they'll set fire to the entire building.'

'Have you been *drinking*?' gasped the manager.

'I've been having a Bacchanalian bleeding orgy.'

The man was aghast. 'You have women in the room?'

'No. Send a few up.'

He put the phone down and disconnected the lead.

'You sure know how to sweet-talk the staff around here,' said Des with a grin. 'Anyway, I'll blow. I can see you'd rather be left on your own.'

'No, no. Don't go, mate. I need a friendly face. And it's nice to meet one other person who thinks I was set up.'

'No question about it. Somebody wanted an excuse to cut you out of that tour. Any ideas who it could be?'

'Have to see the full team first, Des. I was so narked at being left out, I didn't notice who'd been selected.'

'I can help you there,' said the American, opening his briefcase to take out a sheet of paper. 'This is the press release. Came through on my fax.'

Butty took it from him and pored over it with interest. Sixteen players had been selected for the short winter tour of Karistan. He ran his eye down the list with envy.

J. H. Fotheringhay	(Hams.) (captain)
M. D. Mancini	(Middlesex)
P. F. Pilgrim	(Surrey)
D. W. C. Elgin	(Leics.)
W. L. Rodger	(Hams.)
H. M. Smart	(Hams.)
G. O. Day	(Yorks.)
B. V. Jenkins	(Glam.)
P. E. N. Coyne	(Lancs.)
W. E. Winslow	(Kent)
J. J. Cromwell	(Hams.)
P. B. Brooksby	(Essex)
E. T. Montgomery	(Notts.)
C. C. Ings	(Warks.)
R. M. Ryman	(Lancs.)
T. H. Horgan	(Hams.)

'Well?' prompted Des. 'What do you think of it?'

'Bleeding diabolical!'

'All the experts say it's a balanced team. Six recognised batsmen. Six recognised bowlers. Three all-rounders and a wicket-keeper.'

Butty was scornful. 'Recognised batsmen! Recognised bowlers! Their own mothers wouldn't recognise some of these wankers. As for the all-rounders, Monty is the only one who really qualifies. He's as round as a beach ball.'

'Coyne is a genuine all-rounder, isn't he?'

'Old Penny? He's an all-round shit. Wouldn't be at all surprised if he's the bugger who fitted me up last night. When I drop out, he steps in. Typical of Penny Coyne.'

'Any other suspicious names?'

'Three or four. Back-stabbers Supreme.'

'The team seems weighted in favour of Hamcester.'

'What do you expect when Fothers is captain and his uncle is chairman of the selectors? Bleeding nepotism. I suppose we ought to be grateful they didn't pick Fothers' Grannie to open the bowling.'

Butty launched a vitriolic attack on the team. Des listened with fascination. He'd been assigned to write a series of articles about English cricket for his Boston newspaper and still had much to learn. He hadn't realised how much political intrigue lay behind team selection. The commentary was a revelation.

'This is barmy!' concluded Butty, plugging in the telephone once more. 'I'm going to tell him straight.'

'Who?'

'Fothers. That loonie they've put in charge.'

'He topped the batting averages last year.'

'Yeah,' said Butty, dialling the number. 'He caused a record number of run-outs as well. Fothers is always ready to sacrifice someone else's wicket. Stay in longer and you score more runs.'

The receiver was picked up at the other end of the line.

'James Fotheringhay,' he announced.

'Fothers, you cretin! Butty here. Just seen your team.'

'Were you impressed?'

'That lot couldn't win a game of snakes and ladders. Let alone three Test matches against Karistan. I should have been selected.'

'Couldn't agree more, old chap,' lied Fothers. 'I pushed hard for you but the tide went the other way. You did rather tarnish the image of English cricket last night.'

'I was framed.'

'Come off it, Butty. This is not the first time you've been caught with your pants down. You've got previous.'

'You *need* me in that team!'

'Too late. No room for you. On reflection, I don't think you'd have fitted in with the chaps. You've got sterling qualities, I grant you, but you lack true patriotic spirit.'

'Bollocks!'

'Any good will message for the tour party?'

'Yes,' said Butty. 'Bon Fucking Voyage!'

FOUR

A month is a long time in cricket. Two months can effect major changes in the game. Three can seem like an eternity. While the British media turned its attention to noisy soccer pitches and rowdy rugby fields on a Saturday afternoon, cricket was played with competitive zeal in warmer climes around the world. Reputations were made and lost. Careers were developed or ended. Fledgling nations learned to walk on their own feet. Alarming progress was made in the most unlikely arenas.

Tombo was thrown into a complete and gibbering panic.

'Have you read this?' he asked, holding up the newspaper with trembling hands. 'Anyone seen this report?'

'What report?' said Snatcher.

'Here. In the *Karistan Daily News*.'

Snatcher was sarcastic. 'Oh, yeah, Tombo. My favourite reading. Never miss it. As soon as I've had a goggle at Page Three in the *Sun*, first thing I always reach for is the *Karistan Daily Spews*.'

'*News*!' corrected Tombo. '*News* – not *Spews*.'

'Wait till you've tasted their grub!'

'This is serious, Snatcher.'

'Why?' asked the cadaverous Penny Coyne, ambling over to them. 'How did you get hold of that rag, anyway?'

'I sent away for it. Wanted to size up the opposition.' He glanced at the newspaper. 'Wish I hadn't bothered now.'

'What do you mean, Tombo?'

'Look at the headline on the back page.'

Penny leaned in to read it aloud. 'RECORD SCORE BY KARISTAN. So what?' he said with a dismissive shrug. 'It

37

probably means they reached double figures at last.'

'22 all out!' mocked Snatcher.

'Including 15 extras!'

Tombo waited patiently until Penny and Snatcher had finished sniggering. Both of them took a very unflattering view of lowly Karistan. Tombo paid them a lot more respect.

'You were close, Snatcher,' he said. 'It wasn't 22 all out. It was 722 – for 5. Bad light stopped play.'

'You're having us on!' claimed Snatcher.

'It's here in black and white.'

'Who were they playing? The local leper colony?'

'A provincial team.'

'Of what? One-armed war veterans?'

'Karistan scored 722 runs.'

'I don't believe it,' said Penny, taking the newspaper from him to study the report. 'There's nobody in Karistan who can count up to that number. Must be a misprint.'

'Their captain got a double century.'

'Zaki Meero?'

'He's a class player. We've seen that over here.'

'Yes,' conceded Penny grudgingly, 'but Zaki is the only one they've got who can hold a bat straight. Everybody else is village-green standard. Karistan is a one-man band. Well-known fact, lad. Bunch of bloody amateurs.'

'Not according to that report.'

'Cunning propaganda,' decided Snatcher. 'Complete lies. They're simply trying to frighten us.'

'It's worked. I'm terrified.'

'Calm down, Tombo,' said Penny. 'It's a load of guff. These potty little countries always talk big. Anyway, 722 was not the number of runs scored on the pitch.'

'Wasn't it?'

'No,' agreed Snatcher. 'It was the number of spectators who made a dash for the khasi. That lethal food of theirs. One mouthful and you join the Karistan Sprint.'

Penny Coyne joined in the laughter and tossed the paper back to Tombo. Penny and Snatcher treated the whole thing with contempt but Tombo remained on full anxiety alert. One article had guaranteed him endless nights without sleep.

'Come on, chaps!' called a voice. 'Join in.'

Fothers was trying to rally the troops. They had met for a practice session at an indoor cricket school in Outer London but there was a lackadaisical air about the whole proceedings. James Henry Fotheringhay put his faith in what he called an unstructured session, which, in broad terms, meant that the bowlers took it in turns to give him plenty of practice in the nets. Only when one of them toppled his wicket would he even consider making way for another batsman.

'We're a team!' insisted Fothers. 'Let's act like one.'

He sounded less like a cricket captain than a head prefect, rebuking a group of recalcitrant first-formers for talking in chapel. Nobody paid the slightest attention to him. Fothers took his stance in the nets once more and clipped a ball off his pads. It was his idea of Leading By Example.

Penny Coyne, the emaciated Lancashire all-rounder, was less than impressed. The session was too lifeless and disorganised for him. He pointed a bony finger at Fothers.

'Look at that berk,' he said. 'Been stuck in there for hours. Doesn't he give anyone else a chance?'

'No,' sighed Snatcher. 'He likes to refine his technique.'

'What about the rest of the bloody team?'

'Fothers will run us out one by one.'

'That's no joke,' said Mick Mancini, striding over to them. 'I open the innings with Fothers for Hamcester. Hogs the bowling and calls every sodding run. Stranded me in no-man's land a hundred times.' He handed his bat to Tombo. 'Wield the willow, old son. Go on.'

'But I'm a bowler,' protested Tombo.

'You're also a tail-end batsman, matey. So get your tail-end over to that crease and start lashing.'

Tombo nodded disconsolately and moved off. Mick Mancini removed his batting gloves and began to undo his pads. He'd been taking strike in the net parallel to Fothers. The contrast between the two men was remarkable. While Fothers looked like an illustration from the coaching manual, Mick seemed to have strayed in off the set of *EastEnders*. Short, dark and flashy, he had a jaunty manner and a ready line of patter. Mick was the team's fixer. He could get anything for anybody at any time. They called him Dealer.

'You looked sharp in there, Dealer,' said Snatcher.

'Thanks, old son. Gave up before Fothers ran me out.'

'Is it always this dead?' complained Penny.

'Dead?'

'We take our cricket seriously up in Lancashire. Nets are almost as important as matches. We're *keen*.'

'Fothers prefers the laid-back approach,' said Snatcher. 'He practises while the rest of us lay back.'

Penny Coyne looked around with disgust. All sixteen players from the tour party were there but only a handful of them were actually engaged in the practice. Most of the team were lounging around in groups and trading gossip. Derek March was in the far corner, still trying to convince the Colonel that Karistan was not in the Isle of Wight. Bowlers' feet drummed on the floor and bats cracked balls into the netting but these were only fleeting signs of life in a mausoleum.

'Bleeding disgraceful!' decided Penny.

'You'll get used to it, mate,' said Dealer, scratching his pencil-moustache. 'Grit your choppers and bear it. We all know what's really wrong with this set-up.'

'Yes. That frigging Fothers is in charge!'

'No. Butty's not here.'

'I go along with that,' agreed Snatcher. 'Butty would ginger things up around here. Boost our morale.'

'And take Fothers down a peg or two,' noted Dealer. 'I mean, take a butcher's at our esteemed skipper, will you? Big Ben is bowling to him but only off a short run-up so there's no bite in his deliveries. If Butty was here, he'd send down screamers from a standing position. Fothers couldn't handle them. His wickets would go down more often than a whore's drawers. That's why Butty's not in the team.'

'Thank goodness!' said Penny.

Dealer bristled. 'What you on about?'

'Butty. He'd be a bleeding liability.'

'Balls!'

'He would, Dealer. Bull in a china shop.'

'We need someone to crack the fucking crockery.'

'Yes,' said Snatcher. 'Butty'd be the life and soul of the tour party. Never a dull moment with him around.'

'He's a piss-artist!' sneered Penny.

'So what?' retorted Dealer. 'Every man should have a hobby. On a cricket pitch, he's Captain Bloody Marvel.'

'Only when he's sober.'

'Shut your cake-hole, Penny.'

'Butty is the kiss of death.'

'He certainly gave Lancashire the kiss of death in the Roses Match. Bowled you out dirt cheap then knocked seven bells out of your attack.' Dealer gloated over him. 'Butty took you to the cleaners.'

'No, he didn't!'

'When you came on to bowl, he scored a boundary off almost everything you threw at him. Saw the highlights on telly. Wear brown corduroy trousers next time you take him on, Penny. Then you can shit yourself without it showing.'

'Watch it, Dealer!' warned Penny.

'Butty wiped the floor with you.'

'He got lucky, that's all.'

'There speaks a sportsman!'

'Butty would ruin the tour to Karistan.'

'He'd put the kibosh on *your* tour, old son. I know that. If Butty went, then you wouldn't even have been considered. It's only because those gin-swilling sods at Lord's squeezed him out that you got a look-in.'

'That's not true!' yelled the other.

'Calm down, lads,' said Snatcher.

'Then tell Dealer to shut his gob and give his arse a chance. Not that there's much difference between the two.'

'D'you want a punch on the hooter?' threatened Dealer.

'Who've you got in your cricket bag? Mike Tyson?'

'You're asking for it!'

'I got the vote over Butty because I'm better.'

'What at, though? Needlework?'

'Cricket!'

'You're not in the same fucking league as him.'

'Yes, I am!'

'Aw, go and spend a penny!'

'I warned you, Dealer.'

The lanky all-rounder flung himself at the Cockney batsman and wrestled him to the floor. Snatcher tried to pull them apart but he was dragged head first into the fight. All three of them were swearing volubly and exchanging wild punches. Fothers ran across to try to break up the free-for-all.

'Stop it!' he ordered. 'Stop this horseplay at once!'

The rest of the players dived in to yank the combatants out of each other's reach. Blood was coming from Penny's nose. Dealer's eye was already swelling. The gap-toothed Snatcher had just sacrificed another tooth in the name of cricket.

'What on earth were you fighting over?' demanded Fothers.

'Butty,' they said in unison.

Their captain blenched. He waved an admonitory finger and looked as if he were about to make them stay in after school to write out a hundred lines. Instead, he opted to take the sting out of the whole incident.

'Practice over, chaps!' he announced. 'Take a shower and head for the bar. First round is on me.'

The players slowly dispersed. Dealer, Penny and Snatcher licked their wounds and headed for the changing rooms. Derek March and Fothers watched them go.

'You handled that well, James,' said Derek.

'Even when he's not in the team, Butty causes trouble.'

'Precisely! Think how much worse it would be if we had him in Karistan. He'd cause a flaming riot out there.'

'Ah!' said the Colonel, marching up to them. 'You've read it as well, Derek. Disturbing news, eh?'

'What is, Colonel?'

'This riot out in Karistan. Deeply unsettling.'

'But they've had no riot.'

'Yes, they have,' insisted the Colonel. 'I was taking my binoculars out of the paper in which they were wrapped and this article caught my eye. Chaos in Karistan, it said.'

'That was three years ago,' explained Fothers. 'They had a military coup. Since then, it's been one of the most stable governments in the world.'

'Are you sure, James?'

'Yes, Colonel. Take my word for it. I've been to the country. There's no hint of trouble out there now. Karistan is as friendly and placid as Tunbridge Wells.'

The bullet-proof Rolls Royce turned into the car park of the cricket ground at Nova Tunbridge Wells and came to a gentle halt. Police outriders accompanied the cars on the drive north from the Karistan capital. Military helicopters tracked the cavalcade from above. Members of the elite presidential bodyguard had been sent on ahead to reconnoitre. Trained marksmen had been placed in strategic positions around the ground. Nothing had been left to chance. Even the sun had needed written permission to shine.

When the rear door was opened by a flunkey, General Idi Ott, President of Karistan and Supreme Commander of Armed Forces, stepped out on to the red carpet with two of his wives at his heels. He beamed royally at the soldiers who flanked the carpet. As the trio headed for the pavilion, the band played the overture to The Mikado.

The President went up the stairs to find the dapper figure of Zaki Meero, cricket captain of Karistan, waiting for him on the balcony. Zaki gave a polite bow. He wore the national blazer over his cricket shirt. His handsome face gleamed with pride.

'Welcome to Nova Tunbridge Wells!'

'Thank you,' said the President, turning to gaze down at the pitch. 'I wanted to see that preparations were in hand. Is the team in good shape, Zaki?'

'Yes, Mr President.'

'You've kept them at it, I hope?'

'Seven days a week.'

'The improvement has so far been quite amazing.'

'We will give England a run for their money.'

'No, Zaki,' insisted the other. 'We must beat them into submission. Nothing less will suffice. We must *win*!'

General Idi Ott was a burly man in military uniform with a chest covered in medals and epaulets like golden scrubbing brushes. As he gazed down at the practice match below, the big, round face was covered by a benevolent smile. Cricket was not just a form of recreation in Karistan. It was a presidential obsession. He gave a rich chuckle.

'You know how much this means to me, Zaki?'

'Of course, Mr President.'

'It will put Karistan on the map.'

'We already have the advantage of surprise.'

'England is expecting to cut us to ribbons. They have no

44

idea what heights we have risen to out here. Karistan will take them completely unawares.'

'I hope so,' said Zaki with guarded optimism. 'My team is ready but it has not yet been tested against quality opposition. England will provide a first real challenge.'

'Not any more.'

'Mr President?'

'Their selection committee has played into our hands.'

'That is certainly true.'

'They've chosen batsmen who can't handle our spinners and bowlers who'll wilt like dead grass in the Karistan heat. We'll destroy them. The one man who might have held them together has not even been selected.'

'Kevin Sowerbutts of Yorkshire.'

'A county cricket team in himself.'

'They are fools to leave out Butty.'

'We will take full advantage of their folly.'

'We will certainly try, Mr President.'

'And *succeed*!' emphasised the other. 'Now, get out on the pitch and hit some boundaries, Zaki. That's what my wives have come to see, isn't it, my darlings?' The ladies giggled. 'Off you go, Zaki. Show them how's it's done.'

'With pleasure,' said Zaki, giving another bow.

'Oh, and pass on a message to the band,' instructed the President as he lowered himself into a seat and took a wife on each fat knee. 'Give them my compliments and ask them to play selections from the Pirates of Penzance.'

'At once.'

As Zaki went off, the President sat back in his chair.

'I am a pirate myself at heart,' he boasted. 'As the tourists will soon find out. The Karistan flag should have a skull and crossbones on it. An *English* skull and crossbones.'

He shook with such mirth that his wives bobbed crazily up and down on his knees and clung to his medals for safety. He hugged them tight. General Idi Ott had always been a family man.

FIVE

Kevin Sowerbutts hated autumn and winter with equal intensity. Hibernation had no appeal for him and rest was something he only allowed himself after sex (unless an absent husband was due home soon). He had far too much energy swirling around inside him to stay idle. It was foreign to his nature.

Huddersfield Town offered him a contract as a mid-field dynamo but, in no time at all, he accumulated more yellow cards than a Chinese gambler and was ejected forcibly by the Football Association for conduct liable to bring the game into disrepute and the Accident and Emergency Department of Huddersfield General Hospital protesting against the stream of patients during home games. Butty was an over-ebullient soccer player. He made Vinnie Jones look like the Good Samaritan. Another sport turned its back on him.

Des Toyovsky rolled up in the spirit of friendship to console him. He had the utmost compassion for Butty.

'So what have you been doing with yourself?' he asked.

'Sod all, mate.'

'No personal appearances?'

'Only at poxy cricket clubs,' said Butty dejectedly. 'The chicken and Beaujolais circuit. Gets you down after a while. Makes you feel like a bleeding dancing bear.'

'What about endorsements?'

'Sore topic, Des.'

'Why?'

'Because I lost some of the sponsors I already had and all of the ones I was lining up. Everything turned on

Karistan. If I'd been in the team, I'd have signed some lucrative deals by now and been rolling in it. Karistan has cost me a frigging fortune.'

'All because of that business in the Volvo Estate.'

'There *was* no business!' howled Butty. 'I never had so much as a cigarette off that bimbo, let alone a quick shag.'

'I believe you.'

'Thanks, Des.'

'Unfortunately, nobody else does.'

It was a cold day in December and Butty was back in a London hotel. He'd been on the town most of the night with some of the touring team, giving them a lively send-off and drowning his own sorrows at the same time. The morning after found him queasy and dispirited. While the happy tourists flew off to Karistan that afternoon, Butty would be left behind to face a bleak and cricketless winter.

'Hey,' he remembered. 'You're part of the press corps on that tour. You'll miss the plane.'

'Coupla hours to go yet,' said Des easily. 'Couldn't leave without saying goodbye. And I had two other reasons for calling.'

'What are they?'

'First, I've got some good news.'

'I could certainly use it, mate.'

'My detective work finally paid off.'

'Fantastic!'

'The bimbo's name was Mindy Hibbert,' explained the quiet American. 'Leads a double life. By day, she works as a Post Office clerk in East Finchley; by night, she sells cigarettes at the Harpo Club in Soho.'

'What *else* does she sell?'

'Mindy's as clean as a whistle, Kevin. I checked her out. Kid's never been on the game. She's a devout Methodist.'

'How did she end up in the Volvo Estate?'

'Same as you. Someone bought her a drink and spiked it. Mindy passed out. When she opened her eyes, she was lying next to the most famous cricketer in England. She was real flattered, I tell you. Turns out that Mindy's a great fan of yours. Under other circumstances, she'd have asked for your autograph.'

'On which tit?'

'She was in the same boat as you, Kevin.'

'But I was the one who drowned when it capsized.'

'Price of fame,' said Des with a sigh. 'Anyway, the point is that Mindy's not to blame. She was just a pawn.'

'In whose grubby hands?'

'That's what I haven't found out yet but I'm still working on it. Bear with me.'

'Did you trace that photographer?'

'Yeah. Name of Flash McGovern. Freelance. Works for the tabloids and the sleazier girlie mags. Admits he had a tip-off but won't say where it came from.'

'He'll have another tip-off if I get hold of him,' said Butty vengefully. 'From Waterloo Bridge. With his feet in a barrel of bleeding concrete. I'll count the bubbles as he goes down. Give me Flash McGovern's address.'

'Forget him. He's only a link in the chain.'

'A conspiracy, you mean!'

'Now we come to the Volvo Estate.'

'Did that give you a lead?'

'Not really,' confessed Des, shaking his head. 'Owned by a classy lady called Annabelle Jansen-Jones. Lives in a beautiful cottage near Windsor. The car was stolen over-night from her garage. She was not pleased to see photos of it splashed all over the front pages.'

'Nor me, Des. I was *in* the thing at the time!'

'That fact was not lost on her, Kevin. She's having the vehicle fumigated. And sanitized. As a precaution.'

'Against what?' said Butty indignantly.

'Who knows?' The American gave a diffident smile. 'The trail ends there, I'm afraid. Mindy Hibbert, Flash McGovern and Annabelle Jansen-Jones are only bit-players in this sordid drama. Someone links all three of them together and that someone is the guy who set you up.'

'Penny!' guessed Butty.

'Coyne of Lancashire?'

'Or it might be Wanker.'

'Winslow of Kent?'

'Then again, it could even be Marbles.'

'Elgin of Leicestershire?'

'Bloody hell!' howled Butty. 'It could be any of 'em!'

'I'll track him down in the end,' promised Des. 'However long it takes. I'm slow but I'm real thorough.' He glanced at his watch. 'Jesus! Must be off. Gotta get across to Heathrow to catch that plane.'

'Thanks for calling in, anyway. You're a real mate.'

'Pleasure.'

'Enjoy the trip.'

'I'll send you a post card.' He moved to the door. 'See you around, Kevin. Hang in there.'

'Hold on a tick!' shouted Butty, recalling something.

'Why?'

'You said you had two reasons for coming here.'

'Yeah. That's right. One was to update you on my private eye activities. Sherlock Toyovsky.'

'What was the other one?'

'To make certain you stay in this room when I go.'

'Stay here?' asked Butty. 'Why?'

'You'll soon see.'

Des Toyovsky gave him a wave and let himself out. Butty was mystified. He sat on the edge of the bed and scratched his head. What did Des mean? Why was his tone so noncommittal? Was it some kind of practical joke? Butty was still meditating on the possibilities when there was a firm knock on the door. He ran to open it and stood back in utter amazement. His jaw dropped like the back of a removal van.

'Barbara!'

'Aren't you going to invite me in?' she said.

'Yeah, yeah. Of course,' he said, stepping aside to let her past. 'What are you doing here? How did you know where to find me? Are we still speaking to each other?'

'The answer to all three questions is Des Toyovsky.'

'Eh?'

'We had a little chat.'

'What about?'

'A girl called Mindy Hibbert.'

'Ah.'

'And a man called Flasher McGovern.'

'Oh.'

'And a lady named Annabelle Jansen-Jones.'

'Then you know as much as I do,' he said, appraising her properly for the first time. 'You look terrific, Barbara.'

'You look terrible.'

'Withdrawal symptoms.'

'What was her name?'

'I was out on the beer with the lads.'

Barbara laughed. 'Des told me. Pub crawl around London. Men only.' A wistful note came into her voice. 'You've gone to pieces since you broke up with me, haven't you?'

'Yeah. Old story. Didn't realise how much I loved you till you'd gone. Been bloody miserable without you. Every time I see a Volvo Estate, I come out in a rash.'

'I'll have to put cream on it for you,' she said with a knowing wink. 'Where does it itch most?'

Butty revived instantly. 'All over!'

'Let Nurse Ollerenshaw take a look.'

'You bet!'

Sweeping her up in his arms, he gave her a long, guzzling kiss before throwing her on to the middle of the bed. Her skirt rode up to show that she had somehow forgotten to put on any pants that morning. The combination of suspender belt, black stockings and white thighs galvanised

Butty into action. Steam began to rise from his jockey shorts. His moribund manhood was resurrected with the speed of an Apollo spaceship.

After months of trudging alone across a sexual desert, he had stumbled upon an oasis. It was no time to scoop up a genteel handful of water to slake his thirst. He needed it all. Tearing off his clothes, he dived straight in. The splash could be heard throughout the hotel. Butty didn't care. It was a deafening reconciliation.

Let the whole world know!

Afterwards, luxuriating in happy fatigue, they lay in each other's arms, locked together by the Bostik of their perspiration and by the urgency of their mutual needs. All the anguish of separation had been swept away. Butty felt real contentment for the first time since the fatal night in the Volvo Estate. Barbara was his. For ever.

It was she who first thought about the formalities.

'Have you still got my ring?' she whispered.

'No, love.'

'You gave it to someone else?'

'Yeah. Pawnbroker. We're getting married Easter.'

'Don't tease,' she said, punching him. 'Where is it?'

'Got it on me somewhere. Have a good search.'

'Fifthy beast!'

'That's why you love me so much.'

'It's part of the reason.'

'On again, then, is it?'

'What?'

'It. Us. B and B. Ring-a-ding-ding.'

'I'll think about it.'

'After *that*?'

She giggled. 'All right, Kev. You've talked me into it.'

He rolled on top of her, kissed her on the mouth then tickled her under the arms. She went off into a fit of laughter then pushed him on to the floor. Butty crawled to his suitcase and fished around inside it. His hand came out with a small box in it. He held it up to show her.

Barbara was delighted. 'You kept it!'

'Only the box. I threw the ring away.'

'You're teasing me again.' He flipped up the lid of the box for her to see the ring. 'It's there. I had a horrible feeling you might have found someone else.'

'I did,' he said airily. 'Two a night. But they didn't need an engagement ring. All it took was a blast on the whistle and they jumped straight in the bed.'

'I had offers as well, you know,' she said proudly.

'Who from?' he demanded as jealousy pulsed.

'Dozens of men.'

He was hurt. 'Is that true?'

'No, you silly fool. The only offer I had was from that lezzie P.E. mistress who used to twang my knicker elastic during netball. She read in the paper we'd broken up. Asked me round to her flat to discuss Men over a bottle of Bailey's Irish Cream.'

'Did you go?'

'No. I only drink Bacardi and Coke.'

They burst out laughing and rolled over on the bed together. When she'd fitted the ring back on her finger, she snuggled right up to him. They were back in the groove again.

• 'I owe you an apology, Kev.'

'You should have trusted me.'

'I see that now. Do you forgive me?'

'Not yet. But I'm open to persuasion.'

'Must have been rotten for you. Everyone going up in smoke. Everyone turning against you.'

'It was, Barbara. Losing you was the worst.'

She was touched. 'Was it, really?'

'Yes!' he affirmed. Apart from not going to Karistan, that is. And losing my sponsors. And getting my membership at the Harpo Club revoked . . . But you were right up there in the top ten, honest!' He held her wrists as she tried to pummel him. 'You *know* you're number one. And always will be. Got it?'

Violence turned to passion, then she relaxed again.

'It was kind of you to see the lads off last night.'

'Some of 'em are great mates.'

'Yes, but they're going on tour and you're not.'

'Thanks to Fothers! The slimy toad.'

'I bet he wasn't on the pub crawl with you.'

'No, Barbara. He's got more sense than to get anywhere near my orbit. But I haven't forgotten him, don't worry. The lads had their send-off last night. Fothers will get his this afternoon.'

'What do you mean?'

'I've arranged a little leaving-present for him.'

'Present?'

'Yes,' said Butty with a grin. 'She answers to the name of Fifi. Quite a girl!'

Television cameras were waiting to see the team off at Heathrow and an impromptu press conference was held. Derek March and Fothers did all the talking while the others pulled faces in the background. When it was all over, they pushed their trolleys towards Customs. Derek was in a buoyant mood but Fothers was a trifle sad. His uncle understood the problem.

'Missing her already, James?' he said.

'Antonia and I haven't been apart this long before.'

'She's coming out to Karistan for Christmas.'

'Yes,' said Fothers with a wan smile. 'There is that.'

'Antonia might only be a distraction in the early part of the tour. Cricket must come first.'

'I've been telling her that for a year, Uncle Derek. But the excuse is wearing thin. She said that she's getting very frustrated. I'm having a job to control her.'

'She'll calm down when you're out of the country.'

'I hope so.'

The intimate problems of James Henry Fotheringhay were interrupted by the polite voice of a Customs Officer, who invited the England captain to wheel his trolley across to the table along the wall.

'We have a plane to catch,' complained Fothers.

'This won't take a moment, sir.'

'Do you know who I am? And *what* I am?'

'Of course, Mr Fotheringhay.'

The man was short, stocky and unimpressed by reputation. A job was a job. That's all that mattered. He asked Fothers to lift his cricket bag on to the table and undo the straps.

'This is absurd,' said Fothers, obeying the instruction with irritation. 'My kit usually gets waved through without a hitch. What are you expecting to find inside? Cannabis in a hollow cricket ball? Heroin in the handle of my bat?'

'Very droll, sir. Just take everything out, will you?'

Protesting loudly, the England captain did as he was told, unaware of the fact that Dealer and Snatcher had stopped to watch. They had bought shares in the event. It was Dealer who had gained access to the cricket bag and Snatcher who had made the anonymous call to Customs. The major shareholder in the practical joke, however, was Butty. It was his idea.

'And the rest, sir, if you please,' insisted the man in uniform when the bag was almost empty. 'What's that down there underneath your white flannels?'

'Where?' said Fothers.

He dug his hand in and disaster was set in motion. Fifi lay in wait like a cobra. The moment Fothers touched her, she began to self-inflate with a resounding hiss. Her head shot out of the bag with eyes glowing and red lips invitingly apart, then came an arm, then a breast, then a second

54

breast, then a second arm. She was as naughty and naked as an enthusiastic amateur.

When Fothers tried to press her back into the bag, she responded with even greater eagerness, filling to maximum size and leaping out of the bag to clap her rubber arms around him and knock him to the floor. Fothers wrestled in vain with the hissing temptress. The gathering crowd began to cheer him on, delighted by this pornographic performance thrown in for their amusement and admiring the incredible flexibility of the woman's antics.

While Fothers tried to master the billowing sexuality beneath him, the Customs Officer took due note of the sticker on the left buttock of the inflatable doll.

I'M FIFI. WILD, WILLING AND WASHABLE. MADE IN TRURO.

She was too wild for the England captain and far too willing. When she clapped her thighs around his waist, he broke out in a cold sweat. What was happening to him? He could take no more humiliation. Acting on impulse, he bit her right nipple hard and she exploded with a beatific smile. Fothers was left on the carpet in a pool of sharded rubber, all passion spent and all hope of a second session punctured beyond recall. The appreciative audience broke into applause.

Dealer cupped his hands to call out a question.

'Did the earth move for you, too, Fothers?'

His captain did not hear him or the jeering that followed. He was slowly coming to terms with a hideous and unavoidable truth. A plot had been laid against him.

Butty had struck again.

SIX

Karistan was a small island in the middle of the Indian Ocean. When they caught their first glimpse of it from the air, it looked like a yellow leaf, floating on the water. The England touring team could not believe that their jumbo jet was actually going to land on such a tiny and insubstantial strip of *terra infirma*. It was akin to bungee-jumping from the top of Everest. A unique experience that would have a favourable mention in your obituary.

Hysteria spread quickly throughout the plane. The more suggestible members of the team began to draw up their wills. Snatcher bequeathed his wicket-keeping gloves to his country cricket club. The Colonel left his Wisden to his regiment. Dealer prayed for the first time in eighteen years. Penny searched under his seat for a parachute. Tombo, the eternal pessimist, fainted. Even the level-headed Des Toyovsky had palpitations.

When the aircraft lost height, the ashen faces at the windows saw that the island was, after all, stationary and not bobbing about on the waves like a lily-pad. It increased its size with every minute. Karistan looked like a cricket ball which had been bent out of shape by persistent tampering. The thick seam down its centre was the Pindi Mountain Range. Scuffing on the eastern side represented the Caves of Niah. The depression to the north-west was Mingoon Bay. Fingermarks at the southern tip denoted Port Lemmon.

Dealer was the first to spot another geographical feature. Directly below Port Lemmon, like a piece of leather which had come adrift from the ball, was an even smaller outcrop of land, rising craggily out of the foaming breaks.

'What's that?' he said.

'Shark Island,' said Fothers.

'They have *sharks* here?'

'Only in the Dyre Straits. Bathing is forbidden there.'

'How do we get to Shark Island from Karistan?'

'We don't, Dealer.'

'Why not? I thought we were going to see everything.'

'*You* might end up on Shark Island but it won't be to play cricket. Their laws are very strict here so watch your wheeler-dealing. Or they'll arrest you for marketeering and give you a one-way trip on the ferry to Shark Island.'

'Why?'

'It's a prison. Their version of Alcatraz.'

'I thought you said they had a very low crime-rate.'

'They do,' confirmed Fothers. 'Shark Island is the reason. Big deterrent. Nobody's ever escaped from there.'

'Blimey! Thanks for the warning.'

Fothers was glad of the chance to show off his knowledge of Karistan. The long flight had been a continuous embarrassment for him with Fifi jokes being fired at him like pellets from catapults. His only consolation was that his beloved Antonia had not been there to witness the attempted rape of an England captain by a runaway rubber doll in the grip of erotomania. The thought that he might one day have to endure such a savage encounter with Antonia herself made him think twice about the wisdom of proposing to her. In the case of his fiancée, he feared, a bite on the nipple would be no means of ending the ordeal. It might only incite her to wilder passion.

The alert Snatcher noticed a worrying development.

'We're going round in circles!' he yelled.

'So we are!' said Dealer. 'We've lost control and we're going into a spin.'

'We're caught in a black hole!' gasped Penny.

'Rubbish!' reassured Fothers above the hum of disquiet.

57

'We're in a holding pattern, that's all. Air traffic control is not ready to bring us in.'

'No,' said Dealer, 'they haven't built the runway yet. They've probably got a chain gang from Shark Island working on it right now.' He nudged Snatcher beside him. 'What's the first thing you're gonna do when we land?'

'Catch the next plane home.'

'I'm going to have a swim. Unwind a bit.'

'What about you, Fothers?' asked Snatcher, raising his voice so that the whole party could hear him. 'I bet I know the first thing you'll do in Karistan.'

'Take a bath, old chap.'

'No. You'll send a post card back to Fifi.' He waited until the laughter died down. 'And I know what you'll put on it as well. "Wish you were here. Love you to bits."'

Fothers sank down into his seat and put his hands over his ears as another fusillade of Fifirama went off. He hoped that the plane would soon land so that the concerted attack on his masculinity would stop. It undermined his authority and was damaging to his image as the clean-cut, clean-living captain of all he surveyed. When he dared to listen again, the talk had turned inevitably to the Missing Member.

'Poor old Butty!' said Snatcher. 'Should be with us.'

'Yeah,' said Dealer. 'Can't help feeling sorry for the geezer. He'd have a whale of a time with those sharks.'

'What's he doing these days?'

'Nothing!' sneered Penny Coyne.

'He is,' defended Dealer. 'Told me about it only last night. Butty is planning to go on a charity walk.'

'Yes,' said Penny. 'From his home to the nearest pub.'

'From Huddersfield to Karistan so that he can clobber any Lancashire gits he finds there. Get those brown trousers out, Penny. You may need 'em, old son.'

'Only to wrap around your stupid head!'

'Butty's got a big heart. Raises a lot of money for charity. He's always ready to help others in need.'

Penny sniggered. 'He's helped us by staying at home.'

'One Butty is worth ten Pennies.'

'Then why was I chosen instead of him, big mouth?'

The argument escalated, then died at once as the aircraft banked steeply and came in to land. Survival was the only concern now. Dealer and Penny forgot their differences and gripped the sides of their seats. Tombo, having revived, fainted again. It was less of a measured descent than a sudden drop from the sky. Karistan came rushing up to meet them with stupefying velocity. When they hit the runway with a hard thud, everyone was jolted, the luggage rattled mutinously in the overhead compartments and the Colonel's bottom set of dentures shot out of his mouth like a guided missile and bit a lump out of the back of the seat in front of him.

Reverse-thrust motors deafened the passengers and slowly brought the aircraft to a juddering halt. The passengers were thoroughly jangled. The captain's voice was deeply apologetic over the intercom.

'Sorry about that landing,' he said meekly. 'They've moved the runway since we were here last week.'

Vehicles converged on them from all directions. A lorry towed a mobile gangway up to the side of the plane. A brass band in red military uniform jumped out of a bus and got in formation with their instruments. Zaki Meero stepped out of a gleaming Mercedes with a batch of government officials. A huge and excitable crowd was standing on the roof of the airport building to wave flags of welcome. They were wanted.

'Looks as if they're expecting us,' said Dealer.

'I'll go first,' insisted Fothers. 'They know me.'

'So does Fifi!'

'Oh, shut up, Dealer.'

'You won't have the same problem out here, Fothers.

They tell me that Karistan has got very low inflation. Fifi would take three weeks to blow up to full combat size.'

Everyone was anxious to get out and stretch their legs after the cramped flight. When Colonel Arthur Totter had reclaimed his bottom set and inserted them into his mouth, he felt able to contribute towards the buzz of conversation.

'We're here, everybody! Three cheers for the pilot! Hip-hip-hooray!' There was dead silence. 'What's the matter with you?'

'We're not cheering a Kamikaze,' said Snatcher.

'I'm as stiff as a bleeding board,' moaned Dealer. 'Haven't moved out of this seat for twelve hours.'

'Never took this long to get to the Isle of Wight before,' said the Colonel. 'But I was much *younger* then.'

The door was opened and Derek March took command.

'Listen, everybody,' he warned sternly. 'When we step out there, we'll be in the public eye. Very important to make a good impression from the start. Put on a bit of a show for them. Smarten up, everybody. Team blazers on. Remember that we're English in a hostile land.'

'I'm used to that,' said Penny. 'I live in Manchester.'

Amid the jocularity, hair was combed, ties were quickly straightened, hip flasks were put away and trousers were hitched up. Even the press corps made an effort to look like civilised human beings. They emerged from the plane into the bright sunlight of Karistan to be enfolded in the cloying warmth of the tropical climate. Photographers flashed away. Zaki Meero stepped forward with the governmental delegation and the band made a brave but doomed stab at 'There'll Always Be an England'.

It did not matter. As they basked in their first taste of Karistan hospitality, the tourists sensed that they were going to enjoy their visit. They were being feted. Bare-breasted girls in grass skirts raced up to hang garlands of flowers around the necks of the newcomers and to give each one a kiss of greeting. Massed schoolchildren performed a sprightly dance. Fireworks went off. A welcoming banner was towed across the sky by a light aircraft.

Colonel Arthur Totter was overjoyed with the reception. Dentures now firmly in place, he exposed them in a smile of comprehensive gratitude.

'Thank you, thank you!' he shouted, lifting his straw hat. 'It's so nice to be back here on the Isle of Wight.'

He took a closer look at his olive-skinned hosts and adjusted to the new dispensation without a flicker.

'Or should I say – the Isle of Off-White?'

Their first day in friendly Karistan was spent settling into their hotel and getting the lie of the land. Accommodation was at the luxury resort of Bukit on the west coast of the island, a place with such a long stretch of golden sand that Dealer immediately christened it Bukit and Spade. At their four-star hotel, which overlooked the bay, Derek March took the list of double rooms and assigned partners with a flourish.

'I'll go in with James,' he began.

'Give him the Fifi treatment, Fothers!' said Dealer.

Jibes and derisive cheers filled the foyer. The England captain squirmed. It would take a long time to live down his two minutes at Heathrow with a nymphomaniac doll.

Dealer shared a room with Snatcher, Tombo was put in with Big Ben Jenkins, the melancholy Welshman, and Penny Coyne was pleased to team up with his Lancashire colleague, Ricky Ryman, the spin bowler. Everybody was satisfied with the arrangements except the Colonel, who, to his intense horror, found himself billeted with Olly Cromwell. It offended his sensibilities.

'I can't share a room with a Roundhead!' he said.

'You won't,' promised Dealer. 'Olly's bonce is shaped like a torpedo. He has to screw his cricket cap on.'

'It's his damn politics that I protest about.'

'Hasn't got any, Colonel. Had 'em removed with his tonsils when he was a kid. No, you'll be fine in there with Olly Cromwell. Hasn't beheaded a king for months.'

The party broke up and went off to their respective rooms. Dealer had three more suitcases than anyone else. He stacked them neatly against the wall beside his bed.

'What you got there?' wondered Snatcher.

'Supplies.'

'Eh?'

'Basic necessities of life,' said Dealer, lifting the lid of the top case to display his wares. 'See for yourself. Booze, baked beans, biscuits, brown boot polish, pork pies, *Penthouse*, pickled onions, Durex, dominoes, Diet Coke, film, fags, jelly babies, Mars bars, mosquito spray, after-shave, chewing gum, crisps and crinkly chips. You name it, I got it.'

'What's in the other cases?'

'Clothes and personal accessories.'

'Mick Mancini Exports!'

'Brought all the things you can't get here, Snatcher,' he explained. 'Okay, maybe nobody will want balloons and funny hats for the first few weeks out here. But when Christmas comes, I'll have a rush on them. And on my mince pies. Laws of supply and demand. Each of these suitcases will be a nice little earner.'

'But you're here to play *cricket*.'

'Like to do a spot of business between overs.'

'Is there anything you don't have in those suitcases?'

'Women.'

'We'll need those, Dealer. Most of the lads have got their tongues hanging out already. Not only their tongues.'

'Leave it to me, old son. I will provide.'

'You always do.'

When they'd changed into tropical wear, the two friends went down to check the hotel facilities. The staff were infinitely obliging and other guests came up to them for autographs. England cricketers were clearly Very Important Persons in Karistan. They lapped up the adulation. It was a far cry from being booed at Headingley on a cold day by a jaded crowd.

Out on the terrace, they bumped into Fothers. He was dressed in a Mexican hat, a Union Jack T-shirt and a pair of white flannels, gazing out to sea through his sunglasses with the air of an Empire-builder. Standing erect beside him was a giant stick insect, which, on closer inspection, turned out to be the Colonel in khaki shirt and shorts. His mottled legs looked like two matching pipe cleaners.

'What do you think of it, chaps?' asked Fothers.

'So far, so good,' approved Snatcher. 'Is every town on the island as luxurious as Bukit?'

'Karistan has its poorer parts but the standard of living is generally high. The island has rich mineral deposits in the north-east. That and the fishing industry are the basis of their economy. By and large, it's an extraordinarily well-run and thriving country.'

'Seems a peaceful enough place,' noted Dealer.

'I hope so,' said the Colonel. 'We don't want any of those Turmoil Separatists to spoil our tour.'

'*Tamil* Separatists, Colonel,' corrected Fothers. 'They're five hundred miles away in Sri Lanka. No political dissent here. When there was a military take-over three years ago, they rounded up all the rebels. Imprisoned them on Shark Island.'

The Colonel was alarmed. 'You mean, they're still there?'

'Safe and sound behind bars.'

'Suppose they escape?'

'No chance.'

'Political hotheads are dangerous. They believe in social revolution. They might swim to the mainland, storm our hotel, hold a knife to our throats and force us to vote Labour!'

'Relax, Colonel,' said Fothers confidently. 'Those rebels will never escape. They're locked up for life.'

They waited until dark before they put the plan into action. Having dug the tunnel carefully over a period of months, they didn't wish to squander all that effort with one false move. The prison guards walked past their cell and shone a torch in to check that both of them were in their bunk beds. Tiki and Verukka seemed to be fast asleep under their rough blankets. The guards moved on to inspect the next cell.

The prisoners jumped out of their beds. They had an hour before the patrol came again. There was no time to waste. Lifting their bunk beds to one side, they got their fingers under the edge of a paving slab and heaved it upwards. A narrow passageway was revealed. It was dank, dark and crawling with insects but that didn't worry them. They were ready to suffer any discomfort in their bid for freedom.

Tiki slapped his friend on the shoulder and Verukka dived head first into the tunnel like a human mole. After a minute's wait, Tiki went after him, crawling on elbows and knees through the subterranean cavity. It was a journey they had made every night of the week so far. This time it was different. They would not be going back to their cell.

Verukka surfaced in the bushes and looked up at the high prison wall. Searchlights raked the surrounding area but Verukka was too well-concealed to be picked out. He put a hand down the hole to pull Tiki from the tunnel then scrambled through the undergrowth with him. The shore was only a few hundred yards away and they could hear the waves breaking in the stillness of the night. The sound encouraged them.

Their raft was in its hiding-place. It had been hastily

assembled from driftwood during their earlier nocturnal trips. Now it would be put to the test in the Dyre Straits. They dragged the raft across the sand to the water's edge. This was it.

Verukka began to shiver with fear but Tiki had enough courage for both of them. As the leader of the rebel forces, he was used to instilling confidence. He put a hand on his friend's shoulder and looked him deep in the eye.

'Forget the sharks, Verukka. Think of Karistan.'

'Yes!' agreed the other. 'Our country!'

'Seized from us by the army. They are the *real* sharks.'

'Freedom for Karistan!'

'That's our mission. Let's go.'

They were soon paddling steadily across the water.

SEVEN

There was only one ball left and Karistan were still five runs ahead. Victory for the home team seemed a formality. Butty had other ideas. Taking his stance, he watched the bowler begin his run and gripped the handle of his bat even tighter. When the full toss hurtled through the air straight at him, Butty was ready for it. Clubbing the ball with ferocious power, he sent it high into the stands to the acclaim of the England supporters and of his teammates on the balcony of the pavilion. Kevin Sowerbutts had rescued his country once more with a towering six.

When he came out of his fantasy, Butty saw that he was not playing in a Test match in Karistan at all. He was in the new Sports Centre in Huddersfield, giving a demonstration of raw power by smashing balls into the nets. The bowler was a pimply youth with an Adam's apple so big that Butty at first thought he'd swallowed the ball in fear.

Generous applause came from the small crowd who'd gathered to watch their sporting hero open the new centre. Butty grinned in acknowledgement but there was wistfulness in his eyes. Much as he loved his home town, he would rather be in Karistan. That was where the centre of the action was. Butty would never be happy on the outer periphery. He was wasting away through inactivity.

With a conscious effort, Butty went through the niceties with the organisers then posed for photographs with the pimply youth. After signing dozens of autograph books, he slipped out of the Sports Centre with Barbara Ollerenshaw. They made for the nearest pub and took their drinks across to a table in a quiet corner. Butty saw off half a pint with one gulp.

'Thanks for coming, love,' he said.

'I always like to support you, Kevin.'

'I need it just now.'

'Still feeling low?'

'Suicidal.'

'Don't let it get to you.'

'But I want to be in Karistan.'

'You had your chance,' she pointed out. 'Earth TV wanted to send you out there as part of their commentary team. Not the same but at least you'd have got to *see* the games.'

'It would've been slow torture.'

'What if I was in the commentary box with you?'

Butty laughed. 'That'd be different!'

'You'd be ideal,' she argued. 'You know cricket inside out and you've got strong opinions. You're controversial.'

'That's exactly why they didn't pick me for the team, love. I know too much and open my trap too wide. Fothers can't cope with that. Gives him the shakes. Once told me I had a serious attitude problem.'

'Attitude to what?'

'Him.'

'Do you?'

'Yeah. Can't accept his leadership.'

'Why not?'

'Because he doesn't give any,' said Butty. 'Not the kind I can respect, anyway. Give the lad his due. He's a useful batsman on his day. Real stroke-maker. But he knows as much about captaincy as a hole in the arse. Probably less.'

Barbara did her best to lift his spirits but with only mixed success. She hated seeing him so despondent. Butty was usually bubbling with vitality, indeed, that was one of his abiding strengths as a cricketer. His exuberance could ignite even the most depressed changing room and send players out on to the field with a new self-belief and sense of purpose. It was now Butty himself who was in need of a boost to his shattered morale.

'Why don't we go off for a holiday?' she suggested.

'Nice idea,' he murmured.

'Then sound a bit more enthusiastic.'

'Sorry, love. Not sure I deserve it.'

'What d'you mean?'

'Being in that Sports Centre reminded me just how unfit I am. I mean, look at me, Barbara. Flabby as a pregnant hippo. What I really ought to do is to get round to the Sports Centre every morning for a good work-out.'

'Come away with me and I'll give you the best work-out you've ever had! We'll soon get that flab off you.'

He perked up at once. 'Can you get the time off work?'

'I can try.'

'You're on!'

He gazed at her with beery fondness. Barbara was perfect for him. Sexy, strong-willed and endlessly supportive. Marrying her would give his life a direction and stability it had always lacked. Even if it involved some sacrifices on his part. One of those sacrifices walked past their table. Butty could not resist a lecherous glance at the vivacious barmaid.

'*That* will have to stop after the wedding,' she said.

'What?' he asked innocently.

'Sizing up every pair of tits that wafts by.'

'I'm an arse and legs man.'

'They're off the menu as well.'

'Where do I get my recreation?'

'From me.' She blew him a kiss. 'Now, cheer up, will you? Okay, you're not going on tour. So what? It's not the end of the world. You've still got me, haven't you?'

'Yeh!' he said with feeling. 'Who cares about Karistan? Waste of time going all that way. They're only beginners. Be like playing French cricket on the beach at Scarborough.

No, love. I should feel relieved I'm not in the team. Karistan is a bleeding joke. They have to clear the sheep off the pitch before they can play.' He finished the rest of his beer. 'Wouldn't go to Karistan if they paid me!'

The pitch was in excellent condition and the wicket was superb. Fothers carried out an inspection with Derek March. After a couple of days acclimatising themselves at Bukit, the team had driven north to Nova Tunbridge Wells. It bore little resemblance to its namesake in England but they could not fault its cricketing facilities. Pitch, pavilion and stands were of the highest order. It was almost like being back at Lords.

England were having a practice session on the eve of their first match, a limited-overs game against a President's XI. They had no idea what to expect. Zaki Meero was the only name they recognised from the team to play them. Everyone else was an unknown quantity.

While the rest of the players were practising in the nets, the captain and tour manager discussed selection for the morrow. Both had an unassailable confidence.

'I think we should treat it as a warm-up,' said Derek. 'No point in putting out our strongest side until the First Test.'

Fothers nodded sagely. 'I agree, Uncle Derek. This match will be an ideal time to give some of the lesser mortals a crack. As captain, I'll have to play, of course. Zaki would never forgive me if I sat this one out. But we don't have to bring the heavy artillery in.'

'Right. Let's talk names. You and Dealer to open?'

'No. Why not rest Dealer and give Pilly Pilgrim a shot at opening? He'll never make the Test team but he might score a few runs against this rabble.'

'Good idea.'

'We can put Marbles down at number three.'

'Then move Snatcher up to number four. He's in as wicket-keeper, anyway, but we could push him up the order and let him have a slog.'

'The crowd will like that. If we have one.'

'No doubt about that, Uncle Derek. President Idi Ott will be here himself. Where he goes, Karistan follows. Come tomorrow, every seat in this ground will be taken.'

'In that case, we'll put on a real exhibition!'

While nephew and Uncle were engrossed in selection, the players themselves were able to put in some serious practice for once. Olly Cromwell was bowling his medium-pacers at Penny Coyne. Big Ben was hurling down his thunderbolts at Dealer. And Peebee Brooksby was tantalising Wanker Winslow with his cutters. Other players were enjoying some catching practice, others again were limbering up before taking a turn with bat or ball. It was a scene of purposeful activity.

Des Toyovsky looked on admiringly with Snatcher Smart.

'Those guys are working real hard,' observed Des.

'We enjoy our cricket when Fothers is out of the way.'

'But he's such a fine player, Snatcher.'

'Fine player, dodgy captain.'

'I was told he was a brilliant tactician.'

'Oh, he is,' conceded Snatcher. 'He used the perfect tactics to become captain of England. Went to the right Oxford college. Got his uncle installed as chairman of the selectors. Scored lots of runs against rubbish opposition. Hobnobbed with the geriatrics down at Lord's. That's tactics for you.'

'His record so far has not been too inspiring,' admitted Des. 'Since Fothers took charge, England have lost twelve games and won only three. Dismal statistics.'

'The Windies murdered us last winter and the Aussies slaughtered us this summer. That's why they were so keen to send us out here to Karistan,' explained Snatcher. 'They finally found a team we might actually beat.'

'You're not that bad.'

'With Butty we're not. Without him . . .'

Snatcher liked the American journalist. Des wasn't a typical member of the press corps. They divided equally into genuine cricket correspondents and feature-writers from tabloids in search of lubricious stories. Des fell into neither camp. He was a quiet, honest, conscientious professional whose readiness to learn the intricacies of the game was very touching. Some of his questions were still naive but he was no longer a complete novice. Des learned fast.

'Heard a rumour?' asked Snatcher.

'Rumour?'

'They reckon two convicts escaped from Shark Island.'

'When?'

'Couple of nights ago. Dug a hole out of their cell.'

'What happened to them?'

'Nobody knows,' said Snatcher. 'There was nothing in the papers about it. I just overheard gossip among the staff at the hotel. Two prisoners got out. If they tried to swim across those straits, they must've ended up as shark food.'

'Poor guys!'

Des wanted to press for detail but their conversation was terminated by Tom Horgan. He still looked as if he carried the worries of the world on his shoulders. Tombo revelled in misery.

'Is it true, Des?' he asked breathlessly.

'Is what true?'

'All these tales we've heard about Karistan.'

'Search me.'

'But you're a journalist. You should know.'

Des laughed. 'Don't you believe it, Tombo. My journalism is two-thirds fiction and one third bourbon. All I've heard on the grapevine is that the players out here might be a little better than you expect.'

'A little! They sound like world-beaters.'

'Take it easy, Tombo,' urged Snatcher. 'You're supposed to be on *our* side, remember? Stop scare-mongering.'

'I'm not scare-mongering. I'm just scared!'

'Of what?' asked Des.

'Having our arses kicked on a cricket field again.'

Snatcher was adamant. 'That won't happen. So belt up. We don't need a Doom and Gloom Merchant.'

'What about that score of 722 they made?'

'They were playing darts at the time.'

'Zaki really *did* hit a double century.'

'So? No cause to get your knickers in a twist. Fothers hit a double century against Kent last season. Dealer got 211 against Derbyshire. We've got our run-makers as well, you know. And they scored against quality bowling.'

'I still feel something terrible will happen, Snatcher.'

'It already has. We brought you.'

'I'm only trying to be realistic.'

'Right,' said Snatcher. 'If you want realism, here it is. England is a giant cricketing nation. Karistan is a pygmy. Unless they blow poison darts at us, they're in for one hell of a hiding. Got it, Tombo? We, Tarzan. Them, Jane.'

'I suppose so.'

'Stop looking as if your balls have dropped off.'

'Sorry,' said Tombo, trying to brighten. 'We've got nothing to be afraid of, Snatcher. You're right. We'll probably annihilate them. We've got the experience.' His face fell. 'But those 722 runs still worry me.'

'Boy!' said Des with amusement. 'You certainly know how to psych yourself up, Tombo. Think positive.'

'Better still,' advised Snatcher. 'Do something to take your mind off all this bloody nonsense. Get a ball. Bowl at someone. Prove yourself. *Fight*, Tombo. *Fight, fight!*'

Tombo responded with determination. He strode across

to the nets to take over from Ben Jenkins. Tombo was not as fast as the Welshman but he could swing the ball with more venom. Dealer was going to treat him with the utmost respect.

Fothers drifted across to join Des and Snatcher. He waited until Tombo had sent down his first ball, a cunning outswinger which beat the bat and left Dealer bemused.

'Glad to see old Tombo is on form,' said Fothers. 'He's in the team against the President's XI. And you, Snatcher.'

'Thanks.'

'We don't anticipate any trouble.'

'You will if you listen to Tombo.'

'Why?'

'He reckons they'll flay us alive.'

'Yeah,' added Des. 'He sounds as if he's the PR agent for the Karistan Cricket Federation.'

'Take no notice of that,' said Fothers airily. 'Tombo is one of Nature's panic pants. When the chips are down, he always comes good. Just look at him.'

Tombo came in off a longer run-up to bowl a yorker. Event the Dealer, a man with an impregnable defence, had great difficulty in keeping it out.

'Well bowled!' shouted Fothers. 'Try a faster one.'

'Righto, skipper,' replied Tombo.

There was no sign of defeatism now. With a ball in his hand, he was brimming with confidence. If he could trouble a veteran opener like Dealer, he could worry any batsman in the world. Egged on by Fothers, applauded by Snatcher and driven by his own inner desire to improve, Tombo lengthened his run and increased his pace ball by ball. It was a stunning display of sustained aggression and the whole team stopped to watch.

Tombo had bowled three consecutive overs when the catastrophe came. Confidence spilled over into arrogance. He believed he could go faster still. Taking the longest run-up yet, he came in with gathering speed until he was level with the wicket and bowled the fastest ball of his life. Dealer swung at it and there was a loud crack. Everyone expected to see the ball thud into the side-netting but the batsman had made no contact whatsoever. It was Tombo who had provided the sound effect.

'Arghhhhhhh!'

The crack was followed by a howl of pain as he rolled on the ground. Mistiming his release of the ball, he had lost his footing and turned his ankle over. No doctor was needed to diagnose the fracture. Tombo's cry was self-explanatory.

His tour was over before it had even begun.

Butty was naked in bed with an enticingly naked Barbara when the telephone rang. He tried to ignore it but the persistent ring put him right off his stroke.

'Sorry, love,' he said, rolling off her. 'Let me get rid of this.'

'What time is it?' she asked.

He flicked on the bedside lamp. 'Christ! It's three o'clock in the bleeding morning. Who *is* this?'

'Find out. But be quick. I'll go off the boil.'

'Right.' He snatched up the receiver. 'Yes?'

'Is that you, Butty?' said a faint voice.

'No, it's the Huddersfield Fire Brigade. Who the hell wants to know at this time of the morning?'

'Me.'

'Who?'

'Snatcher. Snatcher Smart.'

'Thought you were in Karistan.'

'I am, mate. Just got up. Shit's really hit the fan.'

'What are you on about?'

'Problems.'

'Come back, Kevin,' purred Barbara, stroking his arm.

'Hold on, love. This could be important.'

'And I'm *not*?'

'No – yes – I mean, of course!'

'Then get off that sodding phone.'

'You still there, Butty?' asked Snatcher.

'Yes. But make it snappy.'

'Right. Pack your bags. We may need you.'

'Eh?'

'Tombo broke his ankle yesterday afternoon. Olly went down with malaria last night. Wanker Winslow woke up this morning with dysentery. We've lost three strike bowlers.'

'Wowee!'

'Put that phone down and come here!' demanded Barbara.

'Two seconds, love.'

'You told me I come before anything.'

'Keep your fingers crossed, Butty,' said Snatcher.

'I will. Thanks for the tip-off.'

'We're all rooting for you, mate. Cheers!'

'See you in the sunshine.'

Barbara sat up. 'Look, do you want me or don't you?'

'Do I *want* you? Oh, yes! Yes, yes, yes!'

Easing her on to her back, he parted her thighs and slid straight into her, bucking and twisting before settling into a steady rhythm. As his bum rose and fell in the light of the bedside lamp, he sang in tune with each wondrous thrust.

'Karistan! Karistan! Karistan! Kar-is-tan!'

It worked better than Huddersfield.

EIGHT

Uncle Derek looked less than avuncular as he stared down at the list of names on his lap. He was as mad as a March Hare with dandruff. Frustration had turned his face puce. When he bit on his pencil, he snapped it in two and inadvertently swallowed one half. A fit of coughing and a slap on his back helped him to regurgitate it but there was still a nasty taste in his mouth. He feared it might have nothing to do with the pencil.

Fothers went through the list of bowlers again.

'What about Huggy Reynolds of Derbyshire?'

'Gone in for a prostate operation.'

'Jumbo Edwards of Kent?'

'Got a playing contract in Australia.'

'Won't they release him?'

'No,' sighed Derek. 'And they won't release Charlie Frogg of Hampshire either. He's serving three years in Parkhurst for aggravated burglary. Pity. Charlie's a great seam bowler. Wonder if they have a Prison XI. He'd be a cert for that.'

'There's always Miff Matthews of Somerset.'

'Not any more. Retired last summer.'

'Get him out of mothballs. This is an emergency.'

'No point, James.'

'Why not?'

'Miff's been in a permanent alcoholic haze since his benefit match brought in £50,000. All he could bowl these days is medium pace belches.'

'There's *got* to be someone else!' said Fothers.

'We've tried everyone.'

'Except Gobby Osborne of Worcestershire.'

'Now you're *really* scraping the barrel.'

'He's played for England before.'

'Only that once,' recalled Derek with a shiver. 'How many did the Aussies take off his three overs? Was it sixty or seventy? He was atrocious.'

'Gobby is fast. You have to admit that. Really fast.'

'But he's got no sense of direction. He bowled so many wides at Worcester last season, they moved the pitch five yards to the left. Gobby Osborne is not the answer.'

Fothers snapped his fingers. 'Viv Leek. Northants.'

'Now there's a thought!'

'Viv is only medium pace but reliable as they come.'

'Let me give him a ring.' Derek dived for his address book and thumbed wildly through it. 'I daren't think what my phone bill is going to be and I haven't managed to speak to my wife yet. She'll demand at least an hour.' His eye kindled. 'Here we are. Viv Leek. Northampton 423557 . . .' He dialled the international code before the number. 'I just hope Viv comes through. He's our last hope.'

'Viv won't let us down. Never has before.'

'We've never *picked* him before.'

'That's true.'

'Just pray that he doesn't hold grudges.' His voice took on a jocular note as the phone was picked up at the other end of the line. 'Viv? . . . Derek March here. England tour manager. Ringing from distant Karistan . . . It's a sort of Northampton with real sunshine . . . Listen, Viv, I wanted to ask you a special favour that would get me and James Fotheringhay out of a very big and very dirty hole . . .'.

He recoiled from a string of obscenities that came hissing down the line like steam. Dropping the receiver as if it were red hot, he backed a few yards away.

'What happened?' asked Fothers.

'He *does* bear grudges.'

'Ring him back and appeal on behalf of queen and country.'

'Viv wouldn't play for us if the whole royal family went up to Northampton to beg him. I've never heard such appalling language.'

'Does he hate you that much, Uncle Derek?'

'He wasn't talking about me – but about *you*.'

'Viv is surely not still angry because I ticked him off in a county game, is he?' Derek nodded slowly. 'Oh, dear! Cross him off the list, Uncle Derek.'

'I already have. Along with the other fifteen names.'

'There has to be a top-line bowler left in England.'

'Yes!' groaned Derek. 'Kevin Sowerbutts.'

'Over my dead body!'

'Nobody else is willing and available.'

'I'm not having Butty in my team and that's that.'

'Fate is working against us here, James. We've lost three strike bowlers and we take the field against the President's XI in two hours. All we need is for Big Ben to pull a muscle during the match and we've surrendered all our fire-power. We must have someone sent out. Immediately.'

'I agree – only not Butty.'

'Then find me a credible alternative.'

'Anybody is a credible alternative to Kevin Sowerbutts. Even the Colonel. He could wear those khaki shorts and mesmerise the opposition with his floating kneecaps.'

'A genuine bowler. That's what we want.'

'Then we can rule Butty straight out,' urged Fothers. 'He's not a genuine bowler. He's an all-rounder.'

'When you top the bowling averages as often as Butty has done these past five years, it's a bit churlish to quibble over words. Call him an all-rounder, if you must. Fact remains that he can out-bowl anybody in the team.'

Fothers paced the room like a caged lion. There had to be a means of escaping the ignominy of sending for his arch enemy. When the brainwave came, it made him leap a foot into the air.

'The very man! Why didn't we think of him before.'

'Who?'

'Shagger Andrews of Surrey.'

'No, James.'

'I know he's getting on. But maturity counts in the game. We'd just have to use him sparingly, that's all. Shagger is our man. Long Test career. Plenty of wickets. Lethal with the new ball. My vote goes for Shagger Andrews.'

'Waste of time.'

'Let me speak to him. He responds to leadership.'

'He's responding to treatment at the moment, James.'

'What's that?'

'Shagger Andrews had one shag too many. Heart attack a week ago in mid-poke. He was still smiling when they rushed him into hospital. Needless to say, the barmaid in question wasn't.'

Fothers slumped into a chair. 'Oh. That's it, then.'

'We send a distress rocket for Butty.'

'No, Uncle Derek!'

'Desperate situations call for desperate measures.'

'I'd rather bowl myself than turn to Butty.'

Derek glanced at his travel clock. 'Right,' he said wearily. 'Let's leave it there. Main priority is today's game. Who knows? If the ball turns on that wicket, we might winkle them out with our spinners. A pace attack is not so important then. The vital thing is that we *win*.'

'We will, Uncle Derek. Convincingly.'

Signs were ominous from the start. When they reached the cricket ground in Nova Tunbridge Wells, they found it ringed by armed soldiers. Nobody would tell them why. Derek and Fothers were allowed through the cordon and into the pavilion. When they entered the changing room, the atmosphere was charged. The players had held their own selection meeting. Snatcher Smart was their appointed spokesman.

'We want Butty!' he announced.

Vocal support from all corners of the room.

'This is not the moment to discuss it,' said Derek.

'It's not a discussion,' continued Snatcher. 'We're giving you an ultimatum. Get Butty – or else.'

'Or else what?'

'Just get him, Derek.'

'Out of the question,' chimed in Fothers. 'He's the wrong man for a crisis like this. Lower the whole tone. Apart from anything else, he may well not be available.'

'He is, Fothers.'

'How do you know?'

'I rang him first thing this morning.'

'You had no business doing that!'

'I spoke as a friend, not a team selector.'

'You ought to be disciplined for this, Snatcher!'

'Go on, then,' taunted the other. 'Discipline me. What do I have to do? Stand in the corner with my hands on my head?'

Derek dived in to ease the friction. 'There's no need to get worked up about this. We have a game to play. That comes first. Even Butty couldn't get out here in time to face the President's XI today.' He eased Snatcher away from Fothers. 'Let's have a truce until afterwards, eh? I promise you'll be allowed to have your say. James and I will give you full consultation.'

Under protest, Snatcher and the others agreed. When they all started to change, there was a grim and unforgiving silence. It was finally broken by Big Ben Jenkins's involuntary fart, a noise so loud and threatening that it brought two armed guards rushing in to investigate. One of them levelled his rifle at the sheepish Big Ben.

'You have trouble in here?' he asked.

'Yes, boyo,' admitted Big Ben. 'And down there.'

'We hear gun go off.'

'Both barrels,' complained Dealer, holding his nose.

'Nobody hurt?'

'No,' said Derek, ushering the guards out.

Everyone burst out laughing. Big Ben's lapse of control had restored a measure of normality to the room. They could begin the serious business of talking about the game. Even with a weakened team, they were still convinced that they would trounce inferior opposition without breaking sweat. The old camaraderie was back.

'Why all the security?' asked Penny.

'The President is coming to the game,' said Derek.

'What's he gonna do?' quipped Dealer. 'Invade the changing room and occupy our cricket bags? There must be four hundred soldiers out there.'

'Bleeding intimidating,' agreed Snatcher. 'What happens if we beat the buggers? Do we face a firing squad?'

'That'll only happen if you lose,' warned Derek. 'And the firing squad will be made up of members of the British cricketing press. You all know how good their aim is.'

They took his point. Only a decisive victory would vindicate their tarnished reputation. The press corps could be blistering critics. Their fire had to be deflected.

Another bad omen followed. Fothers lost the toss. Zaki Meero, the courteous captain of the President's XI, put England in to bat. Fothers returned to the pavilion to put on his pads. When he and Dealer came out again to open the England innings, they knew instantly that something was wrong. The vast crowd was uncannily silent. Umpires and players in the field were frozen like standing statues. It was only when the two batsmen reached the pitch that they realised what had happened.

General Idi Ott, President of Karistan, had arrived.

Flanked by his elite bodyguard and wearing an even more resplendent uniform than on his last visit, the President came out on to the central balcony above the pavilion and gazed around the spectators with a benign smile. His medals glittered like diamonds. Only when he lowered himself into the armchair did everyone spring back to life. And anticipatory buzz went up. It was going to be a real cricket match, after all.

Fothers noticed a strange departure from the rules. About to take strike, he checked the field placing with great care and gulped. He beckoned Zaki Meero across.

'Problems?' asked the obliging Zaki.

'Yes, old chap. We're playing the President's XI.'

'I know.'

'Then why are there fifteen of you on the field? Wrong game. Wrong number. If you want to field a President's XV, you should have invited a rugby team out here.'

'We only have eleven players, James.'

'Then how come I counted fifteen?'

'I will tell you,' said Zaki, lowering his voice to a con-spiratorial whisper. 'Four of them are members of our Secret Service. They will not take part. They are only on the pitch to act as additional sentries for our President.'

'Then why are they dressed like cricketers?'

'So that nobody will realise who they are.'

'They're interfering with play.'

'No. They will not do that.'

'This is ridiculous, Zaki. Look – you've got five men on the square leg boundary. How do I know which ones are the genuine cricketers?'

'They can catch. The others can't.'

Fothers protested but the umpires insisted that play should start. Ruffled and resentful, Fothers took his stance and waited for the first ball. Expecting a fast bowler, he was disconcerted to find himself facing a spinner, the tall Inta Walliconi, an ungainly character with a curious bowl-ing action. His hand seemed to disappear behind his back and emerge again through the top of his head. Fothers completely lost the ball in flight and was relieved when it missed his bails by an inch.

He quickly adjusted to the new phenomenon. Though he didn't actually manage to lay a bat on any of the six deliveries, he did pad the remaining five away with comparative ease. Pace was reserved for the other end. Orin Logos was a short, bustling man with sleeves rolled up to expose his Popeye forearms. He'd certainly had plenty of spinach for breakfast that day. The first ball that Dealer faced was a sizzler. It was quite invisible. He had no awareness of its existence until he heard the wicket-keeper pouch it in his gloves.

Dealer dug in and stiffened his resistance. After blocking four balls, he got an outside edge off the last delivery and they took two runs. The spectators clapped politely. The England team cheered. The President beamed.

But the pattern had been set. Inta was a spinner of exceptional skill and Orin was a fast bowler with real fire. They kept the openers pinned down for over after over. Hurried singles and a fluke boundary were the only scores. They were barely into double figures when Fothers produced a classic piece of Fotherism. Opting to take Inta on, he came down the pitch to hook a delivery for four runs. It did wonders for his confidence. Inta himself was unperturbed.

Fothers then stroked a ball past mid-wicket and called for a run but the fielder reacted like lightning. He retrieved the ball in a flash. Halfway down the pitch, Fothers changed his mind.

'Go back, Dealer!'

'Not again!'

'I can't throw away my wicket.'

'Bastard!'

Dealer was yards out when his wickets were knocked over by a perfect throw. He trudged back to the pavilion, mouthing the familiar curses against his captain. The crowd hailed him as if he'd scored a century, and that pained him even more.

The rest of the England innings was a farce. No batsmen really came to terms with Inta's spin or Orin's pace. Runs came more by freakish accident than design. It was the tail-ender, Big Ben Jenkins, who was top scorer, flailing away like a windmill in overdrive and riding a lucky streak. His robust 41 put a pale sheen of respectability on the score by easing it into three figures. England had no illusions. They knew that 104 all out would be nowhere near enough.

'What happened out there!' wailed Derek March.

'Teething troubles,' said Fothers.

'You batted like zombies.'

'Home pitch. They had all the advantages.'

'At least put up some kind of a fight. This is a ragbag team put together for a single match. You should be able to tear them into tiny strips.'

They underwent the post-mortem while they were still alive and conscious. Derek March used rusty scalpels.

When they went out to field, England suffered an even worse blow to their pride. Zaki opened the innings with Orin, the tireless fast bowler. They were in no mood to dally. The England attack was pasted around the field with relish. Zaki was a small, compact but powerful man with a flawless technique. Orin was a destroyer, equally devastating against pace or spin, smashing balls to the boundary with terrifying regularity. Zaki was the real craftsman but it was Orin who worried the England team.

A true all-rounder. Karistan had its own Butty.

It was left to the captain to score the winning run off a loose delivery from Penny Coyne. The President rose to applaud and the entire crowd followed suit. England had been outplayed in every department of the game. Fatigued, fed up and completely disheartened, they dragged themselves back to their changing room and dropped down gloomily on to the benches.

'We were putrid!' said Snatcher.

'Shameful!' confessed Penny.

'Pathetic!' offered Big Ben.

'No,' argued Dealer, reaching out to grasp the nettle of honesty. 'We weren't bad. They were good. We did our best. They happened to be a hell of a lot better.'

'We've got a lot of work to do,' said Derek, trying to control his temper. 'Otherwise, this whole tour will go up in smoke and we'll be the laughing-stock of the cricket world. This was a scratch team you played and they crucified you. Imagine what their full Test side will do to you.' He thumped the table with a fist. 'I want you all in the nets first thing tomorrow. We need practice.'

'We need commitment,' added Fothers, standing beside him.

'We need professionalism.'

'We need runs.'

'Pride.'

'Passion.'

'Skill.'

'Courage.'

'Stamina.'

'Patriotism.'

'We need an England team worthy of the name,' said Derek.

The players surrounded them in a menacing circle. They had their own agenda. It was time to enforce the wishes of the majority. Snatcher Smart was once again their mouthpiece.

'We need Butty,' he said quietly.

All eyes turned to Fothers. The sheer weight of their communal opinion pressed down on him. Uncle Derek wasn't able to help him this time. Fothers gloried in captaincy but there was no kudos in leading an England team into the valley of certain death and disgrace. He was forced to think the unthinkable.

With his back to the wall, Fothers finally capitulated. 'I'll ring Butty today,' he promised.

NINE

When the call came, Butty already had his bags packed in readiness. He had even sent his white flannels to the One-Hour Dry Cleaners to have the beer stains removed. All recriminations were cast aside. England needed him. That was enough.

A tearful Barbara waved her fiancé off at Heathrow.

'You're leaving me,' she complained bitterly. 'Just when we were getting back into the swing of things.'

'I couldn't refuse, love.'

'You swore that you would.'

'That was before Fothers came to the phone and started eating humble pie. Hearing him grovel like that was wonderful. Warmed the cockles of my heart.'

'What about me, Kevin?'

'You warm the heart of my cockles.'

'Aren't you going to miss me?'

'Like hell!'

'D'you really mean that?'

'Of course.'

'I'll miss you!' she said, clinging to him. 'The bed will seem empty without my Kevin beside me.' A warning note came into her voice. 'Don't go off the rails, will you?'

'Off the rails?'

'You know what I mean. Birds, booze, betting.'

'Wouldn't dream of it, love,' he said, artlessly. 'I'm only going out there to play cricket. Won't even look at another bird. Don't need to. Got you.'

'But I won't be in Karistan until the New Year.'

'Then I'll have to lie fallow.'

'You'd better,' she insisted. 'Next time, I won't just throw the ring back at you. I'll shove it where it belongs. You'll need surgery to get it out.'

Butty laughed. 'That's my girl!'

'Your *only* girl. Remember that.'

'How could I forget?'

Four stunning air hostesses walked past, looking like beauty queens in British Airways uniform. Butty goggled at them and twanged like a tuning fork. Barbara brought him down to earth with a punch in the chest.

'Hands off, Kevin. I won't tell you again.'

'You won't need to, love. No chatting up the birds in the cabin crew, honest. I brought my Gideon Bible to read. That'll keep my mind on higher things.'

'See you in the New Year!'

'Can't come soon enough for me!'

Their passionate embrace lasted for five minutes. Airport staff had to prise them apart with tyre levers. Butty waved a wondrous piece of Yorkshire farewell and sprinted through the concourse towards Karistan.

English cricket was once again beleaguered. A touring side was trapped in its fort with ammunition running low. The bugle sounded. Butty was coming like the cavalry.

No expense had been spared. They were flying him First Class. The moment he settled into his luxurious seat on the upper deck of the aircraft, he became a different person. Kevin Sowerbutts of Huddersfield disappeared in a puff of smoke and Butty the Bum-Fancier materialised in his place. He had never seen so many pert posteriors waggling about in British Airways skirts. It was a riveting spectator sport.

One of these birds of paradise approached with a tray. Her smile dazzled him and her voice caressed him all over.

'Champagne, sir?'

'Thanks, darling,' he said, taking a glass.

'Can I get you a newspaper?' she said sweetly. 'We have a wide selection. *Times, Telegraph, Independent* . . .'

'*Daily Mirror*. It's the only crossword I can do.'

'What about lunch?'

'Yes, please! Where shall we meet?'

She giggled politely. 'I merely wanted to know if you have any dietary preference.'

'Food.'

'What kind?'

'The stuff you eat.'

'No other special requirements?'

'None,' he said, running an eye over her figure. 'Unless you have a Yorkshire county cap and a pair of cricket pads you could slip on for me.'

'Will you take wine with your lunch?'

'I take anything's that's going.'

'Red or white?'

'Whichever's the most expensive.'

'Everything is complimentary, sir.'

'I'll remember that when the lights go out.'

'Enjoy your flight.'

Butty grinned. 'It's like being on a magic carpet.'

When the aircraft landed in Muscat to refuel, the passengers were allowed to get out, explore the palatial airport buildings and shop in the Duty Free area. Butty was grateful for the chance to walk around and let his erection go down. Even in the Middle East, he was a well-known face and scores of airport employees pounced on him for autographs. Butty wallowed in the adulation. It was his natural habitat.

During the first leg of the flight, the seat beside him had been empty. When he rejoined the First Class cabin, he saw that he now had a companion. She was reading a copy of *Horse and Hound* as he took his seat. Her perfume was subtle and entrancing. He threw her a casual glance and gaped in amazement when he saw who it was. She also recognised him.

'Hello!' she said in a high, brittle voice. 'What a lovely surprise! You're Kevin Sowerbutts, aren't you?'

'Er, yeah. Sort of.'

'I believe that they call you "Butty", don't they?'

'Sometimes.'

'I'm Antonia Titwillow.'

'I know.'

'James and I are getting married in the New Year.'

Butty had never actually met her before. Eager to keep her away from the ribald comments of his team-mates, Fothers rarely invited his fiancée to watch him play. But they'd had glimpses of her at posh dinners and she was always on their captain's arm in press photographs. Never having seen her this close before, Butty was at first quite overwhelmed.

Lady Antonia Titwillow was a tall, graceful young lady, willowy, in fact, and with exquisite points of interest for Butty's wandering eye. She wore an elegant white dress with a gold brooch on the lapel. Diamond earrings shone through the long, lustrous fair hair which shimmered every time she tossed it. She was breathtaking. Butty's first thought was that she was completely wasted on Fothers. The England captain wouldn't know how to begin to sample the manifold delights of his thoroughbred fiancée. She deserved a more seasoned practitioner. Like Butty himself.

'Are you going to Karistan?' she asked.

'Hope so. Don't think we stop at Huddersfield.'

'What will you be doing out there?'

'Playing cricket.'

'Oh.'

'I'm not flying all that way just to sell programmes.'

'I thought that James told me you were omitted from

the team because of some serious breach of etiquette.'

'Her name was Mindy Hibbert.'

'James has such a high moral code.'

'And such a low opinion of me.'

'Not at all,' she said, laying a hand on his thigh. 'He spoke very well of you. Once. He said that you were unique. Not in so many words, perhaps, but that was the gist of it. Let me see if I can remember . . . Ah, yes. James said – "Thank God there's only one Kevin Sowerbutts!" Then he crossed himself.'

'Fothers . . . er, James and I have always got on well.'

She laughed tinnily and removed her hand. Butty warmed to her. Lady Antonia Titwillow was all woman underneath the silk underwear and the Benendon accent. The second leg of the flight might turn out to be even better than the first. When the champagne came, they clinked their glasses.

'To success in Karistan!' she said.

'We may need your good wishes.'

'I'm so glad you've been recalled to the team. Not that I know anything about cricket. Hockey was my game at school. The rules are so much easier to understand. When someone has the ball, you simply crack them on the shin with your stick.' She sipped the champagne. 'It was terrific fun!'

Butty was excited by this hint of well-bred brutality. He had a vision of Antonia in full flight, racing around a pitch and felling all who got in her way. She'd look very fetching in hockey kit. And out of it. Butty would never have believed he could feel so jealous of Fothers.

'What were you doing in Muscat?' he asked.

'I was there with Daddy.'

'Daddy?'

'We breed horses. We sold some to the Sultan. I had the most marvellous time at the Royal Stud. Do you know anything about horses, Kevin?'

'Yeah,' he said. 'Some run faster than others. I always seem to bet on the others.'

'I meant breeding. Do you know how it's done?'

'I think I can work it out.'

'Bloodstock is a world of its own. Highly complex.'

'Looks pretty straightforward to me.'

'The Sultan only buys the best. That's why Daddy was so thrilled when he chose us. We spent two days at the Royal Stud in Seeb.' She tossed her hair gaily. 'Since I'd got as far as Oman, I thought it might be a hoot to fly on to Karistan. It will give James a wonderful surprise.'

'He doesn't know you're on your way?'

'I wasn't supposed to come until Christmas.' Her face suddenly clouded. 'Gosh! I won't be in the way, will I?'

'Not a bit of it,' he assured her. 'From what I hear, he'll welcome you with open arms. England are in such a terrible state, you'll probably be asked to open the batting in the First Test.'

'That would be divine!'

She whinnied happily and he worked out her age from her teeth. Lady Antonia Titwillow was growing on him. In the fiancée stakes, she was a long way behind Barbara and he'd never think of saddling her for a permanent ride. Daddy wouldn't approve. But in the fillies' handicap, she'd be a joy to mount. Butty began to have ideas above his station. He crackled with electricity.

Antonia, too, felt the attraction of forbidden flesh.

'You're not at all as James described you,' she said.

'Oh?'

'He told me that you were unbearably uncouth.'

'Me? Never! I'm noted for my table manners.'

'James was just being snobbish. He looks down on anyone who didn't go to Harrow.' She finished her champagne. 'Where *did* you go, Kevin? Eton, Rugby, Marlborough?'

'Huddersfield Bisexual School.'

She wrinkled her nose. 'Is that in the north somewhere?'

'Between Luton and Inverness.'

'Foreign country to me.'

'Come and see us some time. I'll show you around.'

'*Would* you?' A radiant smile blossomed. 'That would be lovely! What should I wear?'

Butty laughed. Clothing didn't feature at all in his plans for her visit. As long as she brought the hockey stick.

'I'll give you a guided tour of Yorkshire and you can teach me the finer points of horse-breeding. Is it a deal?'

'Yes!' she said, whinnying merrily. 'Oh, I'm so glad that we met at last, Kevin. I just *knew* that we'd get on famously. I can't wait to tell James that we bumped into each other.'

'Neither can I.'

The limousine swept along a dusty road before turning into the drive of a mansion. Fothers was welcomed by Zaki Meero himself and taken through to the verandah. The England captain was still seething with polite rage. As soon as he sat down, Fothers uncorked the bottle of his ire and poured it out.

'Why on earth didn't you warn me, Zaki?' he demanded.

'Warn you?'

'About the President's XI. We were hoping for a gentle baptism and you throw that lot at us. I thought you told me that Karistan cricket still had a long way to go.'

'It does, James.'

'Then how come you beat the pants off us yesterday?'

'We didn't.'

'Well, it certainly felt as if you did!'

'Let me explain,' said Zaki patiently. 'Our President is a wonderful man. He has made Karistan what it is and designated cricket as our national game. But we are still some way behind the leading cricketing nations.'

'You could have fooled me, old chap!'

'I'm afraid that we had to, James. It was the only way to make sure that the President's XI won the game. We could not possibly lose in the presence of General Idi Ott. It would have been an insult to him. We had to compromise.'

'In what way?'

'The President's XI was an invitation team and so we scattered the invitations far and wide. We borrowed players from Sri Lanka, India, Pakistan, even Kenya. Only three of us were actually from Karistan.'

'That's a relief!'

'You'll never see eight of those players again.'

'Good.'

'From now on, you'll only face Karistan players.'

'A huge boulder has just been lifted off my back.'

'Apart from myself, the only home-grown cricketers in the President's XI were Inta Walliconi and Orin Logos.'

Fothers winced. 'The boulder is back in place again.'

'They're one-day specialists, James,' said Zaki. 'Neither of them has ever played a Test match. You caught them at their very peak yesterday.'

'I'll say! Orin even had Mick Mancini in a pickle. Dealer wasn't in the original team but we drafted him in when we lost three of our players. He can keep the fastest bowlers in the world at bay but Orin tied him in knots.'

'Orin is still young and untried.'

'I hope you've got nobody else like him tucked away.'

'No, James. In the next game, you'll see the true strength of Karistan cricket. Our teams will do their best to beat you, of course, but I suspect that you will out-gun us. Especially when Butty arrives.'

'How did you know that he was coming?'

'Our President told me. He knows everything.'

Fothers relaxed. The situation was not quite as calamitous as he'd feared. It might still be possible for the England team to redeem itself and for Fothers to bat himself triumphantly into the record books. A servant brought cooling drinks out to them. As he took a first sip of his pineapple juice, Fothers actually began to enjoy himself. He even allowed himself a moment to feast his eyes on the spectacular view of the Pindi Mountain Range. It was awesome.

Karistan was a country of great natural beauty. Its spell started to work on Fothers once again. Only one tiny seed of doubt lay at the back of his mind.

'We're still hearing these strange rumours, Zaki.'

'What about?'

'Shark Island.'

'I've heard nothing.'

'Some prisoners broke out of there.'

'Impossible!'

'Then where do these stories come from?'

'I don't know, James,' admitted Zaki. 'But I'd ignore them if I were you. Karistan has one of the most stable regimes in the world. You've seen that for yourself.'

'What I saw was an army protecting your President. He didn't have such a massive bodyguard when I was here before. What's going on, Zaki?'

'Nothing.'

'Is General Idi Ott under threat?'

'Only from his six wives,' he said with a laugh. 'Our President is first and foremost a soldier. He loves to have an army around him for show. That's all. He's also mad about English cricket, which is why you're the first team to be invited here. Rest assured of one thing. The President is here to stay. There isn't a whisper of opposition to him.'

'We heard a different tale.'

'Go on.'

'The men who escaped from Shark Island were political prisoners. Rebel leaders. Revolutionaries.'

'We have no revolutionaries, James.'

'Can you give me your word on that?'

'Yes,' said Zaki with obvious sincerity. 'Now stop worrying about something that doesn't even exist. Do what you came here to do. Show us the greatness of English cricket. And treat our lovely country like your own.'

General Idi Ott rose from the table and kissed each of his six wives in alphabetical order. It was the only way to avoid a domestic squabble. Individually, each of his spouses was a joy to behold and he relished his moments alone in bed with them. Collectively, they were a different matter. Rivalry brought out darker qualities and demarcation disputes were a daily problem. The alphabet was his salvation.

Blowing them a final kiss with both hands, he left the dining room and went out into the hall. Four uniformed soldiers were waiting to escort him to the barracks opposite the Presidential palace. His medals jingled as he kept in step with his quartet. When they went through the main gate, he was conducted across the courtyard until he came to a large tarpaulin draped over something low but bulky.

The guard beside it gave him a respectful salute.

'Let me see it,' said the President.

Taking a corner each of the tarpaulin, the members of the escort lifted it off to reveal the battered remains of the raft. Thick timbers had been crudely lashed together with creepers but the sea had pushed some of them apart. Deep cracks and heavy scoring on the bark showed that it had been buffeted by rocks, but the most satisfying clue for the President was the jagged bite which had been taken out of one of the timbers.

'Where was it found?' he demanded.

'Five miles out to sea, sir,' said the guard.

'No sign of them?'

'None at all.'

The President took one last look at the raft.

'The sharks had them,' he said with a grin. 'Tiki and Verukka were fools. They deserved their fate. Burn the raft and put the ashes in an urn. I'll keep them as a memento.'

TEN

Karistan's only airport was in the capital city of Aragusta. It lay near the southern end of the Pindi Mountain Range and prided itself on its modernity. Delighted that Butty was joining the tour, most of the team drove to the airport to give him a proper welcome. Dealer even acquired a bare-breasted lovely in a grass skirt with a spare garland of flowers for the belated tourist. Butty would appreciate that. He liked grass.

Fothers was reluctant to join the reception committee until Derek March reminded him that it was his duty to be there in order to stamp his authority on the whole team. Derek went along as well and Colonel Arthur Totter accompanied them. After a few days in the sun, his mottled legs had taken on an alarming redness but he made light of any discomfort. Old soldiers never complain. Except about young soldiers.

When the aircraft touched down on the runway and taxied to a halt, they were driven across the tarmac in a bus. They poured out and stood at the bottom of the gangway. The cabin door was open and the passengers came down the steps with their hand-luggage. The team waited with growing impatience.

'Come on, Butty,' urged Snatcher. 'Get a move on!'

'Are we sure he's *on* this plane?' asked Dealer.

'Should be. It's the only one today.'

'Unless he changed his mind about coming.'

'Butty? Miss out on a jamboree like this? Never!'

'Then where is he?'

'Still shagging one of the air hostesses, probably.'

The last of the passengers trickled down the runway and there was still no sign of Butty. Serious disquiet now spread through the team. Had he let them down? Got lost in Muscat? Bailed out in transit? Snatcher was about to board the aircraft in search of their missing friend when one of the cabin crew appeared at the top of the steps.

'Are you waiting for a Mr Sowerbutts?' she asked.

'Yes,' they chorused.

'He'll be down in a moment.'

'What's keeping him?' said Ben Jenkins.

'He's having difficulty with his luggage.'

Fothers turned to his uncle. 'Butty is pissed. What an example to set to the rest of the team! We brought him out here to play cricket not to get paralytic on the flight.' He stepped forward to take charge. 'I'll give him a rocket for this. I must have the highest standard of personal conduct from everyone. Moral turpitude will not be tolerated.'

'Here he comes,' announced the air hostess.

'Catch him when he falls,' joked Dealer.

'Leave him to me,' ordered Fothers. 'I'll handle this.'

But when Butty finally emerged, he was not reeling from too much alcohol. Responsibility had sobered him. Slung around his shoulders were two flight bags and a suit carrier. But it was the luggage in his arms which produced the raucous cheer from his team-mates.

Butty was carrying the inert body of a gorgeous woman in a white dress. He descended the steps with caution and gave his friends a grin of acknowledgement. Snatcher was green with envy.

'Trust old Butty. He knows how to pack for a tour.'

'Why didn't *I* bring one of those?' moaned Dealer.

'This is utterly disgraceful!' said Fothers, thrown into a moral frenzy. 'I will not have this lewd behaviour in my team. What on earth do you think you're doing, Butty? You can't bring one of your pick-ups here!'

'She's not my pick-up, Fothers – she's *yours*!'

'What?'

'Here. Take her.' He handed the body over to his captain. 'Say hello to your fiancée.'

'Antonia!' gulped Fothers.

'She said you'd be surprised.'

Fothers was petrified. 'What happened to her?'

'Too many glasses of champagne.'

'But what's she *doing* in Karistan?'

'Sleeping in her beloved's arms.'

'This is utterly disgraceful!' said Snatcher, mimicking his captain's voice. 'I will not have this lewd behaviour in my team. Drunken women, indeed! Moral turpitude of the worst order!'

Derisive laughter went up from the players and Fothers felt the egg all over his face again. There was worse to come. The others fell on Butty to give him a hero's welcome and the topless beauty bestowed a kiss of greeting on him before putting the garland of flowers around his neck. At that moment, Lady Antonia Titwillow opened her eyes and looked up into the face of the man who was holding her. A smile of joy lit up her features as she recognised him.

'James, darling! How are you?'

'How are *you*, Antonia? That's more to the point.'

'I feel wonderful. Had the most fascinating flight from Muscat. I met Kevin on the plane.'

'So I see,' said Fothers grimly.

'He told me *so* much about you, James. I was entranced.' As she came fully awake, a memory came flooding back. It put an unaccustomed sharpness into her voice. 'Entranced but peeved. Tell me about her yourself!' she snapped.

'Her?'

'The other woman in your life.'

'There is no other woman in my life, Antonia.'

99

'Yes, there is. Kevin mentioned her. She was at Heathrow to send you off with a farewell embrace.'

'Oh . . . her.'

'Fifi.'

The blush turned his face into a Belisha beacon. This was the kind of situation for which Harrow and Oxford had somehow failed to prepare him. He tried a casual laugh but it came out like a death rattle. Perspiration gushed.

Antonia suddenly weighed about two and a half tons.

Butty's arrival put zest back into the whole team. When he'd reclaimed his luggage, they piled into taxis and headed back to the hotel. Butty found himself squeezed between Snatcher and Des Toyovsky. Dealer sat beside the driver and threw in the occasional comment over his shoulder. The team had now moved to Port Lemmon on the south coast so it would take them the best part of an hour to get there. That gave the inquisitive Butty plenty of time to catch up on all the team news.

'Did the President's XI really clatter you?' he said.

'It was a massacre!' sighed Dealer. 'They made mincemeat of us. Their bowlers went through us like a dose of bleeding salts, then their batsmen kicked seven barrels of shit out of us. Right, Snatch?'

'Yes,' agreed the wicket-keeper. 'I didn't take one flaming ball behind the stumps. They hit everything that moved.'

'Those guys were pretty impressive,' said Des. 'But they had the crowd behind them and the President up there on the balcony. Big psychological advantage.'

'How many on the sick list?' asked Butty.

'Three,' said Dealer. 'Tombo flew home this morning with his foot in plaster but we've still got Olly Cromwell down with malaria, Wilton Rodger out with sinus trouble and Wanker Winslow nursing a sprained wrist.'

'I thought Wanker had dysentery.'

'He did, Butty. Recovered from that yesterday.'

'How did he sprain his wrist?'

'How do you think? Stick Wanker in bed for a couple of days with nothing to do and his hand wanders. Overdid it. Wrist fatigue set in. He's out for the next match.'

'Who's that against?'

'Port Lemmon. They're no great shakes, apparently.'

Snatcher groaned. 'That's what we thought about the President's XI. I'm never going to underestimate the other team again. It was humiliating.'

'Isn't there any *good* news?' said Butty.

'Yes, mate. You're it.'

'Something nice must have happened out here.'

'It did,' said Snatcher, brightening. 'She works at the Bueno Vista Hotel in Bukit. One of the chambermaids.'

'Tell him the hot news,' suggested Des. 'It only broke this morning. If I was in the team, I'd be really pumped up.'

'What are you on about?' said Butty.

'The Presidential decree.'

'Come again.'

'General Idi Ott was so thrilled with the opening fixture that he wants to reward the England team for their kindness in coming to Karistan.'

'So?'

'He's putting up two awards, Butty.'

'What for?'

'Best Bowler on the Tour – and Best Batsman.'

'How much are we talking?'

'Twenty-five grand,' said Dealer. 'Worth winning.'

Butty's interest quickened at once. 'Fan-bloody-tastic! That's the nicest thing I've heard since Antonia told me about her sex life with Fothers.'

'Fothers has a sex life?' said Snatcher in disbelief.

'Only when he's not playing cricket. And he always is.

Says it would only sap his vitals and cost him precious runs. Has to keep himself pure. Antonia's being horrendously under-fucked.'

'Is that what she told you?'

'Her phrase was "going through a period of inter-personal neglect" but it comes to the same thing. She's throbbing with frustration. Anyway, come back to this money. My fingers are all a-tingle. Who's in the lead for the Bowling Award?'

'Nobody,' said Dealer. 'We didn't take a single wicket.'

'What about the Batting Award? You? Fothers?'

'Big Ben.'

Butty was incredulous. 'You're having me on, Dealer!'

'True, old son. Big Ben top-scored with 41.'

'Are those runs or farts?'

'Both. But he's the man to catch.'

'Twenty-five thousand quid!' mused Butty. 'That'd come in real handy just now. I'm a bit strapped.' He chuckled and shook his garland of flowers. 'I have the feeling that this is going to be one hell of a bloody good tour.'

'It is now, Butty. We've got a team.'

'No, Dealer,' said Snatcher. 'We've got something even more important now Butty's here. Team spirit.'

They sang all the way back to the hotel.

The three-day game against Port Lemmon restored their faith in themselves as cricketers and gave the press an all too rare opportunity to say something pleasant about them for once. Port Lemmon were a competent side but only on a level with an English county second XI. Put in to bat for the first innings, they struggled manfully to reach 163 all out.

Fothers and Dealer really came into their own against tame bowling. Their opening stand was worth 114 and it was only halted by a bizarre umpiring decision, which saw

Fothers dismissed LBW when the ball had hit his midriff. He accepted the decision like a gentleman and strode back to the pavilion in silence. His sparkling 70 put him decisively ahead in the chase for the Best Batsman Award.

Though still suffering from jet-lag, Butty had bagged a couple of wickets. He was now looking forward to opening his shoulders and hitting some boundaries. Port Lemmon were very eager in the field but there were several gaps that could be exploited. Butty sat on the balcony, padded up and ready for action. When the fifth wicket fell, he went charging down the steps to get on the field.

Fothers was blocking the door of the pavilion.

'Forget it, Butty,' he said. 'I've just declared.'

'But I haven't had a knock yet.'

'You don't need to, old chap. 321 for 5 is a plenty big enough target for this shower. No point in grinding on just for the sake of it.'

'We need all the batting practice we can get.'

'It's your bowling you need to work on. You were a bit sluggish in their first innings. Take your pads off.'

'I want to bat, Fothers!'

'Too late. I've signalled to the umpires.'

'Can't I just have a swing until close of play?'

'No chance,' said Fothers, peremptorily. 'If we declare now, we'll have twenty minutes to bowl at them. Might get a couple of quick wickets.'

Butty raged but his captain held fast. England had declared and Port Lemmon were put in to bat for their second innings. It was only at close of play that Butty got an insight into the strategy which had been used against him. Des Toyovsky might know little about the mysteries of cricket but he could recognise political manoeuvring.

Over a drink in the bar, he took Butty to one side.

'Mind if I make a comment?' he said diffidently.

'As many as you like.'

'I'm not trying to stir up trouble, mind you.'

'That's okay, Des.'

'I don't think Fothers did you any favours out there.'

'He never bloody well does.'

'All the guys in the press box said the same. You bowled from the wrong end. And as soon as you built up any real momentum, Fothers took you off.'

'I know. I complained like mad.'

'Stop, start. Stop, start. Stop, start. It was almost as if he didn't want you to bowl at your best. It must've played havoc with your concentration.'

'It did, Des. I still got two, though.' He drained his glass and put it on the table. 'It's not the bowling that annoyed me. It was the declaration.'

'That was deliberate.'

'Yeah. Getting his revenge for what I told Antonia.'

'I don't think she comes into this at all, Butty.'

'Then what does?'

'Twenty-five thousand pounds.'

'The Best Batsman Award?'

'Fothers wants it. You're his biggest rival.'

'But I was brought out here as a bowler to replace Tombo. The highest I'll go up the order is number six.'

'If you were the last man in, you'd still be a threat to Fothers. He'll never forgive you for what you did to him in that Benson and Hedges Final.'

'One of the reasons he didn't pick me for the tour.'

'I like the guy,' said Des seriously. 'Great player. Lot of good qualities. Full of honest endeavour. But he worships the game. Cricket is his life-blood. It flows through his veins.'

'Eh?'

'The way he sees it, Kevin Sowerbutts is a vampire. That's why he'll do everything to hold you back. So that you don't sink your teeth into his neck.'

Des Toyovsky's comments were all the more persuasive for being delivered in a quiet, friendly voice. When the

American took his leave, Butty was given much to reflect upon. He came to a firm decision. Big Ben Jenkins was the first to hear about it.

'You bowled well today, Butty,' he said, ambling up.

'I'm still rusty, Ben. You were much better. Hardly a stray ball. You deserved your five wickets.'

'I'll enjoy it while I can.'

'It?'

'My lead, boyo. Best Bowler. I had hopes of the twenty-five thousand quid until you showed up. No contest now. It's yours for the taking.'

'Don't give up, Ben. You're still in with a shout.'

'Not if you set your mind on it, Butty.'

'But I'm not concentrating on the Best Bowling Award.'

'You're not?' Big Ben's moon face was puckered with surprise. 'Are you saying you're not after the award?'

'Oh, I'm after it, Ben. But it's not my only target.'

'I'm baffled, man.'

'Don't be. I've just made a vow. The Best Batsman Award carries twenty-five grand as well.' He patted the Welshman on the shoulder. 'I'm going to win *both* of them!'

When the woman brought in the bowl of water, Tiki was slowly unwrapping the blood-stained bandage. She winced when she saw the deep gash on Verukka's arm. The wounded man was lying on a mattress in the cellar of the house. Pain brought him briefly awake and he let out a moan.

'He needs a doctor, Tiki,' she said in alarm.

'He's got one – me.'

'Verukka should be in hospital.'

'They'd ship him straight back to Shark Island in chains. And I'd go with him. We have to lie low, Pikso. It's our only hope. They may still be searching for us.'

'The patrols have eased off,' she said.

'We stay in hiding nevertheless. When Verukka is well enough to move, we'll make our way to the mountains to join the others.'

'There are not many of us left, Tiki.'

'There are enough.'

Pikso was a short, thin woman whose attractive face had been disfigured by deep suffering and loss. Tiki was her younger brother and she was delighted to see him again but she knew only too well the risks she was taking in hiding him. On the night of the escape, hers had been the first house to be searched. She prayed that the soldiers would not come back again now that she was harbouring fugitives.

Disillusion had taken a heavy toll.

'What is the point?' she asked sadly. 'We can never win.'

'We must, Pikso. For the sake of freedom.'

'The government is too strong. We are too weak.'

'In numbers, perhaps. But not in spirit.'

'Most of our members are still locked up in prison.'

'Verukka and I are not. We dared to believe.'

'The two of you cannot take on the whole army.'

'We do not need to,' said Tiki, as he bathed the wound. 'If we kill the President, we remove his administration. One man. That is an easy enough target.'

'But you will never get near him,' she sighed. 'He is closely guarded at all times. Even his six wives are armed. He spends most of his time inside the Presidential palace. You'd never get inside that.'

'He has to come out sooner or later.'

'The only time he has stirred outside the palace recently was to watch a cricket match. You know how mad the President is about cricket.'

Tiki looked up and smiled for the first time.

'Cricket?'

ELEVEN

After a spirited opening stand of 94, the Port Lemmon
batting collapsed in the second innings. A three-day game
was over by the second afternoon and the England team
were able to pride themselves on their achievement.
They'd won in style by an innings and 13 runs. Though
Butty was only given a few overs to bowl, he collected four
wickets from the tail-enders and seemed to have shaken off
all the lingering effects of jet-lag. Lady Antonia Titwillow
watched him through binoculars from the stand and
applauded excitedly when he clean-bowled one batsman
and shattered the middle wicket into tiny pieces.

After the game, Fothers hustled her back to the hotel.
He was anxious to keep her away from the rest of the
players.

'He's such a magnificent animal!' she cooed.

'Who is?'

'Kevin Sowerbutts.'

'He's an animal. I agree about that, Antonia.'

'Such power. Such pace. Such delicious aggression.'

'But such a complete lack of finesse,' said Fothers with
disdain. 'That's what annoys me about Butty. He's too
rough and ready. Cricket is a game of elegance. He
plays it as if he's brawling in a pub. No notion of the finer
points.'

'I liked him,' she admitted.

'Antonia!'

'Not as much as you, darling. You're the best. James
Henry Fotheringhay is a pure thoroughbred whereas Kevin
Sowerbutts is only a mongrel. But he has such throbbing

energy. He reminds me of a stallion I saw at the Royal Stud in Oman. Splendid beast!'

'I want to forget all about Butty,' he said testily.

'Those rippling haunches of his!'

'Antonia – please!'

'I felt almost jealous of those mares.'

She gave a whinny of arousal and put a hand on his arm. They were alone on the hotel verandah while the rest of the team were still celebrating back at the cricket pavilion. The brisk victory over mediocre opposition had given them an unexpected day off. Lady Antonia Titwillow had ideas of how it could best be enjoyed.

'Why don't we go off somewhere tomorrow?' she gushed.

'Off?'

'Just the two of us, James. You've told me so much about the beauties of Karistan. Show some of them to me.'

'I will, Antonia,' he promised. 'When the time is ripe.'

'It can't be any riper than tomorrow.'

'Other priorities beckon.'

'Over me? I'm your fiancée.'

'I know and I'm delighted with that state of affairs. But I wasn't really expecting you until Christmas and you've rather thrown me into disarray.'

'Don't you *want* me here, James?'

'Of course.'

'Then why don't you prove it?'

'Prove it?'

'Yes,' she chided. 'According to the players, you showed more passion towards Fifi than you ever show towards me.'

'I explained that to you. Fifi was an inflatable doll.'

'Perhaps that's what you prefer.'

'Antonia!'

'Something you can just take out of your cricket bag for five minutes of wild abandon now and again.'

'Fifi was planted on me.'

'Was she?'

'I swear it! I love a real woman, Antonia. You.'

She kissed him on the cheek and snuggled up to him.

'Why don't we go up to my room, James?'

'Now?'

'I want to show you my snaps of the Royal Stud.'

'Another time.'

'Tonight?' She gave a titter. 'That would be much more romantic. I'll knot some sheets together and hang them from the balcony. You can climb up in the dead of night like a secret lover to take me in the darkness.'

'I need my sleep, Antonia.'

'Have it beside me. Afterwards.'

'I'm sharing a room with Uncle Derek.'

'Wouldn't you rather be in bed with me?'

'Yes, but it's not . . . convenient. The essence of these things is timing. Cricket must come first. You know how important this tour is to me. And to you. Our whole future depends on how well I perform.'

Antonia sighed a familiar sigh. 'If you ever do!'

Celebrations continued at the cricket pavilion until well into the evening. The Port Lemmon team were affable hosts and mixed easily with their guests, congratulating them on their win and seeking advice from players whom they clearly thought of as ideal role models for aspiring cricketers. Dealer was asked how he'd perfected his stone-wall technique. Snatcher was questioned about the art of stumping – he'd whipped off the bails like greased lightning to dismiss the Port Lemmon captain – and Big Ben Edwards was asked what inspired him as a fast bowler.

'Chapel,' he told them.

'Greg or Ian?' asked one of the Port Lemmons.

'Welsh Baptist.'

They were astounded to hear that Big Ben's fire was stoked by the minister of his local chapel back home in Pontypridd. Big Ben followed the man's advice religiously.

It was the first time on the tour when the England players really mixed socially with the press corps. The players had taken a veritable pounding in print after their defeat at the hands of the President's XI but they'd put that behind them. Cricket correspondents mingled freely with the team to give their opinions and seek quotable quotes.

Butty was in his element, downing pints as soon as they were put into his hand and scattering his trenchant opinions like handfuls of brass tacks. Darren Grubb of the *Daily Comet* joined in the unofficial press conference.

'Sum up English cricket in one word, Butty,' he said.

'Crap!'

'What's wrong with it?'

'What isn't?' said Butty. 'The people who run the game couldn't organise a hard-on in a brothel.'

'What would you do if you were in charge?'

'Clear out the whole bleeding lot of 'em.'

'Including Colonel Totter?'

'He'd be the first to go.'

'Can I quote you on that?'

'No,' said Des Toyovsky, stepping in quickly. 'Kevin is speaking strictly off the record. It's unfair to quote him.'

Darren Grubb smirked. He was a fat, self-satisfied man in his forties with thinning hair above a bulbous forehead. He loved being unfair to people. It sold more copies of his newspaper. The cricket correspondents could be harsh but at least they confined their strictures to events on the pitch. Grubb had no time for the game itself. He was the leading feature-writer with the most disreputable tabloid in Britain, a specialist muckraker with a nose for the sensational exposé.

110

Now that Butty was tanked up, Grubb could probe at him.

'Why weren't you picked for this tour?'

'No comment,' said Des, trying to shield his friend.

'Let Butty answer for himself.'

'He doesn't want to, Darren.'

'Yes, I do,' said Butty, scorning danger. 'The selectors are a bunch of turds. That's why I wasn't in the original list of sixteen. They wouldn't know a real cricketer if he bit them on the arse.'

'What would you like to do to the selectors?'

'Send 'em back to the Jurassic Park to graze with the other dinosaurs. They're past it.'

'Fothers isn't past it,' taunted Grubb. 'And he helped to select the team. Would you call him a dinosaur?'

'He's more of a frigging giraffe.'

'A giraffe?'

'Keeps his nose about ten feet above the rest of us.'

'How do you rate him as captain?'

Des dived in again. 'Now, that really is an unjust question. Kevin is bound by ties of loyalty.'

'Who is?' said Butty. 'Fothers has never been loyal to me. The only loyalty he's ever shown is to Uncle Derek. How do I rate him? On a scale of one to ten, I'd give him minus three. Fothers couldn't captain a tiddlywinks team.'

Grubb's eyes gleamed behind his horn-rimmed glasses. He could already see his headline. BUTTY SLAMS ENGLAND CAPTAIN. All the Yorkshireman needed was a little more prodding and he'd say something even more irresponsible.

'Who *should* be the skipper, Butty?'

'Me!'

'Why?'

'Because I'd send the lads out breathing fire. They'd never have lost that first game if I'd been there. We'd have eaten the President's Pissing XI for breakfast.'

'What about the social side of the tour?'

'There'd be more of it under me,' said Butty as his tongue ran away with him. 'Players need to let their hair down when they're off the pitch. I'd show 'em how to relax and have fun. Christ! That's what we're in Karistan for, isn't it? Get runs, get wickets, get pissed and get laid.'

Darren Grubb had his story. He went off to write it.

'That was a mistake, Kevin,' warned Des Toyovsky. 'When that guy is around, you should button your lip. Grubb is the grubbiest skunk I ever met.'

'He can't hurt me,' said Butty airily.

'He already has.'

'Eh?'

'Who got the first pictures of you and Mindy Hibbert in that Volvo Estate? The *Comet*. Darren Grubb really did a demolition job on you. He's a vulture.'

'I got to Karistan in spite of the little sod.'

'Yes,' agreed Des. 'But I want to keep you here. So do the team. Shoot your mouth off like that and you'll be flying back to Huddersfield.'

Butty waved a dismissive hand and guzzled more beer.

'Never, Des. They can't touch me now.'

It was twenty-four hours before the next morning's edition of the *Daily Comet* reached Karistan. It exploded like a delayed-action bomb. Up in his hotel room, Fothers was frothing at the mouth.

'I want Butty sent back home in disgrace!'

'Now, calm down,' said Derek March. 'We mustn't do anything too hasty. It might besmirch our image.'

'What image?' howled Fothers, picking up a copy of the newspaper. 'Look at this headline. BUTTY'S REMEDY FOR ENGLISH CRICKET. DRINK, SEX AND A NEW CAPTAIN. I won't stand for it, Uncle Derek. He's gone too far this time.'

'He'll be severely reprimanded, don't worry.'

'Reprimanded? He should be off this island today.'

'Don't over-react, James.'

'What am I supposed to do? Agree with him?'

'Of course not. We just have to mount a damage limitation campaign. I've told the rest of the press that we have no comment to make.'

'No comment? When Butty rubbishes my whole career?'

'Rise above it in public.'

'He can't get away with this.'

'He won't, James. I've ordered him to come up here to our room at once. He'll be here at any minute. This is the place to settle any differences. In private.' He took another glance at the headline, then quivered. 'Last thing we want to get into is a slanging match in the press.'

'I don't want him in my team, Uncle Derek.'

'Your opinion is noted.'

'I'm the captain of England.'

'And I'm the team manager,' reminded Derek, pulling rank for once. 'I have to consider what's best for the entire squad and there's no gainsaying the fact that they've cheered up amazingly since Butty joined us. He's put colour in their cheeks.'

'It's a cricket tour, not a stag party.'

'When he's around, it's a bit of both.' There was a tap on the door. 'That's him. Now, let me handle this. Try to maintain a dignified calm.'

Fothers sank resentfully into an armchair. His pride had been severely wounded and he wanted reparation. Derek was equally furious but foresaw worse publicity if they expelled Butty. Though it was a blistering hot day, they had put on their team blazers and flannels for the disciplinary hearing. Even in the air conditioning, they were sweating.

'Wake the Colonel up,' said Derek. 'We need him.'

Fothers nudged Colonel Arthur Totter, who was snoring

in the other armchair. He came awake with a start and waved a fist.

'Hear, hear, Mr Chairman!' he shouted.

'We haven't started yet, Colonel.'

'Oh. I see.'

There was a louder bang on the door. Derek sat on an upright chair between his two colleagues so that they formed a more imposing tribunal.

'Come in!' he called.

The door opened and Butty strolled in with an amiable grin on his face. He was wearing a Hawaiian shirt, striped shorts and bright red espadrilles. When he saw them lined up together, he gave an irreverent chuckle.

'You look like Rag, Tag and Bobtail.'

'This is a meeting of the highest importance,' said Derek with even more than his usual pomposity.

'As long as it doesn't last too long. The lads are waiting for me to go scuba diving with them.'

'This is not a holiday, Butty! Sit down, please.'

The visitor shrugged and perched on an upright chair. Derek lifted the offending newspaper and waved it in the air.

'It's about this abominable story,' he said.

'Wouldn't have thought you'd read the *Comet*,' joked Butty. 'It's a bum and titty rag. I'd have thought the *Financial Times* would be more your line. Or the *Baldies' Weekly*.'

'You should never have given this interview, Butty.'

'Hear, hear, Mr Chairman!' said the Colonel loyally.

'All comments to the press must come through us. It's the only way to stop this kind of fiasco.'

'Pay no attention to it, Derek,' said Butty cheerily. 'Darren Grubb is a toad. He invented that crap. I didn't give him an interview and I never said what he claimed.'

'There were witnesses,' argued Fothers.

'Eh?'

'Other journalists. They heard you sounding off.'

'It was probably Big Ben, dropping another one. We must stop the hotel feeding him on prunes.'

'Don't try to wriggle out of this, Butty,' said Derek. 'You got drunk and opened your big mouth again.' He flung the paper down. 'This is the result. I've had every member of the Test and County Cricket Board ringing me up from England to chew my ear off. They're demanding action.'

'Hear, hear, Mr Chairman!' said the Colonel.

'James wants you flown back home.'

'I've changed my mind,' said Fothers. 'He should be cast adrift in an open boat with nothing but a compass and a copy of the *Daily Comet*.'

Butty grinned. 'It'd come in useful as shit paper.'

'You've dragged the whole team down into the mire.'

'Come off it, Fothers,' said Butty. 'All I did was have a bit of a beef. Every player does that from time to time.'

'But they don't all blacken the good name of English cricket,' insisted Derek. 'You're a complete bounder, man!'

'In my day,' said the Colonel sternly, 'you'd have been horse-whipped.'

'When *was* your day, Colonel?' asked Butty politely. 'Was it before the First World War? Or the Crimean?'

'Don't mock your elders and betters,' said Derek.

'Then don't make such a song and dance about nothing.'

'You might at least apologise!' snarled Fothers.

'Who to?'

'Me, for a start. I'm your captain.'

'And to me,' added Derek. 'I'm your team manager.'

'I demand an apology as well,' said the Colonel. 'In my day, you'd have been court-martialled for insubordination.'

Butty bit back a cheeky reply and spread his arms in apology. It was the only way he would get any scuba diving in. It was time to toe the line for once.

'Look, I'm sorry,' he said. 'Maybe I did go over the top a bit. Grubb had no right to print that guff. I'll flatten the

115

little bastard when I see him. No offence intended. Why don't we all kiss and make up?'

The Colonel was scandalised. 'Kissing in the ranks? Strictly against regimental tradition. When we caught two subalterns at it, they were stripped bare and flogged.' He remembered a significant detail. 'They were bare already, as it happens, so we just flogged them.'

Butty stood up. 'Can I go now?'

'No!' yelled Fothers. 'You haven't heard our verdict. There has to be a punishment to fit this crime. I know what mine would be but I've been overruled.'

'So the final decision rests with me,' said Derek with judicial ponderousness. 'After taking everything into account, I am going to impose a stiff fine on you, Butty.'

'You can't do that!' protested Butty.

'I can and I will. To encourage the others, we're making an example of you. The fine will be five hundred pounds.'

Butty was stung. 'You vicious swine!'

'Six hundred.'

'You bastard, Derek!'

'Seven.'

'Turd!'

'Eight.'

'Tosser!'

'Nine.'

'You malignant, cross-eyed, shit-faced old fuck-wit!'

'One thousand pounds!' decreed the other, rising from his seat like an auctioneer. 'I can go higher if you like.'

Butty took a deep breath and tried to rein in his temper. 'I'll pay you when I win the Presidential bounty.'

'The Best Bowler Award?' asked Fothers.

'And the Best Batsman Award,' boasted Butty. 'What's a thousand quid out of fifty?' He strode to the door and flung it open before turning back with a grin. 'By the way, you can't send me back to England even if you want to.'

'Why not?' asked Fothers.

'Because I have to stay in Karistan.'

'Who says so?'

'President Idi Ott. Sent me a personal invitation.'

'I don't believe you.'

'It's true, Fothers,' said Butty. 'He thinks I'm the greatest cricketer in the western hemisphere. Wants to spend some time with me. So he's asked me to play golf with him on Sunday.' His grin broadened. 'I'm here by Presidential decree. General Idi Ott wants me to make myself at home.'

He breezed out and left them all open-mouthed.

'Hear, hear, Mr Chairman,' wheezed the Colonel.

TWELVE

The one-day match against Western Province provided the tourists with a stiffer challenge than Port Lemmon had been able to mount. Karistan was divided by the Pindi Mountain Range into two provinces. Players from every team to the west of the mountains were thus eligible. England were not pleased to see that the team would be captained by Zaki Meero and would contain the demon bowler, Orin Logos. They were two extremely good reasons to prepare carefully for the encounter.

Butty was not picked for the game but another bout of amoebic dysentery struck. Instead of serving the Lord by bowling his seamers, Big Ben spent the day on the toilet with a copy of the *Baptist News* to keep his mind on higher things. Only Butty could adequately fill the gap and Fothers had to bow to pressure from the rest of the team. What irked the captain most was the fact that Antonia also urged him to include the Yorkshireman.

Fothers was disturbed. His fiancée's interest in the coarse and lecherous Butty was highly uncharacteristic of her. When they had first met at a Hunt Ball, he had been struck by her aristocratic mien and sense of decorum. Antonia was a superior being. A fit companion for Fothers himself. She would not even have allowed Butty to hold her stirrup, still less carouse with him on a flight from Muscat. Yet she was now exhibiting a weird curiosity about him. What *had* got into her?

Butty's own curiosity centred on Western Province.

'How fast is this Orin bloke?' he asked.

'Like a rocket,' warned Snatcher Smart. 'He got past

Dealer's bat a dozen times and not many bowlers do that.'

'He's twice as fast as you, Butty,' sneered Penny Coyne.

'How would you know?' countered Butty. 'You've never managed to see one of my deliveries when you're at the crease. I could bamboozle you if I bowled ping pong balls.'

'You're as slow as shit!'

'Then we've got something in common at last.'

'Don't you believe it.'

'You only came on tour to make up the number, Penny.'

'At least I was their first choice.'

'First choice prick!'

'Say that again!' said Penny, squaring up to him. 'I dare you. Go on.'

'Aw, fuck off back to Lancashire and eat your hot-pot!'

'Yorkshire bloody tyke!'

'Piss off, Penny!'

Dealer and Snatcher had to hold the two of them apart. They were snarling at each other with murder in their eyes. Fothers came over to give them both a verbal rap over the knuckles. He hated any friction in the changing room.

'Save the fisticuffs for the Roses Match.'

'He may not live that long,' said Butty.

'You're playing for England now,' asserted Fothers. 'Put aside your narrow county prejudices. We've no room for them. Yorkshire and Lancashire don't exist over here. Understand? Now, shake hands like gentlemen.'

They preferred to glower at each other like a pair of fighting cocks. Butty had never liked or got on with Penny Coyne. Their mutual antagonism went well beyond rivalry. In the best interests of the team, it was shelved for now. But it was certainly not forgotten. A head-on collision was merely postponed rather than cancelled.

Butty decided to laugh off the confrontation.

'Slow as shit, am I?' he said. 'If it's the stuff that Big

Ben is producing, I'm twice as fast as you. It's coming out of his arse like mortar shells. I know. I share a room with him. We could sell Big Ben to the Karistan Army if there wasn't a ban on chemical warfare.'

The crude banter defused the momentary tension.

Fothers won the toss and put Western Province in to bat. The match was being played at Yanis, a small town to the north-west of Karistan. The bright sunshine which had blessed every day of their visit so far was once again laid on. A sizeable crowd turned up at the ground, which was in immaculate condition for the tourists. Tribesmen from the surrounding area rubbed shoulders with townees. Cricket blended everyone together. Lady Antonia Titwillow sat with Des Toyovsky in the press box, the two of them drawn to each other by a mutual admiration of Butty and by shared ignorance of the game.

Butty took the field with the wicket-keeper.

'Zaki is the danger man,' he said. 'I had a couple of tussles with him when he played for Essex.'

'He's come on a lot since them,' cautioned Snatcher. 'Very strong off his pads. Like a sun-burned version of Fothers only without the snobbery. Zaki's class. Anything loose will be sent straight to the boundary.'

'Then I'll have to concentrate hard.'

'Line and length, Butty. Those are the secrets.'

'Just like shagging.'

In the interests of quick scoring, Orin Logos again opened the innings with his captain. They were both in commanding form and Butty was shaken when they took eleven off his first over. It was not the kind of indignity he was used to and it spurred him on. He persevered and managed to pin them down for a while but they continued to score freely at the other end. Penny Coyne was their chief victim. Butty rubbed salt in his wounds.

'You're supposed to bowl *at* the wickets, Penny.'

'Big joke!'

'You after a knighthood or something?'

'A knighthood?'

'For your charity work among Karistan cricketers. You've been giving them free runs by the fucking handful.'

'Cobblers!'

After a robust half-century, Orin fell to a yorker from Butty and the partnership was broken. Two more wickets soon followed and England seemed to be getting on top. Zaki Meero responded with some brilliant attacking strokes. He treated Ricky Ryman's spin with scorn, taking nineteen off one over, then he helped himself to three successive fours off the medium pace of Peebee Brooksby. He carried his bat for the whole innings, scoring 137 out of a total of 269 runs.

It was not an impossible target and England began well. Fothers provided the flashing boundaries while Dealer's score advanced by single after careful single, as if he were building a house of cards. The stand was worth fifty when Fothers made a rare lapse and snicked a ball to third slip. From that point on, the tide seemed to turn. Western Province set an attacking field and crowded the bat.

Having achieved the breakthrough, Orin sent the next batsman back to the pavilion for a duck. When he'd finished his stint, the spinners began to mesmerise the England batsmen. Dealer remained at the crease but his scoring rate was modest. Three more wickets tumbled and England were still 150 runs short of the Western Province.

It was Butty's turn at last. Selecting his heaviest bat, he trotted down the pavilion steps to the biggest cheer of the day. Karistan cricket fans had been crushed when he was not selected for the tour because his exploits on pitches around the world had given him almost mythic status. National rejoicing accompanied the news that he was to join the tour.

They'd already watched him bowl and take four wickets

but it was Butty's batting that they really wanted to see. When he held the bat in each hand in turn, rotating his arm like a propeller to loosen up, they sensed that he was in a pugnacious mood.

Dealer was waiting for him between the wickets.

'These two are buggers to score off,' he said.

'We'll see about that.'

'The leg-spinner is the real problem. Watch out for his googly. Fooled me twice.'

Butty walked to the crease and asked for middle and leg from the umpire. When he checked the field placing, his eye travelled to the bright blue dress and wide-brimmed sun hat in the centre of the press box. Lady Antonia Titwillow blew him a kiss of encouragement. It was all he needed to light his touch-paper. When he took his stance, he was smouldering.

Western Province soon recoiled from the explosion.

'By Jove!' said the Colonel. 'Where did that one go?'

'Out of the ground,' said Derek March.

'Another six?'

'His third.'

'Who is this young fellow?'

'Kevin Sowerbutts of Yorkshire.'

'Promising batsman. We must nurture him.'

'This is the man you wanted court-martialled and flogged,' said Derek with mild irony. 'Aren't you grateful we didn't send him back to England?'

'Out of the question. He's the lynchpin of our side.'

'I know. That's the problem.'

Derek was sitting on the balcony between a euphoric Colonel Arthur Totter and a muted James Henry Fotheringhay. Desperate to win the game, Fothers wished it might be by any route other than the dazzling talent of Butty. The bellicose exhibition by the Yorkshireman eclipsed his own fine innings completely. The one pleasing aspect of it all was that Butty's systematic destruction of the two spinners encouraged Dealer to come out of his shell at long last. He, too, accelerated the scoring.

The cavalier attitude which brought him a quick-fire 87 also ensured Butty's downfall. Advancing down the pitch to lambast another ball, he missed it completely and was stumped by swift gloves. He was angry with himself but he'd already done enough to put victory firmly within England's grasp. As he left the field to a standing ovation, he looked up at the press box again. Antonia was dancing on her toes and waving her arms in ecstasy. Her own touch-paper had been ignited.

The sporting Western Province XI clapped him off the field and his team-mates gave him a rapturous reception. But the most enthusiastic applause did not come from the players. Nor did it come from the bright blue dress in the press box. It came from the young man at the very back of the stand. Face shining in wonder and eyes glistening with joy, he clapped his hands until his palms were sore.

Tiki had never seen such extraordinary power before. Butty's performance had set his blood racing. Disguised in the robes of the north-western tribesman, he had no fear that he might be recognised as the rebel leader who'd escaped from Shark Island. All eyes were on the pitch. While Butty was in action, Tiki was completely invisible.

He turned to Verukka, who sat beside him with his arm in a sling. Pain from his wound had vanished completely while Verukka was anaesthetised by the cricketing blitz-krieg known as Kevin Sowerbutts. He shook his head in awe.

'What a man!' he said.

'What a cricketer!' admired Tiki, 'No wonder our black-hearted President admires him so.'

'If only we could have such a person on our side!'

'We do, Verukka. We do.'

* * *

President Idi Ott ran the gauntlet of alphabetical kisses before leaving his wives to finish their breakfast. As soon as he was outside the door, the bickering and accusation began in his wake. He was grateful that there were only six of them. A day of rest was the one thing he had borrowed from the Christian calendar and it was the wisest decision he'd ever made. Number Six was a demanding lover on Saturday nights. Even his superlative strength was tested. A day of recovery was mandatory.

The captain of his bodyguard was waiting for him.

'They are at the clubhouse, sir,' he said.

'Good. We must not keep them waiting.'

'Everything is in readiness.'

'It had better be or heads will roll.'

They left the palace and climbed into the Presidential Rolls Royce. Flanked by two armoured cars, it purred on its way.

'He is a fine golfer, I hear,' said the President.

'The best in the team.'

'Does he know the rule?'

'His caddie does.'

'I must win. Whatever happens.'

General Idi Ott was wearing a pair of bright yellow golf trousers, a blue T-shirt and a red Pringle sweater on which a cunning seamstress had embroidered exact replicas of the medals which adorned his uniform. Even on a golf course, he exuded military prowess. His companion was in more conventional golf wear, though few players on the professional circuit carried such a large revolver on their hip.

The course was only ten minutes from the palace. Butty was waiting outside the clubhouse with Des Toyovsky and their caddie, a taciturn man dressed entirely in black. Des opted for fairly neutral golf wear, while Butty chose flamboyant check trousers, white shoes and purple and gold shirt. The President recognised his hero at once and swept down on him to pump Butty's hand.

'Welcome to St Andrews!' he said effusively.

'Thank you, sir,' said Butty. 'Great course.'

'Modelled on the Royal and Ancient. I tried to buy and have it transplanted here but they refused. So I had my own version built in Karistan.' He turned to smile at Des. 'Now, who have you got with you?'

'This is Des Toyovsky,' introduced Butty. 'He's a good friend of mine.'

'Then he is my honoured guest,' said the beaming President as he exchanged a handshake. 'Welcome, Mr Toyovsky.'

'Pleasure's mine, sir. Privileged to be here.'

As soon as Des spoke, the presidential smile vanished. The big, black, judgemental eyes narrowed suspiciously.

'You are an *American*?'

'I guess so.'

'I had not realised that.'

'You told me to bring a partner,' said Butty, sensing the discomfort. 'There's nobody I enjoy a round of golf with more than Des. Good player. Knocks spots off me.'

The President made an effort to overcome his distaste.

'I am glad to see him,' he said coldly. 'And now you must meet my partner. This is Captain Jammu.'

After more handshakes, they moved across to two waiting golf carts. Each was driven by the respective caddies. Butty had already noted that the man assigned to help him and Des around the course had a telltale bulge around his calf. The other caddie also carried a concealed weapon.

The President insisted on travelling with Butty.

'You batted well yesterday,' he said as the golf cart headed for the first tee. 'Fabulous cricket!'

'But you weren't there to see it.'

'I had a video made of the whole game.'

'Did you? I didn't spot any cameras.'

'They were there, Kevin. I like cricket.'

Butty glanced over his shoulder. 'You don't seem to have the same fondness for Yanks.'

'They have not been allies of this country. We are part of the British Commonwealth – they are not. I have nothing against Mr Toyovsky personally. But I do not trust America.'

'Des is a good lad.'

'Your word is enough.'

When they reached the first tee, the visitors realised that everything had to be on their host's terms. He was a competent golfer with a sound short game but both Butty and Des were better. At least, they would have been had they been allowed to play their normal games during the fourball.

But their caddie sabotaged them at every stage. He gave the wrong advice about shots, the wrong clubs and the wrong yardages. The President, by contrast, had the most enormous assistance both from his caddie and from unseen hands. Drives which seemed unimpressive from the tee turned out to have gone a hundred yards further on when they got there. Approach shots which landed in bunkers were miraculously close to the hole as they reached the green. The President was unbeatable.

Des took it in his stride but the competitive streak in Butty soon came out. After losing the first five holes to the subsidised golf of their genial host, Butty took their caddie aside for a brief conference.

'Stop hampering us, mate.'

'I am helping you, sir.'

'By making sure that we lose the frigging game? What kind of a caddie are you?'

'A considerate one, sir. I am protecting you.'

'From what?'

'The President's anger.'

'I'm getting pretty angry myself, mate!'

'He must win.'

'But this is a contest.'

'With our President. He always wins.' The caddie smiled serenely. 'The reward for you is simply to take part.'

Butty found this version of golf hard to accept but Des took a more philosophical attitude. They were playing with the head of state in a foreign capital. That was honour enough. Butty smothered his ire under a fixed grin and soldiered on.

'When in Aragusta . . .' he said to himself.

It was at the tenth hole that the crisis occurred. Though it was ostensibly fashioned after St Andrews, it had far more gorse bushes and heather than Butty remembered at the Old Course. The thick clump of trees would certainly not be found at the Royal and Ancient. The course architect seemed to have slipped up.

Driver in hand, the President smiled broadly at them.

'My honour again, I think . . .'

'You're beating us hollow,' said Butty.

'Yeah,' agreed Des. 'You're one hell of a golfer.'

'Practice makes perfect, gentlemen.'

With a graceful swing, the President sent his ball two hundred yards down the fairway. Butty went next and found some light rough off to the left. Captain Jammu then stepped up to the tee, hitting a respectable but un-adventurous drive that fell short of his partner's.

When Des came to the tee, Butty anticipated the same reliable drive that he had produced so far at every hole. The American was an excellent golfer. Even when hindered by his caddie, he had played some brilliant strokes. Selecting a 3-iron for control, Des addressed his ball and went into his standard routine. Butty fully expected the ball to go sailing on past that of the President. Instead, it was hooked disastrously into the trees.

'I'll get it,' said the caddie.

'No, I will,' insisted Des, trotting off. 'Bring the cart.'

'Leave it,' ordered the President. 'We will not count it. Play another ball from the tee.'

But his command came too late. Des Toyovsky was already disappearing behind the thick foliage. He seemed to be so annoyed at his bad shot that he was insisting on retrieving the ball himself. Butty was about to climb on to the golf cart when he heard the yell. It was not the sound of a man who had just found his errant golf ball. It was a cry for help. Des Toyovsky was deep in trouble.

Butty reacted instinctively. Sprinting down the undulating fairway, he plunged into the trees at exactly the point where the American had vanished. It did not take him long to locate his partner. Des was on his knees in a clearing. His wrists were handcuffed behind his back and two uniformed soldiers were standing over him with their rifles pointed at his head. It was not a situation he would have met at the real St Andrews.

Des Toyovsky managed a diffident smile for his friend. 'Hello, Butty.'

'What the fuck is going on?'

'I just bumped into the Handicapping Committee.'

THIRTEEN

Basking in the tropical sunshine, it was difficult for the England team to remember that Christmas Day was looming. They spent their leisure hours relaxing, swimming or playing uncompetitive games of tennis, volleyball and golf. Some went shooting, others took the boat out to fish for marlin, others again preferred to do some sightseeing on the island. Temperatures hovered in the nineties and kept them permanently in beach wear. The festive season in shivering Britain seemed a million miles away.

'How many would you like, Wilt?' asked Dealer.

'Twenty at least.'

'Why not take two packs? Dozen in each.'

'How much are they?'

'In the shops, you'd pay seven quid for 'em. I can let you have 'em for a knock-down price of a fiver.'

'Thanks, man.'

Wilton Rodger handed over the money and took the Christmas cards. Dealer always looked ahead. He'd come well-prepared to cope with the team's general amnesia. Panic-stricken colleagues who suddenly noticed the date and remembered Christmas could turn to him for cards, presents and wrapping paper covered in sprigs of holly. Dealer had everything. Even an inflatable Santa Claus who sang 'Jingle Bells' when his belt-buckle was pressed.

'You must be used to all this, Wilt,' he said.

'To all what?'

'This weather. Just like being home in Jamaica.'

'No, Dealer,' said Wilton with a chuckle. 'I was born in Jamaica but brought up in Leeds. And that's nothing like

129

Karistan. When you wake up in the morning in Leeds, you can hear the birds coughing. It can get real cold.'

Wilton Rodger was the only black member of the team. A talented player, he had a relaxed, easy-going nature and was universally popular. Now that he'd got over his sinus trouble, he was keen to get into action on a cricket pitch. But he had family responsibilities as well.

'When do I need to post these, Dealer?'

'Soon as you can if you want them to reach England before Christmas. Today, if poss. Tomorrow at the latest.'

'What about stamps?'

'Funny you should mention that,' said Dealer, fishing a huge roll of them from his suitcase. 'I happen to have a lifetime's supply right here. See? They've got a picture of General Idi Ott on them. You can even count his medals.'

'I'll take two dozen.'

'Sold to the man in the bowler hat!'

Dealer peeled off the stamps and took his money. His one-man trading company was a highly profitable sideline. A barrow-boy upbringing had its advantages. As Wilton Rodger went out of the hotel room, Big Ben Edwards came in. He had now shaken off his dysentery and was back to full booming fitness.

'I need some Christmas cards, Dealer.'

'Then you've come to the right place. What kind?'

'Got any religious ones?'

'What about this card with the three nuns on it?'

'I'm a Baptist!'

'Don't they have Baptist nuns?'

'We're Nonconformist.'

'Of course. One of the Awkard Bleeder religions.'

'Don't be blasphemous, mun!'

'Sorry, Ben. How many do you want?'

'Sixty.'

'Blimey!'

'One for every member of the congregation at chapel,'

said Ben, sifting through the cards. 'Then I'll need some for my family and friends. Better make it a hundred all told.'

'This is my lucky day!'

'Where do I post them, Dealer?'

'They've got a supply of carrier pigeons in Reception.'

'Have they?' said the gullible Welshman. 'Can they fly all the way back to Pontypridd?'

'Yes, old son. First class on British Airways.'

Ben chuckled. 'Go on, mun. You're pulling my leg.'

'Would I do that to you?'

'Yes. You're almost as bad as Butty.'

'Nobody's that bad. Butty's taken the piss more often than the Outpatients' Department at Hammersmith Hospital.' He slapped Ben on the shoulder. 'Choose your cards, buy your stamps then go back down to Reception in the lift. When you get out, there's a glass-fronted post box set in the wall on your right. Can you remember all that?'

'Yes,' said Ben, still browsing through the cards. 'By the way, what are we doing on Christmas Day?'

'Drinking ourselves into a glorious stupor.'

'I thought I might organise a service.'

'To hand the beer round, you mean?'

'No, mun. A chapel service. Carols and that. Do you think the rest of the boyos would like that? I always like to sing carols on Christmas Day. Will anybody else join in?'

'Oh, the lads will certainly join in,' said Dealer with a grin. 'But the songs they'll be singing on Christmas Day won't be in the Baptist Hymnbook. I bet your congregation in Pontypridd has never heard of the four-and-twenty virgins who went down to Inverness.'

'No, mun. I told you. We don't have nuns.'

Dealer cackled. Innocence could be very appealing.

*　　*　　*

131

'What happened then?' asked Fothers with intense interest.

'The President gave the order and they released me.'

'But what were those soldiers doing in the trees?'

'Who knows?' said Des Toyovsky with a grimace. 'But they certainly weren't bird-watching. It was scary. I go into the trees to retrieve a golf ball and get ambushed.'

'What did General Idi Ott say?'

'Very little. Wanted to shrug the whole thing off.'

'How did Butty react?'

'It brought out the Rambo in him. Kevin was all for tackling the two soldiers and rescuing me. Luckily, it never came to that.'

'Thank heavens!' said Fothers. 'It would've caused an international incident. You have to be diplomatic when you're in someone else's country. And Butty is about as diplomatic as a water buffalo with an attitude problem.'

They were sitting alone on the verandah at the hotel and Fothers was interrogating him about the incident at the golf course. The England captain was highly alarmed in case relations with their hosts had been in any way damaged. Des assured him that everything went smoothly once they'd taken the handcuffs off him. He bore the soldiers no ill will.

'In fact,' he said with mild irony, 'the President played better than ever from then on. Nick Faldo couldn't have kept pace with him. He stormed ahead of Kevin and me. General Idi Ott had a hole-in-one at the seventeenth.'

'What a great shot!'

'Phenomenal. It's a par four.'

'That must've been the longest drive in history!'

'Kevin reckoned that the President's ball only went a hundred and fifty yards but, when we got to the green, there it was, nestling in the hole beside the flagstick.'

'That's what I call genius.'

'Gamesmanship.'

'Tell me again exactly what the President said.'

Fothers was not so much talking to Des as de-briefing him. The American could not understand why. If the England management was concerned about what had happened, Derek March should have been in on the discussion but Fothers made a point of cornering Des on his own. A great deal seemed to be at stake for the England captain.

'Are you quite sure it did not sour relations?' he pressed.

'Yeah,' said Des. 'The incident was forgotten and the President took us into the clubhouse for a drink. All he could talk about was his hole-in-one. And the cricket, of course.'

'Did he mention me?'

'Very favourably.'

'Good.'

'He told us to pass on his compliments.'

'That's heartening.'

'Admired your innings against Western Province.'

'How? He didn't see it.'

'Yes he did, James. On video. He had the game secretly recorded for his personal use. Watched it with his six wives. They loved Butty's innings, apparently.' He gave a wry smile. 'Butty does seem to have a way with the ladies.'

'I know,' said Fothers ruefully.

'But the President understands cricket. He could see why Butty grabbed all the glory but he described your innings as the most interesting.'

'Interesting?'

'Textbook play, he said. Classic strokes. He thinks that James Henry Fotheringhay is the epitome of English cricket.'

'That's a relief!' said Fothers, losing his frown of anxiety for the first time. 'I just wish I'd been there myself. To curb some of Butty's infelicities.'

'He was on his best behaviour. Only belched twice.'

Fothers relaxed slightly. He had grown fond of Des

Toyovsky. The American journalist was such a friendly and unthreatening member of the press corps. Des was the perfect antidote to Darren Grubb and his ilk.

'Are you enjoying the tour?' asked Fothers.

'Very much. Give or take the odd arrest by soldiers.'

'Have you learned to like cricket?'

'Love it. What I've seen of it, anyway.'

'Take it up yourself, Des.'

'Not me. Baseball is my game.'

'We call it rounders over here.'

'No similarity at all. If you saw the Boston Red Sox playing at Fenway Park, you wouldn't confuse baseball with rounders. Been trying to persuade Kevin to give it a go.'

'Why?'

'He'd be a natural. All that power and aggression. Got such a great eye for the ball. He could make a fortune as a pro baseball player.'

'What did Butty say to that?'

'No deal.'

'He might be a little out of place in Boston.'

'Wants to stay in Huddersfield.'

'That's more than I would.'

'Kevin is very attached to his roots. There's something about Yorkshiremen, isn't there?'

'Yes,' said Fothers with a sniff. 'There is!'

'Your fiancée obviously thinks so.'

'Antonia?'

'Yeah,' said Des approvingly. 'Helluva girl. You're a lucky guy, James. We sat next to each other during the match against Western Province. Antonia spent the whole match quizzing me about Kevin.'

Fothers was ruffled. 'Indeed?'

'I guess it's an attraction of opposites.'

'Hardly a meeting of soulmates.'

'Antonia just loved his innings.'

'Butty scored some useful runs, I'll grant him that.'

'It was the *way* he scored them that excited your fiancée. She kept saying something about the Royal Stud in Oman.' Des glanced around. 'Where is Antonia, by the way?'

'I don't know. I've been looking for her myself.'

'Then I'll let you organise the search party,' said Des as he rose to leave. 'Oh, one thing. She told me that the two of you were in Karistan as a sort of experiment.'

'Did she?'

'What did Antonia mean?'

'I've no idea,' said Fothers evasively.

'Said she came to "look it over". Is that right, James?'

'No, no. She's quite mistaken. Dear Antonia! She does get hold of the wrong end of the stick sometimes. I'd better find her.' He abandoned the civilities and charged out. 'Fast!'

Des Toyovsky strolled back to Reception. He had work to do and needed a few hours alone in his room. As he waited by the lift, his gaze wandered idly to the glass-fronted post box set in the wall. It was packed with letters and post cards. One envelope bore a name printed in clear capitals.

Annabelle Jansen-Jones of Windsor.

Des thought about a stolen Volvo Estate.

Even someone as compulsively gregarious as Butty enjoyed some occasional time alone. While his team-mates were lounging around the hotel pool or taking a dip in the sea, he felt the pull of a favourite hobby. Hiring the tackle, he borrowed one of the hotel mopeds and followed the directions he'd been given. Twenty minutes of phut-phutting along a winding track brought him to the river. Butty chose his spot with care and settled down to a couple of hours of fishing.

He was soon stretched out on the grass without a care in the world. His line was cast, his rod was propped up on a forked stick and a six-pack of lager lay beside him. It was the nearest he'd got to heaven outside Yorkshire. The peace and solitude were seductive. He felt his batteries being charged in the most satisfying way.

Sombrero over his face, Butty drifted off to sleep. He was still dreaming about his reconciliation with Barbara when the moped picked its way along the river bank. Only when the horn was beeped did he come awake.

'Found you at last!' said Antonia.

'Who has?' he mumbled.

'It's *me*, Kevin.'

Butty sat up with the sombrero in his lap and squinted in the sunlight. Lady Antonia Titwillow was astride a hotel moped which was still throbbing fitfully. She was wearing white shorts, a red cheesecloth shirt and a straw hat that might have done duty at Ascot.

He'd never seen her bare legs before. As his eyes got used to the light, he was hypnotised by them. They were beautiful all the way up. Antonia switched off the engine and removed her designer sunglasses.

'Not interrupting you, am I?' she said.

'Er, no.'

'What are you doing exactly?'

'Fishing.'

'You seeemed to be fast asleep.'

'I was waiting, that's all.'

'What for?'

'A bite.'

'Bite?'

'Yes, Antonia.' He forced his eyes off her naked thighs and nodded at his rod. 'On that.'

'Oh, I see. Derek March went off fishing in a boat yesterday. He said that one of the men caught a shark.'

'Sea angling,' said Butty with contempt. 'Not for me.

136

Too much like hard work. Give me the quiet of the river any day. I'm a coarse fisherman.'

'Yes, that was the word James always uses about you.'

'Eh?'

'Coarse. Not that I agree with him,' she added quickly with a giggle. 'A certain amount of honest vulgarity in a man can be refreshing. At the right time.'

Butty grinned. 'You don't have to be coarse to take up coarse fishing. Simply means we go after non-salmonid fish.'

'You've lost me, Kevin.'

'We catch roach, bream, carp, chub, dace and tench.'

'And what have you caught so far today?'

'Nothing.'

She dismounted from the moped and rested it against a tree, pausing to gaze up and down the river. She did not see the bushes move further along the bank. Butty studied her body. Antonia looked even more gorgeous in profile. Fothers had taste.

'How did you find me?' he asked.

'I saw you talking to the hotel porter earlier on. He was showing you something on a map. After you'd gone, I asked him to point me in the same direction.'

'That was clever.'

'I get bored just hanging around the hotel.'

'Does he know you're here?'

'James? Oh, no!' She put an involuntary hand to her chest. 'He'd be ever so cross if he knew. James told me to keep well away from you.'

'Out of bounds, am I?'

'All the players are, really. But especially you.'

'Why?'

'I don't know, Kevin. Perhaps he thinks I might distract you from your cricket. James is so dedicated. He lets nothing get in the way of his batting practice.'

'Then he obviously hasn't seen you in those shorts.'

Antonia gave her inimitable whinny and took a few steps closer to him. She twirled her sunglasses.

'He won't let me speak to that horrible man either.'

'Horrible man?'

'That journalist from the *Comet*.'

'Darren Grubb. Nasty piece of work.'

'He's been pestering me for an interview since I arrived. James made me swear I wouldn't speak to him. Darren Grubb is on the Forbidden List.'

'Just like me.'

'Well, yes. But for a different reason.'

'So you don't think I'm horrible, then?'

'No, Kevin!'

'Why did you come?' he wondered.

'Because I wanted to speak to you.'

'Aren't you afraid he'll find out?'

Sudden fear. 'You won't tell him, will you?'

'I've got a tape recorder under my sombrero,' he joked. 'When I send him the tape, he'll hear every word you've said.'

'You're teasing me.'

'Yes, Antonia. Your secret is safe with me.'

'I knew I could trust you.' She glanced nervously over her shoulder. 'I can't stay long. James and I are playing bridge with Derek and the Colonel this evening.'

'That sounds like a barrel of laughs.'

'It can be quite thrilling if we manage to keep the Colonel awake. But I did want a moment alone with you, Kevin. I simply have to tell you how marvellous that innings of yours was against Western Province.'

'Thanks.'

'I've never seen such a wonderful exhibition.'

'Stay around. I'm hoping to improve on that.'

'To be honest, I find cricket rather boring.'

'So do I. When it's played boringly.'

'You opened my eyes to the full ferocity of the game.'

'Yes,' he agreed. 'Lot of ferocity in cricket. Especially at selection meetings. I've been on the receiving end of their decisions so I should know.'

'You won that game for England.'

'Don't say that to your fiancé. He won't like it.'

'James did his share, of course. He looks so splendid at the wicket, doesn't he? So noble, so *English*.' She shifted her feet and giggled. 'But it was your day.'

'So is this, Antonia. Thanks to you.'

'I told Des Toyovsky how magnificent I thought you were. He said you'd like to hear that from my own lips.'

'Dead bloody right.'

'So . . . that's it, Kevin. Congratulations!'

Antonia leaned over to give him a peck on the cheek but their lips somehow met instead. It was only a brief kiss but it had a profound effect on both of them. Antonia dropped her sunglasses in excitement and Butty's sombrero suddenly rose inches in the air and rotated at high speed like a demented roulette wheel.

It was at that precise moment that Darren Grubb, lurking nearby in the bushes, took his photograph of the couple.

He was so glad that he'd followed Antonia.

FOURTEEN

Mingoon was the largest city in the north of the island. The team hotel was the most luxurious yet, offering its guests a panoramic view of the bay as well as the most extraordinary range of facilities. But the city was not entirely a tourist paradise. On the speedy drive through the suburbs, the England team caught a disturbing glimpse of another side of Karistan life.

The terraced houses looked like strings of air raid shelters made of crumbling concrete. Graffiti were daubed over every wall. The streets were littered with refuse and the tourists caught the hideous whiff of an open drain through the open windows of the coach. Listless men stood about in groups and watched them race past. Packs of children and dogs seemed to be everywhere. Washing lines were festooned with tattered clothing. Women sat outside their houses and cooked food on wood fires.

The air of squalor and deprivation was all-pervading.

'Christ!' exclaimed Penny. 'I'm back in Manchester!'

'You never bloody well left,' taunted Butty.

Ben Edwards was shocked. 'This is terrible, mun! I had no idea they had places like this here. Makes you feel guilty staying in a big hotel, doesn't it?'

'We'll send you out to do missionary work, Ben,' said Dealer. 'Spread the Word for the Baptists.'

'It's no joke, Dealer. Those are real people out there.'

'I thought everyone in Karistan had a high standard of living,' said Snatcher. 'Who are this lot?'

'The ones they never told us about,' said Butty.

He, too, was offended by the sight of so much poverty

140

and misery. It was depressing. When he thought of the sumptuous Presidential palace in Aragusta and recalled the exclusive mansions of the ruling elite, he burned with anger. Karistan was evidently a country of extremes.

Another surprise awaited them around the bend. A gang of children were enjoying a rudimentary game of cricket on a patch of waste ground, using a cardboard box as their wickets and an old tennis ball. When they saw the coach coming, play was abandoned and they raced to the edge of the road to give a ragged cheer to the tourists. They pointed to a long wall over the the left. The painted slogans were in letters a foot high. Poor spelling did not weaken their impact.

WELCOM INGLAND. WEEL BEET YOU. HELLO, BUTY.

The players were touched. Poor children, who had never been to a cricket match in their lives, were nevertheless hailing them as heroes. There was even a pathetic pride in their own team. The game really meant something to the kids.

Penny Coyne seized on the spelling of his rival's name.

'You don't look like a beauty to me, Butty.'

'Shut it!'

'You're the ugliest bugger in Yorkshire.'

'Know something, Penny?' retorted Butty. 'When God put teeth in your gob, he ruined a good arse.'

Stung by the derisive laughter at him, Penny stood up.

'You asking to get thumped?'

'Another time,' said Butty, walking down the aisle to the driver. 'Stop the coach, mate. I want to get off.'

'You can't!' ordered Derek March. 'This is a rough area. It's far too dangerous, Butty.'

'Who for?'

'We have to get to our hotel.'

'I'll join you later, Derek. Right now, I fancy a game of cricket. And those lads back there seem to like me.'

As the coach squealed to a halt, other players got up.

'I'll come with you, boyo,' said Big Ben.

'Me, too,' said Snatcher. 'They didn't seem to have a wicket-keeper. What about you, Wilt?'

'Right behind you, man,' said Wilton Rodger.

Most of the team got out and strolled back to meet their fans. The boys were ecstatic when the England players joined in the game. A crowd soon gathered and a debris-covered wilderness was turned into Lord's for twenty minutes.

A manic March Hare and a furious Fothers watched impotently through the rear window of the team coach. They regarded the whole incident as a serious loss of discipline. Des Toyovsky, by contrast, looked on in wonderment at the smiling faces of the boys and the joy of the spectators. When Butty hit a ball deliberately to one of the fielders so that he could be caught out, the whole outer suburb of Mingoon was delirious.

Des leaned over to speak into a Fothery ear.

'I thought you said that Butty was as diplomatic as a water buffalo.'

'He is, Des.'

'Not from where I'm standing. That looks to me like the best piece of diplomacy we've had so far. Excuse me, guys,' he added, moving to the door. 'For the first time in my life, I simply have to play a game of cricket.'

The one-day match against Mingoon University was an absurdly lopsided affair. England rested some of their star players and included all those who had not so far played on tour. Even this weakened side was far too strong for the students. They had the enthusiasm of youth and were sprightly in the field but there was a yawning ability gap between them and their visitors.

Fothers captained the side and chose to bat when he

won the toss. Since the Dealer was not playing, he opened the innings with Wilton Rodger. They dominated the bowling from the start and were soon scoring at will from both ends. The Jamaican was dismissed for 83 by a superb diving catch but Fothers went on to make 121. Other batsmen took their lead from the openers and the score surged on. England declared at 349 for 5 with three overs still unbowled.

The Colonel was watching from the balcony with Dealer.

'Men against boys!' said the old man gruffly. 'In my day, the universities could field a first-rate team.'

'Maybe this lot can bat,' said Dealer.

'They're too raw and untutored.'

'Let's wait and see.'

'I wouldn't bet on them reaching treble figures.'

'I would, Colonel. Neither Butty nor Big Ben are playing so Peebee Brooksby is our main strike bowler. If he has a bad day, he can be expensive.'

'They won't score a hundred,' insisted the Colonel.

'What will you bet?'

'My silver watch.'

'Let me see it.'

'Here we are,' said the Colonel, lifting the fob watch out of his waistcoat pocket. 'Inscribed with my name.'

'Right,' decided Dealer. 'I'll take on the bet.'

'What will you set against my watch?'

'Six others.' He rolled up his sleeve to display the six wristwatches strapped there. 'Is it a deal, Colonel?'

'Yes.'

'Great! When I win your own watch, I'll sell you one of mine. Waterproof, rustproof and childproof. Every England selector should have one.'

The Colonel chuckled. 'I intend to have six.'

England took the field and the University openers came out to brave applause from their supporters. They were lambs to the slaughter. Though they held off the bowling for the first few overs, they were distinctly uncomfortable. Wickets began to tumble at random. Dealer soon began to regret his rash wager against the Colonel.

When they somehow crawled into the nineties, Dealer's hopes revived but they were soon dashed. The last three wickets fell in one over and six watches changed hands. The Colonel was not above the lure of commerce.

'Any chance of selling them back to you?' he said.

The Colonel went off triumphantly to the bar. Big Ben, who was perched on the corner of the balcony, looked across at his crestfallen colleague.

'That was a big mistake, Dealer.'

'I know, Ben. I should never have taken the bet.'

'The match, I meant. Mistake to play it. The students will be demoralised because we hammered them and our boyos would have had more exercise in the nets.'

'All part of the plan, old son.'

'Eh?'

'We've got the first Test in a few days and our only preparation is a walk-over against students. See what I mean? The Karistan Cricket Federation wanted it that way. Our fixtures have been carefully arranged.'

'Diu!' exclaimed the Welshman. 'You could be on to something there, Dealer. There's skulduggery at work.'

'No, Ben. Commonsense, that's all. They're keeping their powder dry. Haven't you noticed something about the four games we've played so far?'

'Only that we lost the first and won the others.'

'We've seen very little of the Test side.'

'We've seen Zaki Meero twice now. And Orin Logos. And that spinner of theirs, Inta Walliconi, must be in the team.'

'Three out of eleven, old son. Who else?'

'Dunno, mun.'

'Because they don't want you to know. Two-thirds of the Test side have been deliberately kept under wraps whereas they've now seen everything we've got to offer.' Dealer tapped the side of his nose. 'Karistan are cunning. My guess is they'll spring a surprise on us like the President's XI did. We could have problems on Thursday.'

'Let's hope we put our best team out.'

'As long as it includes Butty.'

'Yes!' Big Ben looked around. 'Where is he, by the way? Thought I saw him out here earlier.'

'Got fed up and went back to the hotel to write his Christmas cards. Just as well. Butty wouldn't have enjoyed watching Fothers get his century. That 121 puts our captain well ahead for the Best Batsman Award.'

'Butty won't like it one little bit.'

'That's why I'm not going to be the one to tell him.'

Sharing a room with a zealous Welshman had its disadvantages. Butty had always had a soft spot for Big Ben but some of the latter's personal habits were a trial. He had got used to the bouts of uncontrollable flatulence and did not mind that his room-mate spent most of the time listening to Male Voice Choirs on his Walkman. What irked Butty was his companion's attempts to bring the wanton Yorkshireman within the pale of the Baptist Church.

Big Ben was constantly giving him sermons or slipping improving pamphlets under his pillow. When he invited Butty to pray with him, they almost came to blows. The man had many virtues, Butty recognised that. He was a kind, gentle and uncritical soul, always willing to think the best of even the worst people. Ben was a loyal friend who took Butty's incessant ribbing of him with smiling tolerance. If only the Baptists did not stand between them.

Taking advantage of Ben's absence, Butty sat on the balcony outside his room with his feet up on the rail. He was on the first floor, directly above the hotel swimming pool, and a few guests were splashing about below him.

Butty penned some affectionate obscenities on his Christmas card to Barbara. It might just reach her in time.

'There you are!' said a disembodied voice.

Butty looked around. 'Eh?'

'Down here!' called Darren Grubb.

'Oh, it's you,' said Butty, seeing him beside the pool. 'Go away, Darren. I'm busy.'

'I wanted to have a word.'

'It's got four letters.'

'They've been hiding you from me, Butty.'

'You wore out your welcome.'

'Derek March has banned any of the players from talking to me. Heaven knows why,' he said artlessly. 'I might be able to give them some useful publicity.'

'Disappear!'

'I will, Butty. I'm on my way up.'

Grubb vanished into the hotel and Butty rose angrily from his chair. Since the damaging article about him in the *Comet*, he'd been forbidden to give interviews to any of the feature-writers but especially not to Darren Grubb. The man was being completely ostracised by the team. When he dared to knock on Butty's door, therefore, he got short shrift.

'Piss off, Grubb!'

'I've got something to show you.'

'Stick it up your arse!'

'Let me in.'

'I prefer fresh air.'

'I want to strike a bargain.'

'The only thing I want to strike is that fat face of yours. Now sod off before I lose my temper.'

'In that case, I'll show the photos to Fothers.'

Butty was checked. 'Photos?'

'You and Lady Antonia Titwillow on the river bank.'

'We were alone.'

'I wasn't. I had my camera with me.'

146

Butty opened the door, grabbed him by the throat and yanked him in. Slamming the door behind him, Butty stood menacingly over the cringing journalist.

'Give me one good reason why I shouldn't bash you.'

'Your place in the Test team.'

'What?'

'Fothers is hardly going to pick someone who tried to get a leg over his fiancée.'

'But I didn't!'

'I know that. But the photos say otherwise.'

'What the hell were you doing there?'

'Following a story by instinct.'

'You're bluffing,' said Butty.

'Am I?'

'Nothing happened between us.'

'D'you call this nothing?' said Grubb, pulling some photos from his inside pocket. 'I'd say that was mad passion myself. Lady Antonia enjoying a bit of rough.'

Butty snatched the photos from him and blenched. The kiss on the river bank was captured with hideous accuracy. His mind was racing. Butty didn't care two hoots about his own reputation but he was keen to protect Antonia from any scandal. All she'd done was to congratulate him.

'Well,' said Darren. 'Do we trade?'

'Trade?'

'I give you the negatives. You feed me the gossip.'

'There *is* no gossip.'

'Sixteen super-fit young men on the loose? Well, fifteen. We can't count Fothers. He's never been on the loose in his life.' He smirked at Butty. 'What have they been getting up to? Dish the dirt. Tell me all.'

Butty bit his lip and appeared to concede defeat.

'You win, Darren. Give me the negatives.'

'I want some spicy scandal first.'

'Promise my name won't come into it?'

'Nobody will ever know.'

'Then get your notepad out. This is hot.'

Eyes glinting, Darren took out a notepad and pen.

'All ready. Who's my first victim?'

'Big Ben.'

'What's his dirty secret?'

'Know what he does every night before going to bed?'

'What?'

'Gets down on his knees and prays.'

Darren was disappointed. 'That's not scandal.'

'Then we come to Wilton Rodger.'

'My readers want the real seamy stuff.'

'Wilt can provide that,' said Butty in a whisper. 'Shall I tell what he does last thing at night?'

'Drink? Drugs? Women?'

'He rings his wife and family at home in Leeds.'

'That's not a story!'

'Then there's Snatcher Smart and Dealer. They play snakes and ladders until all hours. Oh, and don't forget the Colonel. He's a secret Rennies fiend. Sucks his way through three packets a day. Then there's Penny Coyne . . .'

'That's enough,' snarled Grubb, pocketing his pen and notepad. 'You're taking the piss.'

'But I haven't told you about Peebee. He reads copies of the *Beano* after lights-out. With a torch.'

'I've heard enough. Fothers gets the photos.'

He tried to grab them back but he was too slow. Butty jerked his hand away then marched to the balcony, tearing up the photos as he went. He flung the pieces in the air and they floated down into the swimming pool.

'I've still got the negatives!' warned Grubb.

'But you won't use them, Darren.'

'Why not?'

'Because I won't like it.'

'Who cares?'

'I do!'

Butty pounced on him and got a firm grip on his collar.

The journalist struggled but he was no match for Butty. In the middle of their scuffle, Big Ben let himself into the room. He stood back in astonishment.

'What's going on?' he asked.

'Get this loony off me!' howled Grubb.

'You're just in time, Ben,' said Butty. 'You've got one at last.'

'One what?' asked the Welshman.

'A convert to the Baptist Church.'

'Leave go or I'll sue for assault!' yelled Grubb.

Ben was baffled. 'What's this about my Church?'

'Darren is going to be baptised into it.'

Lifting the journalist bodily in the air, Butty spun him around before hurling him from the balcony. With a cry of absolute horror, Darren Grubb fell backwards through space and hit the water with an almighty splash.

Butty waited until his spluttering visitor surfaced.

'Be grateful you found me in a nice mood, Darren.'

General Idi Ott sat in his study at the Presidential palace with the list in front of him. Zaki Meero stood beside him to await approval. The President ran his eye down the twelve names with a smile of satisfaction.

'You have chosen well, Zaki,' he said at length.

'Subject to your ratification, sir.'

'You have it.'

'Thank you.' The Karistan captain gave a bow. 'Our hope is to give England a run for their money.'

'Set our ambition higher than that.'

'That might be foolhardy. We are the novices. We have never played a Test match against them before.'

'It cuts both ways, Zaki,' argued the other. 'They have not played a Test match against *us*. Whereas we know their strengths and weaknesses, Karistan will take the field in a cloud of mystery. They have only seen three of you.'

'That was the agreed strategy.'

'It will work. It must.'

'In your presence, everything is possible.'

Zaki gave another bow and left the room. The President gloated over the names in his team. Each player would be richly rewarded for his services to Karistan cricket. To meet England in a Test match was a signal honour. To beat them would be to send a message out to the rest of the world.

There was a tap on the door and Captain Jammu entered. He was beckoned across and shown the names. He gave a dutiful smile and nodded. The President beamed.

'The Test match will be a joy to behold,' he said.

'I strongly advise against your attending, sir.'

'Miss an event as important as this? Impossible!'

'But unavoidable,' said Jammu. 'A fresh report has come in about the fugitives from Shark Island Prison.'

'Tiki and Verukka?'

'They are alive.'

FIFTEEN

Lady Antonia Titwillow looked back on her day with mixed emotions. It had been a tale of highs and lows. Watching her fiancé score yet another glorious century had filled her with joy and reinforced her conviction that she had chosen the right partner with whom to share her life. Those warm feelings were dissipated when England cut their way ruthlessly through the Mingoon University XI and sent them back to the pavilion with a paltry score. It smacked too much of sadism to be considered a genuine sporting encounter.

Antonia's spirits rose when Fothers took her riding in the early evening and she had the pulsing strength of a stallion between her thighs again. That pleasure, too, was soon vitiated. The England captain was summoned back to the hotel by a distraught Derek March for an emergency meeting to discipline Butty once more. A sodden Darren Grubb was threatening legal action if he did not have a grovelling apology from his attacker and an undertaking from the team management that he would have unrestricted access to all the players.

Even this disagreeable interruption was smoothed over. In an unprecedented romantic gesture, Fothers took Antonia out to a candlelit supper at Mingoon's finest restaurant. Rich food and heady wine brought them closer than they'd ever been before and Antonia was confident that he would at last spend the night in her eager arms. But intimacy stopped cruelly short of the door to her room. All she got was a polite kiss on the forehead.

'Don't you want to come on in, James?'

'I'm feeling tired.'

'I have a king-size bed in my room.'

'Derek will expect me.'

'What about my expectations?'

'Cricket must come first, Antonia.'

His only concession to lust was a kiss on her hand before striding off to yet another night of celibacy. As she flung herself on the bed, Antonia felt that this was the lowest point of her day. Cricket had once again smothered her passion. Writhing with frustration, she longed for the moment when her fiancé would throw all inhibition aside.

If only he'd have a change of heart and come rushing back up to her room. She'd surrender herself to him with whinnying delight. Antonia longed for him to knock boldly on her door with the ardour of a lover.

And that is exactly what he did.

She could not believe it when she heard the banging.

'Antonia!' he said breathlessly. 'Are you there?'

'Oh, yes!' she said, tripping across the room.

'Let me in!'

'You came back for me!'

'Hurry up, Antonia!'

She pulled back the door and stood swooning before him.

'My door, my heart and my body are open to you, James.'

'Over here!'

Kicking the door shut, he guided her roughly across to the bed. Antonia was suffused with delight. Carnality had finally taken over from cricket. He was hers.

The illusion was shattered at once. Instead of hurling her down, he made her sit on the edge of the bed while he fished inside his coat. Out came a large brown envelope.

'This was put under my door!' he said, barely able to contain his rage. 'How do you explain it?'

'It's a thin enough envelope,' she noted. 'It should go under your door with ease.'

'Open it, Antonia!'

'But it's addressed to you.'

'Take out the photograph!'

'I'll do anything you want, if only you'll stop yelling at me.' She opened the envelope. 'I can think of much better things to do than to look at a silly photograph.' She took it out and glanced at it. A brittle laugh. 'Oops!'

'You may well say that!'

'Who took this?'

'Does it matter?'

'Of course it matters!' she said. 'Somebody was spying on us. It's a gross intrusion of privacy.'

'It looks more like a gross intrusion of my fiancée!' he said. 'How *could* you, Antonia?'

'But I didn't.'

'You're actually kissing that Yorkshire buffoon!'

'Yes and no, James.'

'It can't be both.'

'It can. Yes, I'm kissing him. No, not in the way you think.'

'A kiss is a kiss, Antonia!'

'But it was meaningless.'

'Then why is that sombrero up in the air?'

'Oh,' she said, looking at the photo again. 'I didn't notice that. Well, it was rather a hot day, I suppose.'

'You let that yob touch you.'

'I touched him, actually.'

'Antonia!'

'It was all very innocent.'

'I'm not blind.'

'It was, James. Honestly. I just wanted to congratulate Kevin on that spiffing innings he played against Western Province.'

He was crushed. 'What about *my* innings?'

'Oh, well . . . yes, that was even more spiffing in its own way. But, then, I've told you that a dozen times. I never had the opportunity to speak to Kevin until that afternoon.'

'At your rendezvous.'

'No!'

'You had an assignation.'

'Don't be silly. Kevin went fishing.'

'I can see that. Look where his left hand is.'

'I followed him from the hotel on a moped.'

'For a tryst.'

'That's ridiculous!'

'You betrayed me, Antonia!'

'This is all getting rather tiresome.'

'Worse still, you betrayed *us*. A vulgarian like Butty! Of all the people to become involved with! I can't tell you how deeply this has wounded me.'

'It was not intentional.'

'No, I was not supposed to find out, was I?'

'There's nothing to find out.'

'You met him, didn't you?'

'Yes.'

'In secret?'

'Yes.'

'Against my express command?'

'Yes.'

'Then you and he . . .'

'No, James!'

'I'm ashamed of you, Antonia. I really am. I expected more from a head girl of Benendon.' He took the photograph and envelope from her and tucked them under his arm like a cricket bat. 'I need to consider my position,' he said.

Fothers walked away with dignity as if departing the crease after an unjust LBW decision. She went after him.

'Listen,' she said, girlishly. 'Now that I've actually got

154

you into my room, why don't I show you my snaps of the Royal Stud?'

James Henry Fotherighay solemnly opened the door.

'I've seen enough photography for one night!' he said.

When the players came down for breakfast next morning, they were slightly on edge. The Test team was to be announced at noon and they were all hoping to be selected for what was an historic occasion. Whatever the result, the first ever Test match between England and Karistan would have its own niche in Wisden. They were keen to be in on the act.

Wearing his Hawaiian shirt and shorts, Butty sat down at a table with Des Toyovsky. The American put his newspaper aside.

'Hi, Kevin!'

'Morning.'

'Where's Big Ben?'

'He's having room service today.'

'Communion wine and unleavened bread?'

'That's too High Church for him. Big Ben's religion is so low, it's bleeding subterranean. He's having tea and rusks. Determined not to eat anything which'll give him the trots again. Set his heart on a place in that Test team.'

'So has everyone else.'

'Yeah, Des. Me included. I love a big occasion.'

'Seems to lift your game.' He sipped his coffee. 'Talking of lifting, what's all this about you picking up Darren Grubb and throwing him in the swimming pool?'

'The bastard tried to blackmail me.'

'How?'

'With some sneaky photos he'd taken of me and Antonia. Nothing at all happened between us but Grisly Grubb made us look as if we were competing in the World Shagging Championships.' Butty poured himself some

155

orange juice. 'It was like being back in that Volvo Estate all over again. Really pissed me off.'

'Watch him, Kevin. He's the vengeful type.'

Butty grinned. 'So am I!'

'Glad you mentioned the Volvo,' said Des. 'Jogged my memory. Do you recall the name of the lady who owned it?'

'Double-barrelled bird, wasn't she?'

'Annabelle Jansen-Jones.'

'That's her.'

'Somebody in the squad knows her.'

'Eh?'

'At that last hotel, I saw an envelope addressed to her in the glass-fronted post box. Helluva coincidence.'

'Dead right, mate! What's your theory?'

'Maybe her car wasn't stolen, after all. It was borrowed by a friend to set you up. Annabell J-J reported it to the cops as stolen to cover her tracks. And his.'

'His?'

'The guy who framed you. He's here, Kevin. In the tour party. We've established his link with the Volvo Estate. Now we have to tie him into Flash McGovern and the Harpo Club.'

'Just tell me who the conniving swine is!'

'When I find out, I will. Meanwhile,' said Des, raising his cup like a wine glass, 'here's to your selection! You're a cast iron certainty for the Test team.'

'I'd better be. I need runs and wickets.'

'You have to be in, Kevin. The selection committee can't find any more spurious excuses for keeping you out.'

'That's it,' said Derek March, adding the final name to the list. 'The team to meet Karistan for the first Test.'

'But we haven't chosen Sowerbutts,' burbled the Colonel.

'We won't even consider him,' said Fothers grimly.

'Why not?'

'Personal reasons.'

'You mean, he's got bad breath?'

'He's got bad *everything*, Colonel!'

'Really? Shouldn't we get him to a doctor?'

'A vet would be more appropriate!'

'Now, now, James,' soothed Derek. 'Don't be vindictive. The selection committee has deliberated. Let's all look forward to taking the field on Thursday.'

'Without our best player,' groaned the Colonel.

Over breakfast in the bedroom, the three men had picked their team for the big event. Having been shown the offending photograph, Derek was fully behind his captain's wishes to exclude the river bank Romeo. No player was indispensable and they had summarily dispensed with Butty.

'Shall I tell him?' asked Derek.

'No,' insisted Fothers. 'I will.'

'We'll ring down for him.'

'I'll see him alone, Uncle Derek.'

'Oh, right. Best way, probably. We'll send him up.' He rose from his chair. 'Come on, Colonel.'

'Are we all done, then?'

'Yes.'

'What about Any Other Business?'

'Do you have any, Colonel?'

'Indeed I do.' He rolled back his sleeve to reveal Dealer's six wristwatches. 'Can I interest either of you in a cut-price digital watch?'

Derek hustled him out.

Fothers walked to and fro as he rehearsed his speech. He decided to eschew any emotional outbursts. Icy control was the order of the day. He would remain aloof. Fothers was a thoroughbred stallion who could dispose of an insect like Butty with one flick of his tail.

When the knock came on the door, Fothers called him in.

'You wanted me?' asked Butty.

A lordly finger pointed. 'It's on the table.'

'No thanks, Fothers. Just had my breakfast.'

'The team for the First Test. On that sheet of paper.'

'Great! Can I see it?'

'I think you should.'

Butty snatched up the list and read the names.

> J. H. Fotheringhay (captain)
> M. D. Mancini
> W. O. Rodger
> D. W. C. Elgin
> H. M. Smart
> P. E. N. Coyne
> R. M. Ryman
> J. J. Cromwell
> P. B. Brooksby
> B. V. Jenkins
> E. T. Montgomery

'I'm not bloody well here!' he protested.

'You've read the eye chart perfectly.'

'Why the fuck have I been overlooked, Fothers?'

'You haven't been overlooked – just dropped.'

'Aren't I even in as twelfth man?'

'We preferred Willy Winslow.'

'Old Wanker!' exclaimed Butty with incredulity. 'This is a cricket match not a Tossers' Convention. Wanker Winslow is a joke selection.'

'Nevertheless, he gets the nod over you, Butty.'

'How?'

'We have our reasons.'

'Then I'm entitled to know them.'

'That's all I have to say. You may go.'

'Not until we get this sorted out. You can't just drop me like that. I've got fans here. Karistan loves me. My name puts an extra few thousand on the gate.'

'I'd rather play in front of empty stands than include you in my team,' said Fothers grandly.

'Then at least have the balls to tell me why.'

'Yours not to reason why. Yours but to clear off!'

Butty folded his arms. 'I'm staying.'

'Hotel security will remove you.'

'Fine. Send 'em up. I'm in a mood for a scrap.'

'That'd only get even more dreadful publicity for this tour. Don't you think you've created enough already?' He drew himself up to his full height. 'Now, disappear.'

His brain whirring, Butty looked at him shrewdly.

'I know what all this is about, Fothers.'

'I am not prepared to discuss it.'

'Antonia.'

'She is Lady Antonia Titwillow to you.'

'That little turd swore he'd get his own back.'

'This interview is terminated.'

'Darren Grubb. The phantom photographer. Yes,' said Butty. 'That's it, isn't it? Showed you a holiday snap of your fiancée on the river bank.'

Fothers tensed. 'That is irrelevant.'

'Rose above it like a gentleman, did you? Like hell!'

'You're out of the team, Butty.'

'That suits me!'

'And I might as well tell you that your chances of playing in any other game on this tour are decidedly slim. You're a thorough-going cad! The selection committee agreed unanimously to drop you.'

'No, they didn't,' retorted Butty. 'The Colonel may be senile but he knows what I can do on a cricket pitch. So does Uncle Derek. Much as he hates me, he'd have stuck me in the team to give you any hope of winning. No, Fothers,' he said, moving to the door. 'This is all your doing. You and Darren Frigging Grubb. He's your co-selector.'

'I have no idea what you're talking about.'

'Ask Antonia.'

'Lady Antonia Titwillow to you!'

'Grubb framed the pair of us,' said Butty vehemently. 'I'm past caring what happens to me but I won't see Antonia dragged down as well. Cracking lass. Only one serious defect.'

'Defect?'

'Yes, Fothers – you!'

Butty could have given lessons in door-slamming.

Hullabaloo filled the hotel for the rest of the morning. The players were incensed by the decision to leave Butty out of the team for the First Test. They complained bitterly and fulminated darkly. Showing unusual wisdom, the selection committee kept a low profile and the flak went over their heads. By afternoon, the team was still simmering.

'It's criminal, Des!' lamented Snatcher.

'Looks plain dumb to me,' said Des Toyovsky. 'Kevin's your match-winner. Leaving him out is suicide.'

'The selection committee should be shot!'

'That's the kindest suggestion I've heard so far.'

'Dealer wanted to boil them in oil,' said Snatcher. 'When he's got his watches back off the Colonel, that is. No point in letting them perish as well. Listen, we're having a protest meeting this afternoon. Want to come along?'

'No thanks.'

'Don't you want to see a players' revolt?'

'I'm squeamish,' joked Des. 'Never liked the sight of blood. No, I'm taking the afternoon off to go for a drive. Across to the mountains, maybe. They say the views are terrific from the top.'

'Be careful up there, Des.'

'Why?'

'That's where they reckon the rebels hang out.'

'They won't bother me. I'm a neutral.'

'Those blokes on the golf course didn't think so.'

'No,' agreed Des with a smile. 'They didn't. Retrieve your golf ball and get yourself handcuffed. Anybody'd think I went into those trees to start a civil war!'

'The civil war is taking place here.'

'Players versus selection committee.'

'Us versus them.'

'May good sense prevail!'

'We'll get Butty back in somehow.'

'Hope so. Good luck!'

Des took his leave and went out to the car park. His hired car was waiting for him with a map of Karistan in the glove compartment. After working out his route, he put the map aside and drove off along the main road to the south-east. The Pindi Mountain Range soon rose up in the far distance to act as its own trailfinder.

It was a longish drive but he had plenty of time at his disposal and it was very bracing to glide along in an open-topped car on such a beautiful day. Des soon learned that he'd chosen a scenic route with many geological marvels to wonder at and some superb man-made lakes and parks. The only blot on the landscape was the frequency of police patrols. It made Des keep well to the speed limit.

Snow covered the peaks like ice cream on Christmas pudding. As he approached the mountains, he wondered how close to the snowline he'd be able to get in his vehicle. A rasping noise made him look in his mirror. Another car was haring along the road behind him well in excess of the speed limit. Whoever was driving it was in a great hurry to reach his destination.

When he saw a sheltered lay-by ahead, he pulled off the narrow road to let the other vehicle overtake. It zoomed past him. Crouched over the wheel, the driver paid no attention to Des but the American was extremely interested in him. Though he caught only a fleeting glance of the man, he recognised him at once.

It was Derek March.

SIXTEEN

The unhappiness in the English camp had deepened into open strife by the day of the first Test. Short only of resorting to physical violence, the players did everything they could to persuade the selection committee to reinstate Butty in the team but Derek March, James Henry Fotheringhay and Colonel Arthur Totter held firm. No surrender. Their one supporter from the team itself was Penny Coyne, the most obvious person to be dropped if room had to be made for his Yorkshire rival. Personal animosity and professional pride made Penny defend his position stoutly.

'I was picked on merit!' he insisted.

'You're a good player,' conceded Dealer, 'but let's face it, old son. Butty can buy and sell you as a cricketer.'

'Then why isn't he in the team?'

'Because Fothers won't play him.'

'He wants a superior all-rounder. Me.'

'Bollocks! Butty is light years ahead of you in every department of the game, Penny. But you got one big advantage over him.'

'What's that?'

'You didn't shaft Lady Antonia Titwillow.'

Penny seethed with envy. 'You mean, Butty did?'

'No. But Fothers *thinks* he did and that amounts to the same thing. Get the message, Pen? You didn't play yourself into the side. Butty shagged his way out of it.'

'He never could keep his trousers on!'

'This time, he did. Oddly enough. He's an innocent victim.'

'How often have I heard that one before?'

163

The team coach was taking them to the Mingoon Cricket Ground for the match. Having played on the pitch against the University XI, they felt that they knew it reasonably well but overnight rain had dampened it and brought out its hidden ambiguities. The Karistan XI contained only three names they recognised, the other eight players coming from teams in Eastern Province. In every sense, the Test match was a journey into the unknown.

'Where is Butty now, anyway?' sneered Penny.

'He'll be along to watch,' said Snatcher.

'Sulking back at the hotel, is he?'

'No, Penny. Had somewhere to go first.'

'Back to the suburbs to play with those kids, probably. That's about his standard. Even Butty can get in the team with that lot of no-hopers.'

'He's always ready to help those in need.'

'That's why he plays for a crap team like Yorkshire. I bet he doesn't even turn up to support us.'

'Oh, he'll turn up. But I wouldn't, in his position.'

'What d'you mean, Snatch?'

'Might as well be hung for a sheep as a lamb.'

'Eh?'

'Right now, I'd be back at the hotel, slipping Lady Antonia a fast one down the leg-side!' Those within ear-shot guffawed. 'I'd win the toss and have choice of ends! Just think of those delicate hands of hers stroking your googlies!'

When they reached the ground, the crowds were already gathering but there was none of the high security seen during the match against the President's XI. Much to his chagrin, General Idi Ott had been forced to cancel plans to attend and was instead watching the Test match on closed circuit television with his six wives in the safety of the Presidential palace. Intelligence reports advised him that the fugitives from Shark Island had made their way to the rebel stronghold in the Pindi Mountain Range. Until

Tiki and Verukka were recaptured, strict precautions were being taken. He was furious. His presence would have been such a fillip to the Karistan team.

Having arrived well before the match, the England side went into the pavilion in a subdued mood. What should have been an exhilarating experience now seemed like a joyless chore. The spark had gone out of the team and the one man who could coax it back into life was not even present.

England were Buttyless.

There were three other absentees from the English changing room. Derek March and Fothers were still at the hotel with Big Ben Edwards. Stricken by his conscience, the Welshman had plunged them into a new crisis at the eleventh hour. The March Hare was hopping around in small circles and even the Harrow-grown sangfroid of Fothers was crumbling at the edges. They'd got the fast bowler as far as the car park but he would go no further until the matter was resolved.

'I'm sorry,' said Big Ben. 'I tried hard.'

'Try even harder,' urged Derek. 'You can't pull out of a Test match *now*. You'd leave us in the lurch.'

'No, I wouldn't. Butty could take over from me.'

'Out of the question!' snapped Fothers as his heart constricted. 'We want you, Ben. We need you. Answer the call of duty. England expects.'

'I'm Welsh.'

'Not when you're out on that cricket pitch.'

'But I won't be out there, Fothers,' he said firmly. 'It's my religion, see? I can't play on a Sunday. An offence in the sight of God. When I came on this tour, I thought the five-day Tests would have a rest day on the Sabbath. Now I discover that these heathens out here watch cricket on the Lord's Day.'

'You've played in Sunday League cricket at home.'

'Only for Glamorgan. That's different.'

'Why?'

'I get a special dispensation from my Baptist minister.'

'Ring him up and get another bloody one!' wailed Derek.

'He's on holiday in Rhyl.'

'Jesus Flaming Christ!'

'Blasphemy will get you nowhere, Derek.'

'Ben,' said Fothers softly. 'I appeal to you. As a friend. As a colleague. As the captain of England. Put your religious objections aside just this once, will you?'

'It won't work. I tossed and turned all night, thinking about it. Honest, mun. I've been racked by guilt. Woke up sweating like a pancake.' He held out a trembling hand. 'I can't bowl like this. I've got the shakes.'

'You've just given us the heeby-jeebies,' said Derek.

Fothers pondered, then shifted his ground slightly.

'There's no problem,' he announced.

'But there is,' argued Big Ben. 'The fourth day of the Test falls on a Sunday and my faith won't let me play. I can't put seamers before singing in Chapel.'

'You won't need to,' Fothers told him. 'Karistan cricket is still in its infancy. They've neither the talent nor the stomach for a Test match. Look at our record so far. We've got progressively stronger while they've got pathetically weaker. Class will tell. We'll win by an innings at least. Probably have wrapped up the game by Saturday afternoon.'

'How can you be sure?'

'Instinct.'

'Mine says they might give us another shock.'

'In that case, we have a fall-back position. You play for three days and pretend you're unfit on Sunday.'

'That'd be dishonest, mun!'

'It's cricket!' hissed Derek.

'What do you say, Ben?'

166

'Against my principles.'

'*Please*. I'm begging you.'

'My conscience won't let me.'

'Ignore it!' howled Derek.

'Get thee behind me, Satan!'

'Ben!' they implored in unison. 'Stay in the team.'

'Sorry, boyos. I must sing hymns on Sunday.'

Fothers became desperate. 'Play for us and sing on the pitch. Every time you come into bowl, I'll make the whole team sing "Guide Me, O, Thou Great Redeemer!" if you like. How's that for a compromise?'

'Hopeless, mun.'

'Why?'

'Not enough tenors to do it justice.'

The two of them gave up. Ben was proof against all entreaty. He refused to play. Musically and theologically, they were stumped.

Tiki travelled alone to Mingoon. It was easier for one man to slip past police and army patrols in search of two. Verruka was left at the cabin high in the Pindi Mountain Range. The cool clean air and the presence of friends would speed his recovery. Tiki, meanwhile, could continue with reconnaissance alone and enjoy some cricket into the bargain. Once again he chose a seat at the back of the stand which allowed him an easy escape.

Like everyone else in Karistan, he was at once amazed and disappointed at the omission of Kevin Sowerbutts from the England team. Such a healthy and powerful man could not possibly have withdrawn because of fitness doubts. He was indestructible. It was inconceivable that they had dropped him. Yet that is what they must have done. Why? Karistan would never be reckless enough to drop their saviour, Zaki Meero. What lay behind England's perverse selection?

Commotion from outside the ground took his gaze to the car park below. Horn sounding loudly, a coach was trying to squeeze between a row of cars. When its way was blocked by a horse and cart, the coach stopped and Butty jumped out. Followed by a horde of children from the poorer suburbs, he weaved his way through the parked vehicles like a Pied Piper. Stewards tried to turn the urchins away but Butty waved a fistful of tickets for them. He had bought each one of the lads a seat in the stand.

When they took those seats in company with their hero, the boys could not believe their eyes. The sheer size of the ground was overwhelming and the atmosphere generated by a capacity crowd was electric. Compared to the manicured grass of the pitch, their own ground was a bomb-site. None of them had ever dreamed of seeing a real cricket match yet here they were, in a prime position, rubbing shoulders with one of the legends of the game.

Other spectators soon spotted the legend. A Mexican wave of greeting went around the ground and he stood to acknowledge it with arms aloft. It was all the invitation they needed. Fans converged on him from every side and he signed autographs for all-comers. It was only a matter of time before there was a pitch invasion. Butty's popularity would endanger the start of the match itself.

A familiar figure came bullocking through the mass of bodies, his bald head flashing like a lighthouse and his face scarlet with exasperation. When Derek March fought his way through, he got a grin of welcome.

'Hello, Derek. Didn't know you wanted my autograph.'

'I don't. Change of plan. You're in the team.'

'Stop joking!'

'I'm serious. Big Ben has pulled out.'

'Why?'

'His religion won't let him play on a Sunday.'

'So that's why he was singing hymns all night! Had to hit him with a pillow to shut him up.' He gave a shrug.

'But why me, Derek? Wanker Winslow is twelfth man.'

'The team want you.' He waved an arm. 'So do they.'

'Wowee!' yelled Butty, standing on his seat to address the entire ground. 'I'm playing!'

Faraway in the mountains, even Verukka heard the roar of approval. Butty was back.

High morale in the England changing room soon fizzled out. Put in to bat, the tourists got off to a disastrous start. Whether from lack of concentration, from irritation at being compelled to recall Butty or from haunting memories of a river bank photograph of his fiancée it was difficult to say, but James Henry Fotheringhay was palpably out of sorts. When Orin Logos bowled the third ball of the day, it was well wide of the off-stump yet Fothers elected to wave a bat at it. He got the faintest of touches and third slip took the catch.

England's captain was out without a run on the board.

The tale of woe was reflected in the dialogue on the balcony of the tourists' changing room. Derek March was soon throwing restorative whiskies down and the Colonel, using a telescope to observe batting technique, was sounding more and more like a frog with constipation.

'Great heavens!' gasped the old man. 'He's out!'

'Wilton should've played a stroke,' said Derek.

'He'd still have missed the bally thing. That ball must have turned eighteen inches. Who is that spinner?'

'Inta Walliconi.'

'They need to get after him, Derek. Smack him down.'

David Elgin, the incoming batsman, tried to do just that and got away with it for an over. Marbles then came to grief at the other end when he met the pace of Orin Logos.

'Well done, sir!' said the Colonel. 'Marvellous stroke.'

'Too risky,' feared Derek. 'In the air.'

The telescope wiggled. 'Where? Lost the damn thing.'

'He's going to be caught by long-on! Urghhhhh!'

England were 25 for 3. Another whisky hit his throat.

Hope stirred when Harry Smart came out to the crease. Famed for his expertise behind the wicket, Snatcher was a more than competent performer in front of it. After playing himself in for a few overs, he cracked Inta for a couple of boundaries then hooked Orin for a third. When the scoreboard ticked over to 50, generous applause rang out.

'Now we're getting somewhere,' opined the Colonel.

'Don't tempt Providence,' warned Derek.

'Dealer is rock-solid and Snatcher is on form. They'll soon teach these fellows what English cricket is all about.'

'They're bringing on a new bowler.'

'That's a ball-boy, surely. Too young to be playing.'

'No, he's in the team, Colonel. Name of Russum. Promising lad, by all accounts. Zaki tells me he's only nineteen.'

'Too early to blood him. Lamb to the slaughter.'

But it was Snatcher who fell to the axe. After taking a boundary and a two off Russum, he tried to hit him up into the stand and looked back to see his bails in the air.

'This gets worse!' said Derek, imbibing yet again. 'This lad is another Inta. Snatcher didn't even smell that ball. Look at the score. 71 for four. What's happening?'

'Nemesis!' croaked the Colonel.

'We're falling like flies.'

'Who's in next?'

'Penny Coyne. At least he won't do anything rash.'

The Lancashire all-rounder confounded their prediction. Out for a duck off the first ball he received. It was an interminably long walk back to the pavilion. Butty, the incoming batsman, passed him on the steps.

'Best innings I've ever seen you play, Penny.'

'Fuck off!'

Butty stepped on to the grass to a thunderous reception. After swinging his bat in alternate arms, he turned to wave up to the children he had brought as his guests. Everyone expected. He vowed to deliver, albeit in a way that nobody quite anticipated.

'What the devil is he doing?' said the Colonel.

'Staying in,' sighed Derek, gratefully.

'That's Sowerbutts out there, isn't it?'

'Yes, Colonel.'

'Why isn't the fellow *scoring*?'

'He is.'

'But only in ones and twos. Where's his artillery?'

Butty was keeping it under camouflage nets until he could read the two spinners with complete confidence. Inta was the real master, varying the flight of each ball and making it turn sharply in both directions at will. Russum had less control but he was still highly dangerous. Butty accorded him respect and pushed his score along with uncharacteristic modesty.

With two tireless fast bowlers and two excellent spinners, Karistan were a formidable team in the field. They were young, fit, fast and wholly committed, but the real secret of their success was the astute captaincy of Zaki Meero. Watching each batsman from the vantage point of first slip, he was able to advise his bowlers between overs and to set fields which made it difficult to score freely.

When the batsmen had negotiated their way into treble figures, Dealer emerged from behind his barricade. As Russum's arm grew tired, the opener took the advantage. Two consecutive balls went for fours. A loose full toss notched up the first six of the day. Belatedly but gloriously, Butty then grabbed a piece of the action.

His bat started to flash and the run-rate galloped along. When spin was replaced with pace again, he became even more piratical. This what was they all wanted to see. Butty at his buccaneering best, pillaging runs from almost every ball that sailed past and taking no prisoners. When 162 runs were on the board, however, he ran aground.

'Not that reverse sweep again!' prayed Derek.

'What's he doing?' said the Colonel, hoarsely.

'Throwing his wicket away.'

'Nobody ever played that shot in my day.'

'I wish Butty didn't.'

Another ovation helped the entertainer off the field but there was panic on the balcony. 162 for 6 with some decidedly unsensational batting to come. Butty had injected some life into the scoreboard but the total was still drastically short of the safety zone.

Zaki returned to spin once more and his duo made short work of the tail-enders. Some useful boundaries and a freak six took them past the two hundred mark but, when Ricky Ryman was stumped to end the innings, England had a mere 209 to their name. On the same pitch they had routed the Mingoon University XI. It was now their turn to be made to look fragile and tentative.

Fothers was understandably bitter about the situation.

'We'd have been no worse off without Butty,' he said.

'We would,' admitted Derek. 'He steadied us.'

'But where were his big guns? Why did he spend two-thirds of the time hiding behind his bat? All right, he produced a flurry of crowd-pleasers towards the end but not nearly enough. Then he plays that fatal reverse sweep again. I've warned him about that a dozen times.'

'Butty did a lot better than most, James.'

A rueful nod. 'We were appalling. Myself, especially.'

'Not to worry,' said Derek with forced enthusiasm. 'All is not lost yet. You still have another innings.'

'Yes, Uncle Derek. But Karistan have two.'

It was a chilling thought. Derek ordered another whisky.

Big Ben Edwards brought his willing honesty into play.

'You were right, Fothers,' he said, coming up.

'About what?'

'The game may well be over by Saturday. But Karistan will have won it.' He pulled a face. 'Wish I'd played now. I'd have had Sunday clear for worship.'

SEVENTEEN

There was still an hour of play left before stumps were drawn on the first day. Fothers decided that it was time to reveal his true worth as a leader. Having played the title role in a production of Shakespeare's *Henry V* at Harrow, he knew how to inspire his ragged army. Standing on a bench in the changing room and brandishing an invisible sword in the air, he gave them his version of the Crispin's Day Speech.

'Listen to me, chaps,' he began. 'This is important. We have not done ourselves justice today. You all know that. We must strike back at once. I want sixty minutes of absolute commitment from you all out there. Everybody must lift their chins and take their hands out of their pockets.'

'Hear that, Wanker?' said Butty.

Good-humoured jeers at the shamefaced twelfth man.

'Don't interrupt, Butty,' chided his captain. 'This is no time for facetious comments. We are involved in a Test match and everything we do will be put under the microscope by the press. Do you want your friends and families back home to read about a feeble and gutless England? Or do you want them to thrill to our triumph in a far-flung corner of the British Empire?'

'British *Commonwealth*,' said Wilton Rodger.

'It will always be part of the Empire to me. We are the colonial masters. Never forget that it was we who taught these chaps the game of cricket in the first place.' Fothers put steel into his voice. 'Are we going to let our pupils make a mockery of us?'

'No,' said the Colonel, lurking in the background.

'Are we going to hand them this match on a plate?'

'I'm damned if we are!'

'*Nil desperandum!*'

'Didn't know you spoke Welsh,' said Butty.

'We must fight *pro patria*.'

'I thought we were fighting Karistan.'

'When we finish this encounter, we must be able to say to ourselves "*Veni, vidi, vici.*"'

Butty grinned. 'I know what that means. "I came, I saw, I had her."'

'We can do without your puerile sense of humour,' scolded Fothers, rising above the laughter. 'Cricket is a serious business. Let's play it seriously. Let's go out there and show them our mettle. We few, we happy few, we band of brothers. Destiny beckons. Let battle commence. We meet a worthy foe. You all know what you must do to vanquish Karistan.'

'Kick the shite out of them!' said Butty.

'Onward and upward!'

Fothers led his men bravely out on to the pitch.

Hopes of an early wicket quickly faded. The openers had sound defences and both were content with a meagre diet of runs. Zaki Meero got the only boundary of the session but his stocky partner, Dulkar, the oldest man in the team at thirty, kept fractionally ahead of him with a series of pushed singles and cautious twos.

When play ended, Karistan had seventeen runs on the board without loss. The partisan crowd were delighted with events so far, though puzzled by the fact that Fothers did not allow Butty to bowl. Unlike the jaded tourists, the spectators departed in high spirits.

The ground was packed again on the next day when play resumed. Zaki was in a more attacking mood but Dulkar remained wary. It was the Karistan captain who took their total past the fifty mark. Fothers shuffled the pack of his bowlers but could make no impact. In desperation, he tossed the ball to Butty.

'Thanks, Fothers. Haven't seen one of these for ages.'

'Just bowl.'

'Change the field first,' said Butty. 'Spread 'em out. If Zaki wants to chance his arm, let's encourage him.'

The strategy paid off. With less players around the bat, Zaki became even more enterprising, sending the ball twice over the boundary ropes and setting off chants of delight in the home crowd. Content to sacrifice some runs by way of bait, Butty got the breakthrough in his second over, tempting the Karistan captain into an uppish drive which was caught by Penny Coyne at mid-on.

'Well done, Pen,' said Butty sarcastically. 'Didn't know you could catch.'

'Didn't know you could bowl.'

'We learn something new every day.'

The new batsman came in and Butty returned to his task.

As the day progressed, it became clear that Karistan were by no means a brilliant batting side. Apart from their captain, they had no superlative strokemakers. What they did possess was a remarkable tenacity. From first to last, the players clung on to their wickets as if protecting the family jewels. They had to be slowly prised out.

Zaki top-scored with 47 and Inta was at the other end of the scale with 16. In between them, the other nine players all contributed solid but unsensational innings. With the whole team throwing runs into the pot, they amassed a total of 327 all out, giving them a valuable first innings lead.

Derek March reached for the whisky bottle yet again.

'This is getting worse!' he moaned.

'Switch to The Macallan,' advised the Colonel. 'First-class single malt.'

'Not the whisky – the cricket.'

'I thought England showed some spunk today.'

'Yes, Colonel. But we're still 118 runs behind.'

'Three days to go yet. Anything may happen.'

'That's what I'm afraid of!'

'Take heart, Derek. I mean, we are going to *win*, aren't we? Our sun-tanned hosts have never played a Test match before. On paper, we should give them a good thrashing.'

'That's exactly what the press will do to us.'

'Keep a stiff upper lip, man!'

'I intend to, Colonel.'

And his lip stayed on the whisky glass all evening.

On the third day, Fothers rose again. Stung by adverse press criticism of his performance and lifted by a touching Best Wishes card from Antonia ('I'm yours alone, James. Remember that and score at will'), he opened his second innings in forthright manner. The Karistan attack was stroked, glanced and hooked without mercy. Dealer supported strongly and a century stand beckoned.

Fothers was on 66 when Karistan unveiled their secret weapon. It had not been required so far in the game but it fired its first telling shot.

'Out!'

The umpire raised the finger of doom.

Fothers was devastated. He padded the ball away in the firm belief that it posed no danger whatsoever. To be given out LBW was worse than being hit by a bouncer. He was held back from making any verbal protest by an innate dignity. Dealer did not suffer from the same handicap. As his captain left the field with great composure, Dealer turned on the umpire as if he'd just stolen two pounds of apples from his barrow.

'Fucking hell!' he exclaimed. 'That was never out. The ball would have missed the stumps by a sodding mile!'

'I am the umpire.'

'Then open your peepers, old son.'

'Are you expressing dissent?'

'No, not me,' said Dealer with mock humility. 'I'm just telling you that that was the worst bleeding decision in the whole frigging history of Test cricket!'

The umpire beamed with gratitude. Ravi Rochester-Smith was a big, muscular man of Anglo-Karistan extraction though his parentage was being hotly disputed on the balcony of the English changing room. In his white coat and hat, Ravi looked less like a cricket umpire than an eccentric decorator who had come out to paper the wicket with Regency stripe. The more Dealer ranted and raved, the more the umpire loved it.

Quiescent throughout the first two days, Ravi now took a more active role. If the decision against Fothers was questionable then the one against Wilton Rodger was unbelievable. A ball which he missed by a foot was adjudged to have come off the outside edge. Dealer was sent into an even wilder frenzy of protest but his own dismissal was at hand.

Inta beat him at last with a ball which struck him in the groin. Once again the finger of fate was lifted.

'It hit me in the goolies!' complained Dealer.

'Out!'

'And it would have cleared the bails by a foot.'

'Out!'

'I demand a television replay!'

'Watch it in the pavilion!' ordered Ravi.

It was minutes before Dealer was persuaded to leave the pitch. What angered him most was the fact that he'd really been playing well, striking the ball hard and often to reach an impressive 80. When he got to the changing room, it took three pints of beer and a cold shower to calm him down.

Legitimate dismissals sent two more batsmen back to the

pavilion. It was 217 for 5 when Butty got his second bite of the apple. His orders were to occupy the crease for as long as possible and build steadily on the score. Those orders were revoked by the crowd before he even reached the wicket.

'Bu-tty! Bu-tty! Bu-tty! Bu-tty!'

They wanted the full technicolour performance.

'Bu-tty! Bu-tty! Bu-tty! Bu-tty!'

They could not spell his name, but the children who were there as his guests could certainly pronounce it. Wanting their own team to win, they were yet longing for some quintessential Buttyama to flash across the sky like forked lightning. It would be cruel to deny them that pleasure.

'Bu-tty! Bu-tty! Bu-tty! Bu-tty!'

Someone else could not be denied. Even in the rippling sea of faces, he could pick her out clearly. Lady Antonia Titwillow was sitting beside Des Toyovsky in the press box, chanting along with the others and waving a small Union Jack. His innings during the Western Province game had earned Butty a kiss which still vibrated in his memory and made his cricket box rattle. Antonia deserved a show of thanks.

Butty struck at once. He took thirteen off the first over and sixteen off the second. Inta and Russum were punished as never before. When Butty took strike again, he was so bellicose towards the younger player that Russum began to falter badly. Orin soon replaced him with pace but he fared no better against the whirlwind attack. Butty belaboured every ball within reach.

He was well into the fifties before Ravi intervened. A reverse sweep brought Butty two easy runs but he was hungry for more. As he turned for the third, the ball was hurled in from the boundary. Butty showed a turn of foot that was surprising and got his bat down in the crease a split-second before his bails were whipped off.

Ravi Rochester-Smith raised his notorious digit.

'Out!'

'What are you on about?' demanded Butty.

'Out!'

'I was there with seconds to spare.'

'Run out.'

'Bollocks!'

'Who is the umpire here?'

'Not you, mate. You're a walking disaster!'

Ravi grinned. 'Thank you.'

'I was home and dry,' insisted Butty, looking around at the Karistan team. 'Ask them!'

Zaki and the others were plainly embarrassed at the decision but they could do nothing to rescind it. The umpire continued to point towards the pavilion like a signpost.

'Anything I can get you while I'm there?' said Butty.

'Get me?'

'Your guide dog, maybe? Your white frigging stick?'

Ravi chuckled. 'I like you, Mr Butty.'

'Well, that's more than I can say for you, sunshine.'

'Run out!'

'Think again, mate!'

'Run out!'

'Stay in!'

'Run out!'

'Stand still!'

'RUN OUT!'

'Sit down!'

And Butty lowered himself to the ground and sat behind the crease like a bull-dog outside his kennel. Both umpires tried to remonstrate with him but he simply took some chewing gum from his pocket and slipped a piece into his mouth. Butty was settling in for a long siege.

Zaki was called over but even his persuasive voice could

not shift Butty. As a last resort, Fothers was brought out on to the pitch to add his authority.

'Come on, Butty,' he said. 'Let's go.'

'I like it here.'

'You were given out.'

'Illegally. So were you, Fothers.'

'I accepted the decision without demur.'

'Well, I've got enough fucking demur for the two of us. If we let Ravioli get away with this, he'll raise his finger every time one of us farts. I don't like cheats, Fothers. And neither do they,' he added, waving an arm at the crowd. 'No doubt whose side they're on.'

The chant of support for him was ear-splitting.

'Bu-tty! Bu-tty! Bu-tty! Bu-tty!'

'See?' said Butty. 'They've heard of the spirit of fair play. Pity that deaf, dumb and blind umpire hasn't.'

'As captain of England, I command you to leave.'

'When they get me out properly, I will.'

'You're causing a terrible rumpus, Butty.'

'Good.'

'Why not discuss this over a beer in the pavilion?'

'Nothing to discuss. I'm not out.'

'But you can't sit here indefinitely.'

'Who can't? Just watch me.'

They were in a complete quandary. It was a situation which had never occurred at Test level before. The two umpires scrutinised the laws of cricket in search of a precedent but they could find no mention of a sit-down strike at one end of the pitch by a batsman with a supply of chewing gum to sustain him.

Marshalls could be called to remove him by force but that could prove dangerous. Butty would not go without a fight and he had already shown his mettle with a bat in his hand. Ravi suggested they shoot a tranquilliser dart into him so that they could remove him without violence but one glance at the crowd quashed that idea. They would never allow their hero to be dragged off a field he had graced with such a monumental display of power cricket.

'For the last time,' pleaded Fothers. 'Leave.'

'I'm comfy down here.'

'You were run out, man.'

'Fancy a piece of chewing gum?'

After another febrile discussion with the umpires in the middle of the pitch, Fothers opted for the only solution that came to mind.

'We declare!' he announced.

Two hours of play still remained and both captains agreed on the need for a prompt resumption. It was the only way to still the volatile spectators. Butty felt so betrayed that he refused to field so Wanker Winslow deputised for him. Karistan were 76 for 1 at the close of play but everyone knew that they had now won the match. They needed less than a hundred runs with almost the whole batting line-up intact.

Butty left the ground as soon as the game ended. Des Toyovsky took him back to the hotel in a taxi then invited him up to his room for a drink.

'Thanks, Des. I need an escape hatch.'

'From what, Kevin?'

'That fiasco back there,' said Butty, taking a first drink of beer. 'They make me sick. Dunno who's worst – the Karistan umpire or the England captain.'

'Fothers was only trying to be tactful.'

'He threw the game away.'

'You left him no feasible alternative.'

Butty bristled. 'Oh, so it's my fault, is it?'

'No, of course not. But the situation did rather get out of hand. You'd have sat there for days.'

'Weeks! Bloody months!'

'Fothers had to use his discretion.'

'Discretion!' roared Butty. 'He was as discreet as a rhino crapping on a snooker table. Did you see what he did out on that pitch? He gave in. All that guff about doing our best and we get the legs cut off from under us by Fothers.'

Des nodded. 'What will happen now?'

'Karistan will come out tomorrow and win.'

'To you, I meant. Will there be repercussions?'

'Yes,' sighed Butty, 'but I'm used to those. Derek March will haul me over the coals. Fothers will try to get me booted out. And the Colonel will tell me that this kind of thing never happened in his day.'

'And the end result?'

'I'll be the Bad Boy of English cricket once more.'

'You were its salvation out on that pitch.'

'That's why he tried to get rid of me.'

'Who?'

'That bastard umpire. Karistan's twelfth man!'

'He's half-English.'

'The bottom half. They got the brains, we got the arse.'

'Some of his decisions were a little perplexing.'

'Bleeding diabolical!' said Butty. 'Ravi Rochester-Smith is a nightmare. Games have rules. You're supposed to stick to 'em, not bend 'em to suit your own team. Ravi probably makes a few bob on the side selling ball-tampering kits to the Karistan bowlers. I'd certainly like to tamper with *his* balls.'

A commotion from below took them both to the balcony. They were two floors up from the swimming pool and well-placed to see the England team walking back into the hotel. Heated argument was going on. While players wanted a firm protest by the management about the standard of umpiring, Fothers was taking a don't-rock-the-boat attitude. The Colonel was burbling about his honeymoon on the Isle of Wight and Derek March was bringing up the rear with a bottle of whisky in each hand.

It was going to be a long and acrimonious night.

A knock on the door drew Des away from the balcony. The surprise visitor was Darren Grubb. He smirked oleaginously.

'I thought I might find Butty up here,' he said. 'Des can act as a witness.'

'To what?'

'Your apology.'

'Get stuffed!'

'I told the team management that I must have it.'

'Oh, did you?'

'Otherwise, I'd take legal action against you for assault.' He walked uninvited into the room. 'They agreed.'

'But *I* didn't,' said Butty.

'That's why I came to apply a bit more pressure.'

'Don't do it in my room, Darren,' warned Des, 'or I'll start applying a bit of pressure myself. To your ass!'

'Another bully boy, eh? Birds of a feather.'

'Leave him to me, Des,' said Butty, advancing on the newcomer. 'I'll tear him limb from disgusting limb.'

'Not if you value Lady Antonia's reputation.'

Butty stopped. 'Eh?'

'It could cause her grave embarrassment.'

'You've already done that, Grubb. You stuck that photo under Fothers' door. He went up the wall.'

'He was an interested party. Deserved to see it. Now,' he said, leering at Butty. 'Give me that apology – or else!'

'Or else what?'

'You and Antonia will get seen by other interested parties. The three million readers of the *Daily Comet*.'

'You'd never print that photo of us!'

'Try me.'

'You're bluffing.'

'Am I, Butty?' taunted Grubb. 'It might not hurt you all that much. Everybody knows you've got a wandering knob. But Lady Antonia is a different kettle of fish. Think how well it'd go down in *her* social circle.'

Butty had to fend off the urge to throttle him with his bare hands. Certain that he held all the cards, Darren Grubb waited patiently. He wanted to make Butty grovel.

'Well? Do I get my apology?'

'Yeah,' muttered Butty. 'Suppose so.'

'Speak up. I want our witness to hear it.'

'He will, don't worry.' He raised his voice and spoke very slowly. 'I'm sorry, Darren. I didn't mean to throw you into the swimming pool from a first floor balcony.' He grabbed the journalist by the arms. 'I really intended it to be from the *second* floor.' He ran him across the room. 'Like this!'

Darren Grubb went head first this time, whistling through the air like a buzz bomb and hitting the water with such force that he emptied half the pool. When he came to the surface, he expelled a gallon of water and floundered wildly.

Des roared with laughter. Butty waved a cheery hand.

'You're really getting the hang of this, Darren,' he said. 'See you up on the *third* floor next time.'

EIGHTEEN

For the first ten miles he didn't say a single word. Antonia began to wonder if he'd fallen into a trance. Her fiancé's eyes were open but they stared unseeingly ahead. His mouth was agape, his face was drawn, his shoulders sagged. Wherever he was, it was patently not a pleasant place to be. She sought to draw him gently back into the real world.

'James?' No answer. 'James, can you hear me?'

'Hmm?'

'It's Antonia. I'm here beside you.'

He let out a low moan and turned his gaze at her as if he had never seen her before in his entire life. Lady Antonia Titwillow was deeply alarmed by his behaviour.

'You look dreadful, James.'

'I *feel* dreadful!'

'Are you in pain?'

'Agony.'

'Where? Head, chest, tummy?'

'All over.'

'Is there anything I can do?'

'No, Antonia.'

'Oh, my poor darling!' she said, stroking his hand softly. 'What on earth is wrong with you?'

The question sent him into a paroxysm of shivering. When he finally stopped, his voice had gone down an octave.

'We lost!'

'I know, James. I was there.'

'England lost to Karistan. It's shameful. I shall never

be able to hold my head up high again in the Long Room. We were defeated by a nation of cricketing apprentices.'

'That umpire had something to do with it,' she said.

'No, Antonia.'

'He cheated!'

'We must expect a certain of amount of that kind of thing among the more untutored countries. Sportsmanship is an alien concept. It is up to us to teach it to them.'

'How can you when you're given out unfairly?'

'By rising above such setbacks. By behaving with poise and dignity. By exhibiting true British aplomb.'

'You certainly did that, James.'

'I did – Butty didn't.'

'Kevin reached that crease in time.'

'That is immaterial, Antonia. He was given out.'

'Unjustly.'

'That, too, is immaterial. Whether a decision is just or unjust does not really come into it. Once again, it must be obeyed. Otherwise, you have anarchy. You have chaos. You have some blithering idiot like Butty taking leave of his non-existent senses and forcing a confrontation.' He winced in pain. 'It's not in the spirit of the game.'

'Kevin was playing so well up to that point.'

'So was I until my dismissal. Did I complain?'

'Not a whimper.'

She kissed him on the cheek and found it moist.

'James,' she said in alarm. 'You're crying.'

He gave a shrug of despair. 'We lost.'

'But that was yesterday.'

'No, Antonia,' he said with sudden passion. 'It's today, tomorrow and every day in the future. Don't you understand? Test cricket is not like a game of snap that you can forget as soon as it's over. Every result becomes part of tradition. In a hundred years, people will be opening their copies of Wisden and looking back in ghoulish horror on our first calamitous Test against Karistan. We can never remove the stigma. I feel *unclean*, Antonia.'

He lapsed back into a morose silence and she did not disturb him again. Being the wife of the captain of England would clearly involve a few radical adjustments on her part.

It was Monday. The early finish to the match – Karistan had won it by noon on Sunday – gave them an unexpected free day. Derek March decreed that everyone should relax and try to get over the trauma of defeat. Needing to get well away from the scene of the crime, and hoping to effect a reconciliation with his fiancée, Fothers had taken up an invitation from the head of state. A car from the Presidential fleet was now driving them to a resort on the north-east coast of the island.

The Pindi Mountain Range was the dominant topographical feature of the journey. Soon after they left Mingoon, they could see its peaks spearing the sky in the distance. Now that they were closer, they could admire the undulating beauty of the foothills but it was only when they plunged into the Golgo Pass that they appreciated the true scale and magnificence of the range.

Black rock rose steeply on both sides of them. Sheep and llamas grazed on patches of grass along the road, and goats could be seen picking their way with sure-footed eagerness on the higher slopes. Eagles hovered over the pass like feathered guardians. The Golgo Pass was so wild, mysterious, elemental and uncompromising that they were made to feel like denizens of some earlier and more primitive era.

It even jerked Fothers out of his gloomy introspection.

'Wonderful!' he murmured.

'I wish I'd brought my camera.'

'This is breathtaking!'

'We needed to get away together, James.'

'I never came through the pass on my previous visit. It

was blocked by an avalanche.' The car began to slow down. There was an obstruction ahead. 'Oh dear! Not another rock fall, I hope.'

'It looks like a barrier,' she said, peering over the chauffeur's shoulder. 'With soldiers behind it.'

'A military road block.'

The car was not stopped. When the soldiers recognised the Presidential emblem on the bonnet of the car, they swung back the barrier and stood to attention, saluting until the vehicle had gone past.

'That was fun!' said Antonia. 'They think we're VIPs.'

'We are.'

'You still haven't told me where we're going, James.'

'It's a surprise.'

'Will I like it?'

'Oh yes. You'll love Jelli.'

'I've always preferred blancmange. Benenden speciality.'

'Jelli is the name of the town. A pretty resort. The house is just outside it.'

'We're going all this way just to see a house?'

'It is rather special, Antonia.'

They came out of the pass, picked up speed and took the Jelli road. Antonia's eyes were pinned to the window. The changing vistas kept her gasping. Trees, shrubs and flowers had even more vivid hues than in the Western Province. Police patrols waved them past even though they were now exceeding the speed limit.

By the time they finally reached the house, Antonia felt that her capacity for awe had been exhausted. She was wrong. The mansion was a split-level work of art, perched on red rock above a private bay and fronted by stone steps which led down to a huge and ornate garden. It was like something out of a Hollywood film. She was entranced.

They got out of the car to examine it more closely.

'Let's go inside,' suggested Fothers.

'Will they let us in?'

'There's nobody at home.'

'How do we get inside?'

'I have a key.'

The interior was even more stunning. Large, light-filled rooms had exquisite furniture and fittings. The kitchen was a masterpiece in itself. Even the wine cellar made Antonia gasp with delight. But it was the master bedroom which really thrilled her to the marrow. A large round bed stood on an even larger round carpet in a room that gave them a perfect view of the bay. Whinnying with excitement, she trotted around the edge of the carpet like a horse in a dressage competition.

'What a super place!' she cooed.

'I'm so glad you approve, Antonia.'

'Why?'

'We're going to spend our honeymoon here.'

'James!'

She flung herself into his arms with a passion that kindled even his flame and they kissed. As their lips met in a moment of burning intensity, they heard a series of loud bangs. They embraced joyously, feeling that they'd achieved earth-moving coition at long last.

When they got back to the car, they still were so absorbed with each other that they didn't notice the series of dents on the bodywork of the car.

The members of the England team spent their rest day in a variety of different ways. While their captain went for a drive with his fiancée, others preferred more solitary pleasures. Big Ben Jenkins went butterfly hunting in the nearby woods. Olly Cromwell curled up in a quiet corner with the latest Jilly Cooper. Pebee Brooksby set up his easel on a hill and painted a landscape in watercolours. Derek March took one of the hotel mopeds for a spin. Colonel Arthur Totter listened to a tape of John Arlott, commentating on a long-forgotten Test match. Wanker Winslow could not be found anywhere.

Spurred on by Butty, the remainder of them had an impromptu barbecue on the beach. Snatcher Smart organised the booze, Wilton Rodger was in charge of the food and Dealer miraculously rustled up a dozen gorgeous young women. He also provided party hats and false noses. With music blaring out of a ghetto-blaster, they were soon having a rare old time.

Drink threw Snatcher into a maudlin mood.

'Never believe it was round the corner would you, But?'

'What's that, mate?'

'Christmas. '

'Yes, I would, Snatch,' joked Butty. 'It's like this in Yorkshire every day. We're always having barbecues in the sun on a patch of land behind the gasworks. Huddersfield's a sort of Mingoon with knobs on.'

'I miss England, mate.'

'Why?'

'The wife, the kids. Christmas and that.'

'Ring 'em up on the big day.'

'Not the same.'

'No,' said Butty, fondling a girl who fell giggling into his arms. 'But there are compensations.'

The girl kissed him and danced away to the music. Her grass skirt rustled and her nipples peeped through the garland of flowers around her neck. Penny Coyne could not take his eyes off her. Butty noticed his enslavement.

'Penny's never seen anything like it before,' he said. 'All this tweakable tit, bouncing around in front of his eyes. Not many of these grass skirts in Manchester, I bet.'

'He probably wishes he brought his lawnmower.'

They traded a laugh, filled their glasses and took a hot dog from the plate which Wilton Rodger offered round. In the happy atmosphere of the barbecue, they could forget their setback in the Test and float on a sea of pleasure.

Butty was therefore surprised when Dealer – normally the first to join a party – became serious for a moment.

'Just want to let you know, Butty. We're behind you.'

'Who is?'

'The whole team – except for Penny, that is.'

'He's always behind me, Deal. Ready to knife me.'

'The rest of us are holding firm.'

'About what?'

'You. Derek says you'll never play again on tour.'

'Try stopping me.'

'That's what we feel. One out, all out. That's our motto. We'll insist that you get your fair share of games.'

'I need 'em if I want to win those awards.'

'Fothers is the real problem. Loathes bad publicity. And we had a bellyful of it in that Test match.'

Butty groaned. 'Don't remind me, Dealer. BUTTY DEFIES UMPIRE. CHAOS AT THE CREASE. RAVI RAVE. SOUR BUTTY. IS THIS THE END OF CAPTAIN MARVEL? Every time I read a bloody headline these days it's more of a headstone for me.'

'You still got some friends, old son.'

'Thanks, Dealer.'

'And the crowd will always be on your side.'

'Yeah. But they don't run English cricket.' He looked around. 'Where did you get all this gorgeous talent?'

'I got contacts.'

'You're not the only one.'

'Eh?'

Butty nudged him. 'Over there. Penny is sneaking off with that skinny one. Where the hell are they going?'

'To the island, probably. Nookie paradise.'

Dealer's guess was correct. Hand in hand with his olive-skinned companion, Penny was sidling towards the boats that bobbed at the jetty. While everyone else was still eating, drinking or dancing, the Lancashire Lothario was rowing the girl to a small island only a few hundred yards out to sea.

Butty's smile turned into a loud cackle of delight.

'You got any brown boot polish with you, Dealer?'

'Masses of it, old son. Up in my room.'

'What about a black wig?'

'Black, brown, blond, ginger and grey. Why?'

'Don't suppose you got a grass skirt stashed away in one of those suitcases, by any chance?'

'No, Butty.' Dealer's eye fell on a fat girl who was dancing frenziedly around the fire. 'But I know where I can lay my hands on one. Let me take her a drink . . .'

Penny Coyne was not a popular member of the squad. They admired him for a skill as an all-rounder but resented his prickly manner. What really isolated him was his animosity towards Butty. Alone of the team, Penny had rejoiced in the way that the cricket press had attacked Butty for his defiance of an umpire's unfair decision. He was fed up with playing second fiddle to the Yorkshireman. Penny wanted his place in the sun.

No sunnier place existed at that moment than the island towards which he was rowing. As he pulled on the oars, the muscles on his lean body tightened and the girl giggled in approval. The movement of the boat made her garland swing from side to side, letting her nipples wink at him. He was mesmerised.

When the boat thudded into the bank, it threw him forward. The girl caught him and they both laughed.

'Let's get you ashore, love,' he said.

'Be careful.'

'I know what I'm doing.'

With his foot on the prow, he tried to jump on to dry land but the pressure on the boat sent it a yard back into the sea and he hit the water with a splash. She giggled again. Wading to the boat, he pulled it backwards until it was halfway up the bank then helped her out.

'Thank you, Mr Penny.'

'My name is Phil.'

'They all call you Penny.'

'Forget them, love. This is about me and you.'

'You said we'd explore the island.'

'We will!'

'Do you know the way?'

'Oh, yes!'

Penny took her hand and led her into the trees. It was important to get out of sight of his colleagues on the shore. They were absorbed in their barbecue. Penny wanted his own private party.

When they came to a sandy hollow, he grinned amiably.

'Perfect! Let's sit down and rest.'

'But we haven't seen everything yet.'

'Now's your chance.'

He sat on the ground and pulled her down beside him.

'That's better.'

'It's cold here,' she said with a mock shiver.

'Let me put my arm round you.'

'Thanks, Phil.'

'These flowers are getting in the way.'

'Take them off,' she said, lifting the garland for him to put to one side. 'Now I'm colder than ever.'

'Come here!'

Penny pulled her close and played with her breasts like a safecracker feeling for a tricky combination. She groaned with pleasure and undid the buttons on his shirt. Time passed in a haze of groping and grunting. When she came up for air, she pushed him slightly away.

'Are you married?' she said suspiciously.

'Me?' he lied. 'Of course not.'

'You seem so experienced, Phil.'

'Beginner's luck.'

'Will you marry me, then?'

'I'll think about it.'

'Will you?' she pressed. 'I love Englishmen.'

'All right,' he conceded, ready to tell her anything. 'Let's get engaged – right now!'

They were soon locked in another pulsating clinch.

'Have you got anything?' she whispered.

'Can't you feel it?'

'You know what I mean.'

'Oh, yeah. Two packets. Bought 'em off Dealer.'

'Two packets? How many is that?'

'Six,' said Penny. 'I'm planning on a long engagement.'

She giggled and pulled off his shirt. His shorts came down in record time. There was a swift rustle of rubber as he opened a packet and slipped on the condom then he plunged deep into the grass skirt like an absent-minded rabbit searching for its hole. The Penny suddenly dropped.

Afflicted by the deafness of lovers, they did not hear the other boat being rowed towards the island. Nor did they hear the bare feet of the man who leaped on to the shore. The naked buttocks of Penny Coyne were still rising and falling with gathering power between the strands of the grass skirt when the interloper came.

'Stop!' he commanded in a deep voice.

'You're joking!' grunted Penny.

'She's my wife – STOP!'

The order was accompanied by a jab in the arse with the point of a spear. Penny's passion dried up instantly. A glance over his shoulder told him that it was time to break off the engagement. Standing behind him, with a spear in the throwing position, was a big, muscular tribesman with the distinctive brown skin and thick black hair. Like the girl, he wore a long grass skirt but Penny did not want to find out what was underneath it.

The angry husband used the spear to prick Penny's testicles. It was all the encouragement that the lover needed.

Abandoning his pride, his clothes and his temporary fiancée, he scrambled to his feet and hared off towards the sea. Red-faced and bare-arsed, he was soon swimming for his life towards the beach.

Back in the hollow, Butty took off the wig and tossed it away with the spear. The frightened girl recognised him and giggled with relief.

'I remember,' she said. 'You're Bummy.'

'Close enough, darling.'

'I knew it was a joke. I'm not married.'

'Good.'

'But I might have been. We were engaged. Until you scared him away.'

'Penny didn't deserve you.'

'Why not?'

'You're too nice for him. Too young, too sexy, too . . .'

Deep in his grass, there was an urgent rustle.

She grinned. 'What have you got in there?'

'A mole.'

'Can I play with him?'

'If you like.'

He lay down beside her and their grass intertwined.

She wanted commitment. 'Will you marry me afterwards?'

'No need to,' said Butty uxoriously. 'I'm your hubby. Remember? How do they say "Welcome home" in Karistan?'

NINETEEN

James Henry Fotheringhay's definitive book on Captaincy was not yet written but it was taking shape in his mind all the time. In the wake of the Test Match against Karistan, he began to frame a chapter entitled 'Coping With Crisis'. Leadership did not just consist of presiding over an uninterrupted series of triumphs. Even in the best-run teams there were bound to be setbacks, and the real captain was the man who could pick his side up again and inspire them to new heights.

Fothers had reached new heights in his personal life. The trip to Jelli had moulded his relationship with Antonia into a more exciting shape. Gone were his doubts about her fidelity. Accepting her explanation of what did and did not take place on a river bank, he saw how hasty and ill-judged his reaction had been to Darren Grubb's apparently incriminating photograph. He and his fiancée were back in each other's arms. Antonia loved him and she loved the house. At least one of the aims of the Karistan tour had been achieved.

The feeling of well-being generated by the visit to Jelli spilled over into his *magnum opus* on Captaincy. He addressed his mind to a chapter on Fraternising With Your Players. Ideas came so thick and fast that he decided to put one of them into practice.

'Who's he taking?' asked Wilton Rodger.

'The senior players,' said Dealer. 'That's you, me, Pilly Pilgrim, Marbles, Penny Coyne and Snatcher.'

'What about Butty?'

'Fothers hasn't invited him.'

'But he's senior to all of us.'

'Makes no difference, Wilt. He's off the guest list. The only other person coming is the Colonel. Don't sit next to him.'

'Why, Dealer?'

'Because he can bore for England. When the Colonel's had a few drinks, all he can talk about is the time he bowled out Denis Compton at the Oval.'

'What year was that?'

'1066.'

They were waiting in the hotel lobby for their captain. Fothers was treating them to a meal at a seafood restaurant further up the coast. It was not their idea of the most exciting way to spend an evening but they could hardly refuse. In the congenial atmosphere of a restaurant, they might even be able to put in a good word for Butty with their captain.

Penny Coyne was the first person to join them.

'Where are we going, lads?' he asked.

'Out to that island,' teased Dealer. 'To see if your girl-friend is still out there with her "husband". Butty tells me you had a nasty attack of *coitus interruptus*.'

'I'll have a nasty attack on him one of these days!'

'Learn to take a joke, man,' advised Wilton.

'Not from Butty.'

Fothers arrived with the rest of the party and they were driven to the Dolphin Restaurant. It had a rather seedy atmosphere with subdued lighting and pounding muzak.

'Are we in the right place?' asked the Colonel.

'It was highly recommended in the brochure.'

Snatcher jerked a thumb over his shoulder. 'The sign of the door said "Under New Management". But I like it.'

The waiter showed them to a table in an alcove and offered them complimentary rum punches. They began to relax. Fothers had to force himself to be sociable. He'd never stepped this far down from Mount Olympus before.

'Treat me as one of you,' he said with condescension. 'This is a night when all the barriers are down.'

'Hear, hear!' said the Colonel.

'It's important for us at the top to keep in touch with the hearts and minds of you lot down at the grassroots. We want to know how you *feel*.'

'Hungry,' said Wilton.

'We can soon solve that problem.'

The food looked good, smelled even better and tasted delicious. Every one of them ordered a second helping of the house speciality, Prawns in Anchovy Sauce. After a few glasses of wine, their reservations about the Dolphin Restaurant evaporated. It was a great meal. The only two items the guests would have removed from the menu were Fothers and the Colonel.

Their captain and host had the fixed smile and frozen posture of a dummy from Madame Tussaud's. His small talk consisted of such throwaway items as the meaning of life, the future of cricket and the history of Harrow School. The Colonel provided no light relief. After bowling Denis Compton out a dozen times for their benefit, he rounded on Dealer and rolled up his sleeve. His wrist was bare.

'You see?' he boasted. 'I've sold all those watches.'

Fothers looked around the well-fed faces of his foot-soldiers and congratulated himself on the success of his Fraternisation policy. It was only when he got back to the hotel that its major defect became apparent.

His stomach began to revolve like a washing machine on fast-spin and the pain was excruciating. He only just made it to the bathroom in time. Fothers spent the rest of the night sitting on the toilet and musing on a new chapter for his book.

How To Provoke A Disaster.

* * *

The full scale of the disaster became clear next morning. All six players who'd been at the restaurant declared themselves unfit for the one-day match against Powlee and Fothers himself would not venture more than five yards from the bathroom. The England team had been decimated. The Colonel was in a coma.

Derek March had to cobble a team together on his own. Faced with the loss of his major batsmen, he had to draft Butty into the team as a last resort. Snatcher was bullied into playing because he was the only specialist wicket-keeper. Penny Coyne, his emergency stand-by, was standing by his own personal emergency. Wilton Rodger was also cajoled into playing. Fed with stomach pills, he and Snatcher were reluctant cricketers.

Butty sat next to them on the team coach.

'What the hell did you eat, Snatch?'

'Prawns for the main course. Figs for dessert.'

'Best pair of openers since Hutton and Washbrook.'

'Dealer's in a worse state than I am.'

'Must've been fun, sharing one bathroom.'

'We were in and out of there on a rota system.'

'Going through the motions, eh?'

'Please, Butty!' he wailed. 'No jokes about it.'

'Sorry, mate. I'll let the matter drop.'

Snatcher and Wilton were in agony.

Powlee was a town on the northern coast of the island. Its cricket team contained three of the Test cricketers who'd helped to humble England at Mingoon. They would be stiff competition. In the absence of Fothers and Dealer, his vice-captain, Butty took charge at the insistence of the other players. He rose to the challenge well. Winning the toss, he elected to bat on what was a perfect batting wicket.

Butty took major responsibility on to his shoulders.

'I'll open with Olly,' he announced.

'Right,' said John Cromwell, padding up.

'Wilt will come in first-wicket down.'

200

'If I'm still alive,' said Wilton.

'What about you, Snatch? Do you fancy Number Two?'

Snatcher sprinted off to the nearest toilet.

The Powlee XI were a competent, well-balanced team but they had no answer to Butty. Captain of England for the first and only time in his life, he was determined to make the most of it. There was no Ravi Rochester-Smith to curtail his innings this time and no Fothers to make a premature declaration. Butty scored 72 in the century stand with Olly Cromwell. It was only when his partner fell to the spin of Russum that the troubles started.

Wilton Rodger could not stay at the wicket for any length of time. The call of nature could not be denied. Butty hogged the bowling to take the strain off him but Wilton could not be protected indefinitely. Facing the first ball, he was in such dire discomfort that he swung wildly at a delivery he hardly saw. The ball went deep into the stands for a six. By the time it had been found again, Wilton had left the field at a canter, staved off humiliation and returned.

Butty was on song. Russum's bowling held no fears for him and the young spinner was overwhelmed by the ferocity of the England captain. By the time that Snatcher replaced the grateful Wilton (caught at mid-wicket), Russum had been knocked out of the attack and England were within sight of the two hundred mark. Butty welcomed the new batsman.

'How're you feeling, Snatch?'

'Terrible.'

'I'll shield you as much as I can.'

'Thanks, mate.'

'Anything else I can do?'

'Yeah – set up a portaloo behind the stumps.'

Snatcher left the pitch six times in the course of his innings but he scored runs whenever he faced a ball. With Butty now into the fast lane, Snatcher bumbled along on the hard shoulder. His progress was slow but sure. At the end of the allotted fifty overs, England were 288 for 2.

Butty was cheered to the echo as he left the pitch. The crowd had seen him at his best. High in the stand, Tiki clapped as loud as anyone. He turned to Verukka alongside him.

'I told you that cricket was the answer,' he said.

'But the President is not here.'

'He'll be back to watch England again sooner or later. He dotes on the game. Butty will tempt him out. We have no player like him in Karistan. The President will simply have to see him in action.'

'When will that be?'

'He will be tipped off well in advance, Verukka.'

'Will we?'

'Yes,' said Tiki with a smile. 'We have a friend in the English camp now. He will help us.'

When Derek March laid eyes on Fothers, he was uncertain whether he should summon a doctor or ring an undertaker. Prostrated by prawns, his white-faced room-mate lay on the bed and moaned. In breaking the bad tidings to him, Derek felt positively sadistic.

Fothers turned a bloodshot eye upon his uncle.

'What's the news?'

'Not good, James.'

'We lost *again*!'

'No,' said Derek. 'We won. To be more exact, Butty beat them almost single-handed. He scored 175 not out then took 6 for 44. We beat them by 27 runs. Exciting cricket.'

'Butty should never have played.'

'He saved our bacon.'

'We agreed to drop him for every game.'

'That was before you and the others did some dropping

202

of your own. Butty simply had to come in. As it was, we dragged Snatcher and Wilton from their sick beds.'

'How did they play?'

'Fitfully.'

'I know the feeling.'

'Worst part was during the Powlee innings.'

'Why?'

'They did more running than the batsmen,' said Derek. 'Butty had Wanker Winslow on stand-by. Whenever Snatcher went off to the loo, Wanker took over as wicket-keeper. And when Wilton charged off, Wanker covered for him at Silly Mid-On. The three of them changed places as if they were in a square dance. There was only one moment of crisis.'

'Crisis?'

'Snatcher and Wilton got the call together.'

'What happened?'

'Wanker stepped into the breach. Trouble was, when they came back on to the pitch, he went haring off to the pavilion himself.'

'I didn't know that he had diarrhoea as well.'

'He didn't. Wanker has his own agenda.'

Everything that Fothers heard only increased his discomfort. All pleasure was taken out of the victory. Derek saved the killer blow until the end.

'It was a team decision, James.'

'What was?'

'The election of captain.'

Fothers was aghast. 'You don't mean . . .'

'Butty took over your mantle for the day.'

'That's appalling. Why ever did you allow it?'

'I had to. The hideous truth is that it paid off.'

'Butty would be the world's worst captain.'

'Not today,' admitted Derek. 'Butty was fantastic. But for him, we'd have been up Shit Creek without an Elsan.'

Leaping from his death-bed, James Henry Fotheringhay

fled into the bathroom as if the German Army was on his tail. It was the speediest evacuation since Dunkirk.

Flushed with his success as England captain, Butty returned to the team hotel in Powlee with the other players. Those who could still look at food wanted to have a celebratory meal in the dining room later on. Butty went up to his room to take a shower. The water was still cascading over him when he heard the loud knocking at the door.

'Is that you, Big Ben?' he called.

The knuckles banged with more urgency.

'You're always forgetting your bloody key.'

Two fists drummed madly on the timber.

'All right!' yelled Butty, walking naked across the room and leaving a trail of wet footprints. 'I'm coming, Ben. So calm down, you Baptist head-banger!'

Opening the door, he expected Big Ben Jenkins to lumber in but it was a Lady Antonia Titwillow who darted into the room before anyone saw her in the corridor. She was carrying a newspaper and wearing nothing but a bikini. Butty suddenly became aware of the fact that he was wearing even less. He snatched the newspaper to hold over his groin and kicked the door shut with a dripping foot.

Antonia was panting with distress.

'I had to see you at once, Kevin!' she said.

'You've seen all there is to see.'

'Something terrible has happened.'

'Yes, I heard about Fothers and those prawns.'

'Something far worse,' she explained. 'That odious little man, Darren Grubb, carried out his threat.'

'Eh?'

'He got them to print that photo of us.'

'Who?'

'The *Comet*.'

'How do you know?'

'See for yourself. You're holding a copy of it.'

Butty lifted the paper to read it, realised that he was naked again and replaced the fig leaf of decency. He began to understand why she was shaking all over.

'I'll drown him next time!' he vowed.

'What are we going to do?' she sobbed. 'Just when I managed to calm James down, *this* has to happen. He'll go berserk. He loathes any bad publicity. So do Mummy and Daddy. They'll be beastly to me about it. But James is the one I'm worried about.'

'Don't let him see the paper.'

'He's bound to somehow. Grubb will make sure of that.'

'When did you get this copy?' asked Butty.

'A few minutes ago,' she said. 'I came straight back after the match to have a relaxing swim in the hotel pool. Before I could dive in, Grubb walked past and slipped this scandal sheet into my hand.'

'Vindictive polecat!'

'The whole world will know about us now, Kevin!'

'But there's nothing to know.'

'It doesn't matter. The damage will have been done. And James is the one who'll be hurt most. He's very sensitive to pain. Help me, Kevin! Please help me.'

Instinctively taking her in his arms, he held her for a few moments to comfort her, looking at the *Comet* over her shoulder and seeing the photograph on the front page beneath the banner headline of KISSES IN KARISTAN. Proximity to a beautiful woman made him stiffen at once and he leapt back in alarm to hide his burgeoning erection behind the paper.

'I hate tabloid papers!' she said.

'Me, too. I need a broadsheet right now.'

'Advise me, Kevin. Tell me what to do.'

'Go back to your room and get dressed,' he said. 'When I've thrown some clothes on, I'll ring you and make plans.'

'We must stop it blowing right up in our faces.'

'Yes!' said Butty, jiggling about and moving the paper to conceal each new pulsing inch. 'Just go. Please!'

'Open the door to make sure it's safe.'

'Like *this*?'

'I can hardly just stroll out in a bikini.'

'Let me get a bathrobe,' he said.

But before he could even move, ruination tapped on the door.

'Christ!' he exclaimed. 'It's Big Ben!'

'He mustn't see me like this!'

'No, Antonia. He'd only call you a harlot and try to convert you to Christianity. Quick – in the bathroom. I'll get rid of him and call you when he's gone.'

'Right.'

As soon as she was safely hidden, he opened the door.

'Sorry, Big Ben,' he said. 'You can't come in now.'

'Why not?' demanded a hostile female voice.

Barbara was standing there with her arms on her hips.

'Barbara!'

'Recognise me, do you? Surprise, surprise!'

'I wasn't expecting you until the New Year.'

'That's obvious!'

'What brought you to Karistan?'

'This,' she said, pushing him back into the room and snatching the newspaper from him. 'This photo of you and Lady Antonia Willowtit.'

'Titwillow!'

'She's nothing but a high-class whore!'

'Let's discuss this downstairs, love,' he said, trying to ease her out. 'Big Ben will be here any moment.'

'I'm staying here with Big Kevin,' she said, looking down pointedly. 'All you have to do is to hold a photo of Antonia against yourself and you get a champion hard-on.'

'That's because of you, Barbara.'

'Don't lie to me! While the cat's away, the mice will

play. While Barbara's in Yorkshire, you're having a bit of Tit-bloody-willow in Karistan.'

'There was nothing between me and Antonia!'

'Shagged her stark naked, did you?'

'No!'

'How long has this been going on, Kevin?'

'It hasn't, love. I swear to you.'

'How many times did you poke her?'

'I hardly know the woman.'

'It looks like it,' she said, holding up the paper.

'I can explain that, Barbara. When you've calmed down. All you need to know is that there's absolutely nothing happening between me and Lady Antonia Titwillow. I haven't seen her for well over a week.'

A noise from the bathroom killed the conversation. The shower had just been switched off. Barbara knew that there was somebody in there and that it was not Big Ben Jenkins. Butty offered his Little Boy Lost grin but it didn't work. Before he could dredge up a lame excuse, the door of the bathroom opened and Lady Antonia Titwillow sailed out with a shower cap on her head and a towel around her body. She might have been crossing the lawn at a royal garden party.

'Thank you so much for the loan of your shower, Kevin,' she said sweetly. 'The plumbers will have finished in my own bathroom now. Oh,' she said, taking the newspaper. 'I believe that's mine.' She gave Barbara a gracious smile. 'So nice to have met you! See you over cocktails?'

And she went serenely out into the corridor.

TWENTY

President Idi Ott lay back in the chair while his valet polished the medals on the huge chest in strict hierarchical order. His six wives looked on, eagerly awaiting their moment of alphabetised affection from their husband, each one knowing – he always made a point of telling them during his marital recreation – that she was his favourite. Excerpts from *Ruddigore* were being sung on CD by the D'Oyly Carte Opera Company. Gilbert and Sullivan were in their heaven and all was right with Karistan.

When his medals were glistening, he dismissed his valet and bestowed six kisses of equal weight and passion upon the twelve waiting lips. Then he swept out of the room and marched towards his study with an armed escort.

Zaki Meero was waiting for him beside the desk.

'Good morning,' he said with a deferential bow.

'Take a seat, Zaki.'

'Thank you, sir.'

After waiting for his lord and master to lower himself into the chair behind the desk, Zaki sat on an upright chair in front of him. The Karistan captain was immaculately dressed in a suit he had bought from a Bond Street tailor in London. Like the President, he admired England and all things English. The mutual passion had forged a bond between them.

'How are preparations for the Second Test?'

'I am very pleased with the way things are going.'

'We must be sure to beat them again,' said the President. 'England can win as many matches as they like against provincial and university teams but Karistan must win the Test series. That is the result which really counts.'

'I've told the players that many times, sir.'

'They are in good heart?'

'Never better.'

'What of the England team?'

'They have internal problems.'

'I heard about those prawns.'

Zaki smiled. 'These problems are connected with ladies. James Fotheringhay was disturbed by some photographs of his fiancée which appeared in a British newspaper. As you might expect, Kevin Sowerbutts was involved again. There was a great deal of friction in the camp for a couple of days.'

'These English,' said the President with a chuckle. 'They are at the mercy of their gutter press. Why expose themselves to the jibes of their journalists when they could censor everything that gets into print?'

'They believe in freedom of the press.'

'Freedom to criticise? Freedom to mock? Freedom to hurt?' He shook his head. 'Idiocy! If anyone dared to publish a photograph of me without permission, I would invite him to have a paid holiday on Shark Island.'

'Talking of Shark Island, is there any news of . . .'

'No,' said the other, cutting him off. 'They have still not been apprehended. But they soon will be. I have doubled the number of patrols and set up road blocks on all the main thoroughfares. Over two hundred soldiers are guarding the Pindi Diamond Mine because that may be one of their targets. They need money to buy armaments. They will not get it by stealing more diamonds.' He sat back complacently. 'When they try to move, we will have them. With Tiki and Verukka back behind bars, the rebels have no leaders.'

Zaki was worried. 'I heard about the Jelli incident.'

'That was unforgivable!'

'How many bullets were fired?'

'Six.'

'James and Antonia might have been killed.'

'No, Zaki,' said the President. 'They were in the house at the time. The sniper was merely making a point. Firing at a car from the Presidential fleet by way of insult. The chauffeur called for help on his mobile but the sniper had gone by the time the patrol arrived.'

'What about James and Antonia?'

'They had no idea that bullets were even fired.'

'That's a relief! What about the house?'

'They loved it, Zaki. It was all in the chauffeur's report. Every word they said on the return journey to Mingoon.'

'That is a crucial bargaining factor.'

'If they stay together, that is?'

'Stay together?'

'You said they had internal problems.'

'They are slowly sorting them out,' said Zaki. 'James and Lady Antonia are closer than ever now. Tomorrow will bring them even closer.'

'What is happening tomorrow?'

'Christmas Day.'

'Karistan does not recognise such nonsense.'

'They will celebrate it in style.'

'Even though the Second Test is on the next day?'

'Even then.'

The President grew pensive. 'Then we should help them to enjoy themselves, Zaki. Karistan hospitality knows no bounds. I will organise a party for them.' He gave a ripe chuckle. 'You will see the effects of it on the next day.'

'We would prefer a fair contest,' said Zaki.

'You will have one.'

'James is a friend. I will not use underhand methods.'

'You do not need to, Zaki,' said the other. '*I* will.'

*   *   *

Christmas Day eased all the tensions within the England team. It was spent at the Excelsior Hotel in Kimm, a large town in the Eastern Province and the venue for the Second Test. Ailments had been comprehensively cured and rifts were largely mended. After several bruising rounds in the ring with her, Butty was reunited delightfully with Barbara. Fothers, too, had come to terms with the perils of fame. The anguish of seeing the embarrassing photograph of Antonia in the *Comet* slowly faded away and he stopped wondering what his old housemaster at Harrow would say.

Some of the other wives and girlfriends had flown out from England to join the squad. Everyone seemed to blend together into one large and happy family.

Butty and Barbara spent most of the morning in bed.

'And this is the last one,' he said.

'Another present? You're spoiling me.'

'You deserve spoiling, Barbara. Open it.'

'I will,' she said, tearing off the Christmas wrapping paper to find a silk nightdress. 'Oh, Kev! It's gorgeous!'

'Hope it fits.'

'Oh, I'm sure it will!' She jumped off the bed and slipped her head through the nightdress, wriggling her naked body until it worked its way down. 'Perfect!'

Butty was sorry to see the wobbling bum disappear but he loved the sheen of the red silk. It showed off every delectable curve of Barbara's body. She came back to the bed and kissed him on the lips.

'Where did you get it?' she asked.

'The local Harrods.'

'I didn't know they had a branch out here.'

'Neither do they, love. It's in Room 214.'

'Eh?'

'Mick Mancini's Emporium.'

'Dealer?'

'He had that nightdress in three colours and five different sizes. Talk about being prepared. Dealer's sold cards and

211

presents to the whole team.' He slipped an arm around her. 'Are you pleased with what you got?'

'Overjoyed!' she said, looking around the gift-strewn bed. 'What about my presents to you?'

'Every one a winner.'

'I wasn't going to bring them,' she confessed. 'When I saw that photo of you snogging with Antonia, I was going to set fire to the lot of them. Then I thought "No. I'll take them with me. I'll need something to throw at the randy rooster!" So they came.'

'More to the point, love. So did you.'

He gave her a long, lingering kiss and held her tight.

'I hope Big Ben didn't mind,' she said.

'Mind?'

'Moving out to make way for me.'

'Well, he could hardly stay,' observed Butty. 'Big Ben doesn't approve of sin. If he'd seen us banging away, he'd have had us excommunicated from the choir.'

'What's everyone doing this morning?' she wondered.

'Same as us if they got any sense.'

'They don't all have a wife or a girlfriend here.'

'Then they're the ones who are probably on the phone to England right now. Talking to their families.' He began to put the presents on the floor. 'Big Ben is sloping off to the island's only Baptist community – all four of 'em. Des Toyovsky was talking about going for a drive. Marbles is a keen fisherman so he'll be out in a boat. And I think Derek March was taking the Colonel on a tour of the Diamond Mine.'

'On Christmas Day?'

'No such thing in Karistan, love.'

'You mean, it's just an ordinary working day for them?'

'Afraid so.'

'How terrible! While we're all having fun, they're still slaving away.' She pondered. 'Mind you, I wouldn't say no to a look at all those diamonds.'

'You've got the only one that matters, Barbara.'

'Where?'

'Here,' he said, holding her hand. 'On your engagement ring. Best investment I ever made – apart from my new cricket bat. Whenever you miss me, just look at this little sparkler and remember what it means and why I bought it for you.'

'It's the nicest thing you ever gave me, Kev.'

'Second nicest.'

'Oh? What was first?'

'This!'

He swept her up in his arms and rolled over on the bed with her, mounting her with one decisive thrust and riding her hell for leather through piles of discarded wrapping paper. Legs waving happily into the air, Barbara urged him on with a yell of pure ecstasy.

'Merry Christmas!'

The tour of the Pindi Diamond Mine was fascinating. They saw how the diamonds were extracted from the alluvial deposits and how they were graded by experts before being sold uncut to foreign dealers. Security was tight. The mine itself was encircled by soldiers and the internal checks on every movement of the precious stones were very thorough. Derek went into the overseer's office to thank him personally for arranging the tour then he drove the Colonel back towards Kimm. The old man was impressed by all he had seen.

'No wonder this is such a rich country,' he remarked.

'Diamonds are the major source of Karistan's wealth. During the military coup, the first thing General Idi Ott seized was the mine. Control that and you control the nation's moneybags.'

'You seem to know a lot about it, Derek.'

'You've forgotten that they flew me out here last year

213

on a fact-finding tour, Colonel. Buttering me up so that I'd recommend that England would tour Karistan. Made lots of friends here. I loved every moment of my first trip.'

'What about your second one?'

Derek pulled a face. 'No comment!'

'Thanks for bringing me, anyway,' said the Colonel. 'Never been to a diamond mine on Christmas morning before. Damned decent of you to bring a crusty old soul like me.'

'I was glad of the company, Colonel. Besides, I was keen to take a closer look at the place myself.'

'Should've thought you'd be back at the hotel today.'

'Hotel?'

'Ringing your lady wife. Giving her the compliments of the season. Women like to be remembered on Christmas Day.'

Derek smiled. 'My wife has been remembered, don't worry. But we're five hours ahead of Greenwich time here. Much as she loves me, she wouldn't like it if I rang her at five in the morning. As soon as we get back, I'll be on the phone to England.'

'Give her my warmest regards.'

'I will, Colonel.'

'Pity you can't take some of those diamonds back for her.'

'Yes,' said Derek with a mirthless laugh. 'Great pity!'

He put his foot down on the accelerator. He was now eager to return to Kimm to join in the celebrations. Derek was far too busy peering through the windscreen to look in his rear-view mirror. It never occurred to him that they were being followed.

A traditional Christmas lunch was served in the dining room of the hotel. Tables were set together to form one long banqueting board. All the players were there with assorted wives, girlfriends and members of the press corps. Darren Grubb had been banned by general agreement. Even the spirit of Christmas did not stretch to that act of tolerance.

Fothers presided at one end of the table with Lady Antonia Titwillow beside him in a pale blue dress. Derek and the Colonel were close by. At the other end of the table, Butty held court with Barbara and Des Toyovsky either side of him and Snatcher, Big Ben, Dealer and Wilton Rodger within earshot.

Drinks were poured, toasts were made, Dealer's crackers were pulled, paper hats were put on, feeble jokes were read out and food was served. Christmas was truly under way. As knives and forks attacked the meal, Butty shouted a warning.

'Watch out for the prawns, lads!'

Seeing that there were none, they laughed with relief. Fothers did not even crack his face. His memories were too bitter. It had been the most costly meal of his life.

'Derek took me to the Diamond mine,' said the Colonel. 'Intriguing place. You must visit it, James.'

'We're going to, Colonel.'

'Are we?' said Antonia.

'Yes. By personal invitation of the President.'

'You never told me, James.'

'I was saving it up until today. As a surprise.'

'How lovely! A visit to a Diamond mine.'

'That's only part of the treat, Antonia.'

'Is it?'

'Yes,' said Fothers, whispering in her ear. 'If we come to Karistan for our honeymoon, the President is going to give you a big diamond as a wedding present.'

'Marvellous!'

She whinnied excitedly like a mare who had just jumped a clear round at the Horse of the Year Show. They heard her at the far end of the table.

'Antonia sounds pleased,' said Des.

'Yes,' explained Butty with a wicked grin. 'Fothers has got his hand on her thigh.'

'But I can see both of his hands.'

'Then it must be something else she can feel on her thigh. No wonder she's getting all worked up.'

'I like her,' decided Barbara. 'I came out here ready to scratch her eyes out. But she's grown on me. Now I know that there was nothing between you two, she and I can be friends.'

'She likes you as well, Barbara,' noted Des.

'How do you know?'

'She told me. Admires your no-nonsense attitude.'

'That's nice.' She looked down the table. 'Antonia and Fothers are well-suited. They look right side by side.'

'Yes,' added Butty. 'Pulling a Hackney carriage.'

The manager of the hotel arrived to announce that the Karistan Cricket Federation had sent a gift of five dozen bottles of vintage champagne and ten crates of beer. When the cheers had died down, the corks popped and the Christmas spirit really took over. They were soon pleasantly sloshed and revelling in the occasion.

Champagne and good fellowship helped them to forget all about the setbacks so far on tour. As the afternoon turned into evening, they spilled into the lounge to sing songs and play games. The generous donation of alcohol from their hosts was turning it into the most riotous day so far on tour. It never crossed their minds that they were being encouraged to drink themselves into a stupor on the eve of a Test match.

Butty was doing his impersonation of Darren Grubb when Dealer sidled over to him. The whisper made Butty chuckle. He was soon slipping out of the lounge.

The three of them met in Butty's room. Dealer and Snatcher had brought the costumes and the boot polish.

Before Butty would change, however, he spotted a temptation that he could not resist. Spurned by the squad, Darren Grubb was spending a lonely Christmas beside the pool, reading a pornographic novel with a snigger as he lay on a recliner. Butty moved fast.

'Where's that jock strap Big Ben left behind?'

'Why?' asked Snatcher.

'Just pass the ammunition, Snatch.'

'Ammunition?'

'Those oranges.'

Finding the jock strap, Butty tied it to the vertical bars of his balcony so that he had a catapult. The orange fitted perfectly. Butty drew the catapult back, took aim and fired. The orange scored a direct hit on Grubb's forehead.

'Aouwwww!' he yelled. 'What was that?'

Butty's second missile hit him smack in the open mouth and lodged so firmly between his teeth that he could not remove it. Standing up to grapple with the second orange, he offered a perfect target for the third. Butty pulled the jock strap back much further to add greater velocity. When he released it, the orange whizzed through the air like a comet before striking Darren Grubb directly between the eyes and sending him backwards into the pool with a plop. His book floated on the water.

Shaking with laughter, they reached for their costumes.

Down in the hotel lounge, there was a slight lull in the general hilarity. Penny Coyne had passed out, Wanker Winslow had wandered off and the Colonel was alternately falling asleep and waking up to confess that he had once attempted to put glue in Denis Compton's Brylcreem and had only been held back by his finer feelings. Thousands of miles away from his family, Wilton Rodger was subdued and pensive. Big Ben was humming 'Mine Eyes Have Seen the Glory of the Coming of the Lord' and Fothers was gathering material for a chapter on Captaincy At Christmas.

The quieter mood was soon shattered. Two armed soldiers made a dramatic entry, marching into the lounge with rifles and barking at everyone to stand up in the presence of the head of state. As they dragged themselves out of their chairs, the burly figure of General Idi Ott, President of Karistan and Supreme Commander of the Armed Forces, came striding into the room with his medals jingling like sleigh bells. So cunning was the disguise and so perfect the uniform, the whole room was at first taken in. Even Barbara failed to recognise him.

It was only when Butty spoke that he gave himself away.

'Free Karistan!' he shouted. 'Home Rule for Yorkshire!'

Everyone collapsed with laughter. It was Butty and his two uniformed henchmen – Dealer and Snatcher – who were now the target for oranges and other missiles. They responded by grabbing whatever came to hand and throwing it back.

Dodging a coconut, Butty was in his element.

'This is the best bloody Christmas I've ever had.'

The hotel management disagreed. They pressed the security alarm and ten uniformed guards appeared from nowhere to pounce on Butty and his two companions before dragging them unceremoniously off towards the exit.

'It was a joke!' said Butty. 'It was all in fun.'

'Tell that to the police!' said the manager. 'It is against the law to impersonate our President. The last man who did that was shot at dawn. Every day for a week!'

TWENTY-ONE

Karistan gave them countless new experiences, but being locked up in the Kimm Police Station was not one they would care to repeat. Dragged out of the hotel by the security guards, Butty and his two henchmen were then seized by the ten uniformed giants who arrived at top speed in the police van. The three felons were expertly fitted with handcuffs and leg irons before being locked in single cells in the rear of the van. Their protests went unheard as the vehicle sped off with its siren wailing like a banshee.

The driver zigzagged his way crazily through a maze of streets, hurling them to and fro in their steel compartments. Butty was bruised, Dealer was knocked almost senseless and Snatcher's stomach decided to remind him exactly what he'd eaten during the Christmas lunch. By the time they reached the police station, they were regretting their few minutes of fun in brown boot polish and hired costumes.

They were hustled into a room and their fetters were removed. Butty rubbed his chafed wrists ruefully.

'Thank goodness for that!' he said. 'You had no right to arrest us. We'll be suing you for unprovoked assault.'

'We *were* provoked,' snarled the sturdy police sergeant. 'How?'

'By these insults,' said the other, pointing to the uniforms. 'Get them off at once.'

Rough hands fell on the prisoners and they were stripped down to their Y-fronts before being handcuffed again. Yelling their heads off, they were taken to a cell block and hurled into a large cage. As the door clanged inexorably behind them, they threatened and pleaded.

'Let us out, you bastards!' shouted Butty.

'I have a wife and children,' said Snatcher.

'It was all a joke,' explained Dealer.

'We demand to speak to the British Ambassador,' said Butty as he rattled the bars of the cage. 'We'll have your guts for garters! We'll have you all sacked! We'll have you expelled from the Commonwealth.'

'Silence!' ordered the police sergeant.

'We didn't mean to upset you,' whispered Dealer.

'No,' agreed Snatcher. 'We were just entertaining our friends. It was our Christmas party.'

Butty nodded. 'They knew I wasn't the *real* Idi Ott.'

'You are all idi-ots!' said the sergeant.

'What will happen to us?' asked Dealer.

'To you, very little. Impersonating a member of the Karistan Army is not such a serious offence.'

'That's the best news I've heard so far.'

'All you will get is five years on Shark Island.'

'Five years!' chorused Dealer and Snatcher.

'What about me?' asked Butty.

'Karistan law is very flexible. It gives you a choice between being hanged by the neck or being burned to death.'

'I'll have both,' joked Butty. 'Now, get these frigging handcuffs off us and let us out before I really lose my temper.'

'The prisoners are becoming unruly!' said the sergeant, pressing a bell in the wall. 'Cool them down!'

Two policemen came running in with a high pressure hose. A jet of icy cold water was directed at the prisoners for five minutes, making them dance around the cell until they slipped on the wet floor and landed in a heap. Their shrieks of protest only made the policemen jeer louder.

Eventually, they were left alone, three sodden figures on the floor of the cell, their hair plastered to their heads and the boot polish on their faces running down their bodies in rivulets.

'What a way to spend Christmas!' groaned Dealer.

'Yes,' gulped Snatcher. 'And next year we may be spending it on Shark Island.'

'One thing,' said Butty, searching the void for a glimmer of consolation. 'At least, it can't get any worse.'

He spoke too soon. The outer door opened and the police sergeant ushered in their first visitor. It was the person they least wanted to see them in their predicament. Darren Grubb came scurrying into the room with a wall-to-wall smirk. He raised his camera and focused.

'Watch the birdie, lads!' he said, flashing away. 'I'm going to make you all famous.'

Back at the hotel, the party was still going on and many of the England squad were still laughing. They thought that the sudden removal of Butty and the others by the guards was all part of the hoax, a carefully rehearsed piece of action to add even more fun. It was only when Butty did not reappear that Barbara began to get worried. She turned to Des Toyovsky.

'Where are they?'

'Upstairs, probably. Getting changed.'

'They've been gone half an hour, Des.'

'There was all that stuff to get off their faces.'

Des sounded more confident than he felt. The security guards had looked very authentic to him and the siren sounded identical to that of the real police force.

'I'll go check with the manager,' he decided.

'Thanks, Des.'

'Just in case.'

While Des slipped away, Barbara crossed the lounge to

221

where Fothers was sitting with Antonia, Derek and the Colonel. Drinks in their hands, all three were basking in the glow of the Yuletide celebration. Barbara's anxiety cut across the mood of inebriated contentment.

'Kevin's in serious trouble,' she said.

'I thought he was absolutely *super*,' gushed Antonia. 'If he ever gives up cricket, he should go on the stage.'

'Fooled me,' admitted the Colonel.

'Yes,' said Derek. 'I thought he *was* General Idi Ott.'

'They've been arrested and taken away,' said Barbara.

Fothers shook his head. 'That was all part of the act.'

'Suppose it wasn't?' she pressed.

'Then the three of them will have a night in the cells and wake up feeling sorry for themselves.'

'And for the England team,' she reminded. 'Kevin, Dealer and Snatcher are all supposed to be playing in the Second Test tomorrow. What sort of state will they be in if they've been locked up all night?'

Fothers was shocked. 'I never thought of that.'

'Well, it's about time you started.'

Antonia was dismissive. 'No,' she argued. 'This has all been deliberately set up to make us feel worried about them. They weren't really arrested. The moment we try to go off to the police station, Kevin and the others will jump out from behind a potted palm and laugh at us for being taken in.'

Barbara was adamant. 'They're locked up somewhere. I feel it in my bones.'

'I'm beginning to have uneasy feelings myself,' said Derek.

'It was that Christmas pudding,' decided the Colonel. 'Too rich for my stomach as well.'

'Do something!' pleaded Barbara.

Fothers shrugged. 'What am I supposed to do?'

'Get your ass into gear quick!' advised Des, walking up to them. 'I've just talked to the manager. That performance

222

we all saw was for real. Kevin, Dealer and Snatcher are now behind bars at the Kimm Police Station.'

'I knew it!' said Barbara.

'There's worse to come,' he added. 'According to the manager, they'll only be held there for a couple of hours before appearing before a magistrate to be charged.'

'With what?' asked Fothers.

'Conduct liable to provoke a riot. Impersonating the head of state is a capital offence in Karistan. That's why the guys were given the strong-arm treatment.'

'Will they be released on bail?' said Barbara.

'No chance. Once they're charged, they'll be held on remand at Shark Island. This time tomorrow, they could be working on a prison chain gang.'

'What about the Second Test?' said Derek in alarm.

'Your chances of winning will go down the tubes,' said Des. 'If you want to field your best team, activate some high-level diplomatic activity. Otherwise . . .'

'What?' gasped the Colonel.

'You're dead in the water.'

Soaked to the skin and shivering with cold, the three prisoners were huddled together in the cell. Being visiting cricket celebrities gave them an enormous amount of kudos and rendered them immune to most dangers. They now learned that there were limits to that immunity. They'd overstepped the boundaries and were being called to account.

'If only they'd give us a blanket!' complained Butty. 'I'm frozen stiff.'

'Choose to be burned alive,' suggested Dealer.

'Yes,' said Snatcher. 'At least you'll die *warm*.'

'Don't go on about it!' yelled Butty. 'It wasn't my idea to dress up as General Idi Ott. By rights, Dealer ought to be up on that bonfire with me.'

'I'll be too busy sewing mailbags on Shark Island.'

Snatcher brightened. 'I suppose we could always escape. Those two political prisoners did.'

'And have the entire Karistan Army on our tail?' said Dealer. 'They'd recapture us in five minutes and double our sentences.' He pondered. 'Maybe we should make a personal appeal for clemency to the President himself.'

'Great idea!' said Butty with heavy sarcasm. 'I'll nip over to the Presidential palace in my look-alike uniform. Use your head, Dealer. How can we appeal to anyone when we're banged away like this?'

'Every condemned man is allowed one last request.'

'Mine will be for a return ticket to England.'

'Put in a good word for us, But,' said Snatcher.

All three fell silent, contemplating a grim future.

When they heard the outer door being unlocked, they braced themselves for further humiliation. More rough handling by the police? Another dose of the water treatment? Transfer to Shark Island? The possibilities were equally depressing. Glowering at them, the sergeant came into the room and opened the door of their cage. He then took out some more keys and removed their handcuffs.

'What's happened?' asked Butty.

'Shut up!' ordered the captain.

'Any chance of a nice hot cuppa?' asked Dealer.

'Get out!'

'Where to?' said Snatcher.

'The firing squad, if I had my way,' said the sergeant. 'But we've had orders from above. We're not to harm you.'

He led them into the next room where two familiar faces were waiting to greet them. Fothers were horrified to see three of his senior players in such an appalling state. Zaki Meero was covered with embarrassment.

'I am sorry about all this,' he said.

'So are we,' said Butty. 'A police cell is not the nicest place to spend your Christmas in.'

'It was all a big mistake.'

'Yeah, Zaki.'

'And you made it,' rebuked Fothers, pointing at Butty. 'They were not amused to see their President mocked by you. Karistan reveres General Idi Ott.'

'Then why are the rebels trying to overthrow him?'

'They are not,' said Zaki, hustling them out. 'And it is, in any case, no concern of yours. The main thing now is to get you back to your hotel.'

'Yes, please!' said Dealer.

Snatcher nodded. 'Anywhere but Shark bleeding Island.'

They were soon heading for their hotel in a car. Zaki drove with Fothers beside him. Wrapped in blankets, the three released prisoners sat in the rear seat.

'Thanks for springing us, Fothers,' said Dealer.

'That was all Zaki's doing.' The three of them mumbled their gratitude. 'I contacted the British Consul and he said it would take a week to go through diplomatic channels. By that time, we might all be attending Butty's funeral.'

Butty winced. 'Now, there's a cheerful thought.'

'Out of desperation,' continued Fothers, 'I rang Zaki and he pulled all the right strings.'

'Not without difficulty,' said Zaki. 'The President was very annoyed at being impersonated but he wanted nothing to stand in the way of the Second Test tomorrow. Don't thank me for getting you out. Thank the President's love of cricket.'

'We'll show our appreciation tomorrow.'

'Yes,' added Butty. 'On the pitch.'

It was a lethal combination. Excessive amounts of food, drink and anxiety over the fate of their three colleagues conspired to give the other members of the team a torrid night. When they awoke on Boxing Day, they were bleary-eyed with fatigue and queasy with hangovers. The donation of alcohol from the Karistan Cricket Federation was having its intended effect.

Even Butty's strength was taxed by a Christmas Day divided between lavish hospitality at the hotel and an ordeal at the Kimm Police Station. When he forced his eyes open next morning, his lids felt as if they were reinforced with lead. Seeing the room in half-darkness, he yawned loudly and closed his eyes again.

'Thank God it's still the middle of the night!'

'It's not,' said Barbara. 'It's eight-thirty and they've just brought breakfast up.'

'The sky is still black.'

'Rain is forecast. Now, sit up and I'll put this tray on your lap. You need some strong black coffee.'

'What I need is to make an attempt on Rip Van Winkle's shuteye record. I could snooze for ever.'

'Not while I'm around.'

She eased him up into a sitting position and plumped his pillows to support him when she brought the breakfast tray across from the table. They were soon sitting side by side with a cup of coffee each.

'Something to eat?' she suggested.

'Not for a week or two at least.'

'You did rather go at that turkey yesterday.'

'What else is Christmas for, Barbara?'

'Us.'

'You complaining?'

'Yes. You were so tired last night, you only managed it three times. What did they give you at the police station? Bromide sandwiches?'

There was a deep rumbling sound and he instinctively put his hand to his stomach. Barbara glanced towards the window.

'That sounded like thunder,' she said.

'We don't want that. It's the Second Test today.'

A flash of lightning suddenly illuminated the sky and

threw dazzling patterns over the floor of their room. It was followed by the sound of heavy rain. Thunder soon rumbled again and more sheet lightning came hard on its heels. Rain took on a monsoon intensity and drowned out any hopes of play that day. A dejected and debilitated England team were saved from certain humiliation by the Karistan weather. Butty went back to sleep.

The deluge lasted for four days and the pitch was still so waterlogged on the fifth that no play was possible. The Second Test was abandoned as a draw. From the balcony of the pavilion at Kimm Cricket Ground, the players looked out at the lake below them. Fothers was heart-broken.

'We missed our chance to square the series,' he said.

'What at?' asked Butty. 'Water polo.'

'Think how it will look in Wisden. Lost 1, Drawn 1, against Karistan. That's an appalling indictment of English cricket. We simply must win the final Test.'

'Weather permitting.'

'Yes,' said Penny Coyne, surveying the ground. 'We don't want another fiasco like this.'

Butty grinned. 'You'd have done really well out there.'

'In all that water?'

'Yes, Penny. You could have taken a bath between overs and played with all those ducks you scored.'

'Sod off, Butty!'

'Best suggestion you've made in ages.'

Butty went into the pavilion and joined the other players at the bar. They were deeply disappointed to have the Test Match wiped out but were putting a brave face on it. Butty was about to order another drink when Des Toyovsky took him aside.

'I think I know who he is, Kevin,' he said.

'Who's who?'

'The link with Annabelle Jansen-Jones.'

'That bird with the Volvo Estate?'

'She wrote to a member of the touring party.'

'How do you know?'

Des grinned. 'Bribery and corruption.'

'Eh?'

'When the mail arrives at the hotel every morning, it's sorted by one of the receptionists into the guests' pigeon holes. I slipped her some dough and asked her to keep an eye out for any letters with a Windsor postmark.'

'That was clever.'

'It paid off,' said Des with quiet satisfaction. 'When the letter came this morning, it actually had Annabelle's name and address on the back.'

Butty's ears pricked up. 'Who was it sent to?'

Des looked around to make sure that nobody was listening. 'Derek March,' he whispered.

'The bastard!'

'Don't jump to conclusions,' warned the other. 'Just because he knows Annabelle Jansen-Jones, it doesn't mean that he was the person who pinched or borrowed her Volvo Estate. It could just be a coincidence.'

'What's your gut feeling, Des?'

'He's our man.'

'How can we be sure?'

'By ringing her up to ask her.'

'She'd never talk to complete strangers like us.'

'That's why Derek himself will phone.'

'The March Hare?'

'Not in person,' explained Des. 'You'll impersonate him. If you can do such a brilliant take-off of President Idi Ott, you'll have no trouble with Derek. The lady won't be able to *see* you, remember. And the long-distance line will distort your voice, anyway.'

Butty was intrigued. 'What do I say to her?'

* * *

Annabelle Jansen-Jones was a tall, slim, handsome woman in her late thirties with a deep pride in her hyphen. Even when lying in a bubble bath, she had the unmistakable aura of the English upper middle class. The telephone rang and she reached out a hand to lift the receiver.

'Hello,' she said. 'Windsor 72395.'

'Is that you, Annabelle?' said a faraway voice.

'Speak up, please. Can't hear you, I'm afraid.'

'Bad line,' apologised the voice, slightly clearer. 'Is that you, Annabelle?'

'Yes. Who is his?'

'Derek.'

'Darling!' she exclaimed. 'Did you get my letter?'

'That's why I rang.'

'Wonderful!'

'How are you, Annabelle?'

'Missing you dreadfully.'

'What about the Volvo Estate?'

'Oh that! I've sold it,' she said briskly. 'I'm still cross at you for persuading me to loan it to you. I had no idea you were going to let that dreadful man, Sowerbutts, get into it. My poor Volvo Estate felt *polluted* after that human oil slick had oozed all over it. Kevin Sowerbutts is an environmental hazard.'

'Fucking hell!' said a Yorkshire voice in Karistan.

TWENTY-TWO

As the chimes of midnight struck, the England team and their entourage joined hands in the lounge of the hotel to sing in the New Year in the traditional way.

> 'Should auld acquaintance be forgot,
> And never brought to min'?
> Should auld acquaintance be forgot,
> And days o' lang syne?
> For auld lang syne, my dear,
> For auld lang syne,
> We'll tak' a cup o' kindness yet,
> For auld lang syne.'

Swaying drunkenly, they exchanged handshakes and kisses all round. The Karistan Cricket Federation had been even more generous this time, contributing an almost unlimited supply of alcohol for the tourists' New Year's Eve party. As the revellers peeled off in ones and twos, they grabbed a bottle to take up to their rooms so that they could continue the celebrations in private.

Fothers and Antonia chose champagne, Butty and Barbara preferred wine, Derek March settled for whisky, the Colonel opted for brandy, Snatcher Smart was a gin man, Wilton Rodger liked rum, Penny Coyne grabbed a six-pack of beer canisters, the normally teetotal Big Ben Jenkins selected a flagon of rough cider and Dealer – alert to the commercial potentialities – waited until everyone else had retired to bed before shifting all the booze that remained to his room with a view to selling it to his colleagues at some future date.

The whole team seemed happily unaware of the fact that they were playing Eastern Province next morning. When they arrived at the Kimm Cricket Ground, the team looked careworn and lethargic. The Presidential strategy of weakening the opposition by means of alcohol seemed to have paid off. Encouraged by the sight of eleven walking wounded, the Eastern Province captain won the toss and chose to bat. When the England team came out to field, they looked like eleven zombies. The umpire had to guide Snatcher to his position behind the stumps like a policeman helping an old lady across a road.

Confident that they were going to score a packet of runs, the Eastern Province openers came out with eager steps and broad grins. Butty was given the new ball by Fothers. Bowling off a short run-up, his first delivery was a full toss which was cracked to the boundary for four before anyone in the field could even move. The second ball met the same fate. Butty stifled a yawn before he came in to bowl the third.

Pushed past mid-wicket, it looked like an easy single and a possible two. When the batsmen set off, however, the England team suddenly came to life. Dealer was on the ball like a flash and it was hurled to the bowler's end for Butty to whip off the bails with a flourish. Eastern Province were jolted. They'd been comprehensively conned.

Three days later, the game ended with the narrowest of wins for England. Sitting on the balcony of the pavilion, the Colonel had no doubt what had given them the slight edge.

'Psychological advantage,' he said. 'We rattled them on that first day. Cunning strategy of yours, Derek.'

'We learned the lesson of Christmas,' said Derek

pompously. 'Thank heaven it rained on Boxing Day because we were in no fit state to compete in a Test Match. James and I were determined not to be in that position again. So we passed the word around on New Year's Eve.'

'Moderate your transports.'

'Yes, Colonel. The eleven players had a good time at the party but they pretended they were drinking themselves into imbecility. They turned up for the game looking like corpses and Eastern Province bought it.'

'Just as well. They were a tidy outfit.'

'Close game. Good cricket.'

'But we *won*. That's the way to start the New Year.'

'The Third Test is the big one,' reminded Derek. 'Nothing less than a decisive victory will do. If we lose another Test match to Karistan, we'll be the laughing-stock of the cricketing world. The press will destroy us.'

'Mustn't let that happen.'

'There've been enough disasters on this tour already.'

'Yes,' agreed the Colonel. 'Had one myself. Seem to have misplaced the lady wife. Can't find her anywhere.'

'You didn't bring her with you.'

'That might explain it.'

'She died five years ago.'

'So she did! I keep forgetting. Damned shame, really. The lady wife would've have enjoyed the way we outthought the wily foreigner. I miss her,' he said fondly. 'She could quote Kipling by the yard.'

While the Colonel launched himself into his marital memories, Derek stole quietly away. Most of the team were still in the bar, celebrating with the abandon they had wisely kept in check on New Year's Eve. They would be there for hours yet. Derek felt that he could leave without being noticed but Des Toyovsky was keeping a close eye on him. The moment that the team manager slipped out, the American went after him.

Collecting his hired car, Derek drove out to a wooded

suburb of Kimm and turned off the main road. He came to a halt in a quiet lane and waited. Des trailed him from a safe distance on one of the hotel mopeds, parking it in the trees and creeping through the undergrowth until he saw Derek's vehicle. Through a pair of binoculars, he watched the transaction with interest.

A second car arrived and pulled up beside the first. Derek got into the other car and talked with the driver for a few minutes. Something appeared to be exchanged. When Derek got out of the car, there was a bulge in his pocket. The other man turned his vehicle round and drove swiftly away. Derek's own car rejoined the main road and headed back towards the hotel.

In the bushes, Des felt a tap on his shoulder. He swung round to find himself staring into the suspicious eyes of Butty. The player had his hands on his hips.

'What's going on, Des?'

'Nothing.'

'I saw you sneak off after Derek. So I followed.'

Des shrugged. 'Just wondered where he was going.'

'Don't bullshit me,' warned Butty. 'I'm not stupid. I was there when you went into the trees after that golf ball, remember. You played that shot deliberately so that you could slope off and snoop, didn't you?' He pointed to the binoculars. 'Just happen to have those with you?'

'Okay,' said Des. 'I'll come clean. Only not here.'

'Let's go back to the hotel.'

Lady Antonia Titwillow was quivering with anticipation. It was about to happen at last. The victory against Eastern Province put her fiancé into a state of polite exhilaration. Fothers had reached the fifties in both innings. When he suggested they go back to her room, she had every hope that his scoring would not be confined to the pitch. Baulked at the New Year's Eve party ('Cricket comes first,

Antonia'), she could now take her turn in the queue.

They came tripping into her room hand in hand.

'You looked so noblesome at the crease today, James.'

'It was a crucial match for me.'

'I thought you led the team superbly.'

'My captaincy turned the balance our way,' he said with a touch of arrogance. 'I outmanoeuvred Eastern Province.'

'Completely, darling!' She kissed him on the lips and he responded with comparative warmth. 'Mind you,' she observed, 'Kevin's century in the second innings did help.'

He eased her away. 'Butty was very fortunate.'

'He's such a devil-may-care player.'

'That's his strength and weakness. When he comes off – as he did today – he can work wonders. But all too often he sacrifices his wicket with a reckless blunder. Control and elegance. Those are my watchwords.' He allowed himself a congratulatory smile. 'True cricket *aficionados* like President Idi Ott appreciate my superiority.'

'The President?'

'Yes, Antonia,' said Fothers proudly. 'My performance against Eastern Province clinched the deal. The President watched it on closed circuit television and authorised Zaki to go ahead.'

'With what, James?'

'The contractual side of things.'

'I'm not with you, darling.'

'But you are, Antonia,' he said, suddenly taking her hand in an uncharacteristic display of affection. 'I'm accepting the post on both our behalves.'

'What post?'

'This is in strict confidence, mark you.'

'Of course.'

'Nobody must know until it's officially announced.'

'Know what, James?'

'When the rest of the team return home, I'll be staying here until the English cricket season starts.'

'Here in Karistan?'

'Yes, Antonia.'

'What about the wedding?'

'I'll come back for that, naturally,' he explained. 'Then the two of us will have our honeymoon at our house in Jelli. You won't just be sharing it with a husband, Antonia. I'll also be Director of Cricket in Karistan. That's the job they've offered me. To develop the game here to the highest standards.'

'What about your own playing career?'

'That will continue uninterrupted. My contract releases me to honour my county contract with Hamcester and any commitments I may have with the England team in winter months.'

'So we'd live in that super house in Jelli?'

'Yes, Antonia.'

'It would be like a permanent honeymoon.'

'Yes, Antonia.'

'The two of us, alone in that paradise.'

'Yes, Antonia.'

'It's divine! What could possibly be better?'

'£250,000 a year. That's my salary.'

'James!' she exclaimed, metaphorically embracing his wallet. 'That's marvellous! Now I realise why you were so keen to come on tour to Karistan in the first place.'

'It was a shop window for me,' he explained. His voice darkened. 'That's why I was so determined to keep Butty out of the team. He was the one person who could've thrown the brick through the window. His impersonation of General Idi Ott nearly ruined the whole deal. Fortunately, Zaki was able to smooth out any wrinkles and all is well.'

'This calls for a celebration.'

'Why don't I take you out for dinner?'

'I'd prefer room service.'

'Order anything you wish, Antonia.'

'Then I'll start with you,' she said, flinging her arms around his neck and whinnying softly. 'I'm yours, James. Take me. Uncage the beast within you and show me no mercy.' She drew him to the bed. 'Possess me.'

'Not before cricket, Antonia,' he said.

'But the game is over.'

'We have another one in two days' time.'

'Don't you want me?'

'Of course, I do.'

'Then why don't you make passionate love to me?'

'Because it would *show*.'

'Sleep the whole night with me, James.'

'What about Uncle Derek?'

'I'd prefer to have you.'

'He'd know. I'm sharing a room with him. What is he going to think if I'm not in the next bed?'

'That you're up here in mine instead.'

'He'd be terribly upset,' said Fothers, detaching himself from her. 'I'm sorry, Antonia. We'll have to wait. Cricket comes first and a cricket team manager comes second. I couldn't possibly upset Uncle Derek. He has such high moral principles.'

Holding the telephone in one hand, Derek March lay in the soapy water and used the deft fingers of his other hand to play with his high moral principles. His eyes glistened and his stertorous breathing echoed around the bathroom. A phone call to Windsor was making it a very Happy New Year for him.

'I picked them up today for you, Annabelle,' he cooed.

'You're such a darling!'

'Only the best are good enough.'

'How will you get them out of the country?'

'Leave that to me.'

'Isn't it dangerous?'

236

'Highly. But I'd take any risks for you.'

'Oh, Derek! You're so resourceful.'

'I know.'

'In bed and out of it.'

A joyous shudder. 'Do you like me in bed?'

'I love you anywhere,' said Annabelle Jansen-Jones.

'What will you do for me?'

'Anything!'

'Tell me, Annabelle.' His hand increased its rhythm. 'Tell me what you'd do if you had me there right now.'

'Do you really want to know?' she teased.

'Oh, please!'

'I'd tie you naked on my fourposter bed.'

'What with?'

'My black tights.'

'And?'

'I'd whip you unmercifully with your Old Harrovian tie.'

'And?' he urged. 'And? And?'

'I'd fetch a jar of Frank Cooper's Oxford Jam.'

'What flavour?'

'Blackcurrant.'

'Oh!' he sighed in ecstasy, moving straight into top gear with a syncromesh that Wanker Winslow would have envied. 'Tie me up with black tights, whip me with my tie, fetch a jar of Frank Cooper's Oxford Blackcurrant Jam. And then? And then?'

'I'd spread it all over you, Derek.'

'And then?' He was almost there. 'Go on. Go on.'

'I'd bend over you.'

'And what would you do, Annabelle?'

'Very slowly, I'd . . .'

'Tell me!' he begged. 'Tell me, tell me, *tell* me!'

'Take you in my mouth and . . .'

'Yes? Yes?'

A sudden memory surfaced at the other end of the line.

'Derek,' she said sharply. 'Why did you swear when you

rang me up the other day? You know I can't stand bad language. It puts me off completely.'

Annabelle Jansen-Jones slammed down the receiver and cut off his fuel supply. With a dramatic judder, his motors went into reverse thrust. The water bubbled furiously for an hour.

Butty was still rather bewildered by what he'd been told.

'So who do you actually work for, Des?' he asked.

'*The Boston Globe.*'

'You just said that was a front.'

'It is and it isn't,' said Des. 'I became a journalist in order to have access to the England cricket team but I do have to deliver the goods. I mean, they print my articles about the game and there's been a great response. They seem to like the kinda stuff I write – especially when a certain Kevin Sowerbutts comes into the action.'

Butty grinned. 'Try keeping me out.'

'Mission impossible.'

They were in a quiet corner of the bar at the hotel. Des was being very cagey but he had divulged a few details about himself and his work. Butty pressed for more.

'So you used the England team to get into Karistan?'

'Yeah.'

'Why?'

'They're not too fond of Americans here.'

'I noticed that when we played golf with old Idi.'

'If I hadn't been a friend of Kevin Sowerbutts, he'd probably have beaten me to death with a six-iron. That game was a big break-through for me,' admitted Des. 'I was sent here to gather intelligence about Karistan and I get to play golf with the President himself. I learned more from playing those eighteen holes than I would have done from a month of poking around.'

'But who do you report back to, Des?'

'My employers.'

'And who are they?'

'The guys that pay my wages.'

'Are you part of the Secret Service or something?'

Des smiled. 'I'm a journalist, that's all. Doing a rundown on sunny Karistan. Until Derek March happened to float across my path.'

'How did you get on to him?'

'By accident. I saw him haring towards the Pindi Mountain Range one day. On his way to the Diamond mine, it now appears. He's got a friend there.'

'A friend?'

'The guy I was watching through my binoculars. He's the overseer at the mine. Derek made contact with him when he did that tour on Christmas Day.'

'Didn't he take the Colonel with him?'

'Yes,' said Des. 'Perfect cover. They looked like genuine visitors and the Colonel is too doddery to notice any funny business going on between Des and his friend.'

'Funny business?'

'My guess is that they're involved in some kind of shady deal. Why else go in for all this cloak and dagger stuff? Your team manager is a diamond smuggler.'

'Derek March?' said Butty in amazement. 'He couldn't smuggle a snowflake through an arctic blizzard. Are you trying to tell me that the Mad March Hare is a major international crook?'

'No,' said Des. 'This may be a one-off and he's only operating in a small way. My guess is that he's smuggling the diamonds out for somebody special. His wife, perhaps.'

'Or Annabelle Jansen-Jones.'

'Exactly. Sort of a peace offering for making free with her Volvo Estate. Those diamonds will mend broken fences.'

'Crafty bastard!'

'He's a smooth operator. You know that, Kevin.'

'Yes. He set me up with that bimbo in the Volvo Estate. I haven't forgotten that, Des. I'm just biding my time until I can take full revenge.'

'Then here's your perfect opportunity.'

'Opportunity?'

'Of course. What Derek is doing is against the law.'

Butty thought about Kimm Police Station and cackled.

The one-day match against the Karistan A team showed the best and worst of James Henry Fotheringhay. Played at Hanio Cricket Ground in front of a capacity crowd which included Tiki and Verruka, it was a game with a result that was never in doubt. England were effortlessly superior even though Butty had been left out. Seizing his chance to overtake his rival in the chase for the Best Batsman Award, Fothers scored a majestic 143, ran out three of his team and declared on an unreachable total of 300 for 5.

The opposition lacked nothing in drive and enthusiasm but they were woefully inexperienced. Big Ben Jenkins went through their batsmen like a combined harvester. It was when they were 118 for 9 that the incident occurred. Fothers was fielding at mid-on, watching the batsmen with the close interest of a man whose job would be to coach them in due course. Big Ben bowled, one of the tail-enders lashed out wildly and the ball went zooming high in the air.

Fothers ran backwards to position himself, losing his floppy hat in the process and suddenly finding himself staring up into a fiery sun. The ball vanished completely. When he saw it again, it was six inches away from his face and travelling at the speed of light. There was an audible crack as it hit him between the eyes and he went down like a sack of potatoes.

Even in the moment of crisis, Fothers evinced a cricketing instinct. He switched to automatic pilot. As the blood began to spurt all over his white shirt, his hands went up to his chest to hold the ball.

It was a good catch. Karistan A were all out.

TWENTY-THREE

President Idi Ott was a great believer in musical foreplay. To get himself in the mood for a supreme physical and emotional experience, he sat propped up in bed, with his six wives disporting themselves around him in attitudes that ranged from the seductive to the grotesque, and sang himself into the perfect mood. His voice was deep and resonant.

'I am a very model of a modern Major-General,
I've information vegetable, animal, and mineral,
I know the kings of England, and I quote the fights
   historical,
From Marathon to Waterloo, in order categorical,
I'm very well acquainted too with matters
   mathematical . . .'

The subtle ironies of Gilbert and Sullivan were lost on him but he sang with a gusto that gained him a battery of titters and a round of applause from his wives. They had not yet mastered the choral work sufficiently well to join in with Major-General Stanley of Karistan.

His attention turned to the huge television screen at the end of the bed and he used his remote control to switch it on. The second match from the Hanio Cricket Ground was being piped through to him but that was not what he and his six wives first saw. Instead, the screen was filled with what looked like a convention of giant rubber balls. It was only when their eyes became accustomed to the frenetic activity in front of them that the six wives realised they were looking at a video recording of their naked husband auditioning a seventh member of his boudoir brigade for a place on the substitutes' bench.

The woman had such generous proportions that it was difficult to decide if her huge breasts were bigger or smaller than his massive buttocks. Since the four trembling appendages were interchangeable every few seconds, it was even more difficult to find a matching pair in order to assign them to the correct owner. Six wives rose as one and screamed their dissent. The remote control was used to eject the video.

What now came on the screen was the cricket ground. The President beamed at his shrieking harem.

'For military knowledge, though I'm plucky and
    adventury,
Has only been brought down to the beginning of the
    century;
But still in matters vegetable, animal and mineral,
I am the very model of a modern Major-General.'

When they saw the name of the Gilbert and Sullivan XI on their tour itinerary, the England team thought that it was some sort of joke, a case of light relief being laid on before the more serious business of the Third Test. They soon discovered their mistake. The one-day game was the toughest they had faced so far. With a weakened side, the tourists were struggling.

'Bloody hell!' said Butty as Nanki-Poo took another boundary off him. 'This bugger can play!'

'Try him with a bouncer,' advised Dealer.

'He hit the last one for six.'

'He seems weaker on the on-side.'

'Yes, Dealer. He only scores threes and fours there.'

Butty took the ball and experimented with a longer run-up.

In the absence of Fothers, it was Dealer who skippered the side. Fothers himself sat on the balcony, the scars of battle still spectacular. His broken nose had swelled to twice its normal size and his eyes were panda-black. Whenever he saw the ball hit up into the sky, his whole face throbbed violently. Expecting an easy win, he was disconcerted to see the Gilbert and Sullivan XI compiling such an impressive total in such a scintillating way.

'Where have all these players *come* from?' he asked.

'D'Oyly Carte,' said the Colonel.

'They're brilliant.'

'Months of rehearsal. That's the secret.'

'I didn't know Karistan had such talent.'

'They're from Savoy.'

What confused the visitors was the fact that the opposing team were all in costume. When they finally got Nanki-Poo out, the Right Honourable Sir Joseph Porter KCB came to the crease. By the time that Jack Point hit the last ball of the innings for three, they'd scored 347 for 5.

Snatcher Smart had divined their mystery.

'They're from all over the bleeding place!' he said.

'What do you mean?' asked Big Ben.

'Well, when Butty hit him in the ribs, Sir Despard Murgotroyd swore with an Australian accent. And the Duke of Plaza-Toro is definitely from New Zealand.'

'He's right,' confirmed Wilton Rodger. 'The Earl of Mountararat is really the captain of the West Indies. We're up against some of the best players in the world.'

'No wonder they wore those costumes.'

'Yes,' said Dealer. 'To remain anonymous.'

Butty had his own complaint. 'I wouldn't mind so much if they didn't play that frigging music over the PA system all the time. What the hell is it?'

'Gilbert and Sullivan!' chorused the whole team.

'Ask a silly question!'

The cricketing prowess of the Light Operatic XI extended

to the bowling. King Hildebrand and Poo-Bah had a pace, power and accuracy which troubled every batsman. When they had finished their stint, the beguiling spin of Princess Ida took over. At 98 for 5, the England team were wondering if they'd reach even half of the target score.

One member of the team at least was prepared to match fire with fire. Acting on impulse, he walked into the changing room of the opposing team and discovered a large costume hamper. It was all the inspiration he needed.

Penny Coyne did well to make a robust 30 but he was eventually stumped by Iolanthe. As he trudged back to the pavilion, the scoreboard was telling a sorry tale. England were still only 139 for 6.

The Pirate King then came strutting out on to the stage. When he loosened his arms in his familiar way, Butty was instantly recognisable and the crowd rose to acclaim him. Tiki and Verukka identified with him immediately. Played over the loudspeaker, the song had a special significance for them.

> 'When I sally forth to seek my prey
> I help myself in a royal way:
> I sink a few more ships, it's true,
> Than a well-bred monarch ought to do;
> But many a king on a first-class throne,
> If he wants to call his crown his own,
> Must manage somehow to get through
> More dirty work than ever *I* do.
> Though I am a Pirate King.'

After checking that his black moustache was still stuck on, Butty took his stance and was given a friendly full toss by Sir Marmaduke Pointdextre. The ball ended up at the back of the stand. From then on, the bowling was more hostile but it found Butty at his most audacious.

He sailed the seven seas of cricket, using his bat like a

cutlass to hack down all who stood in his way. As his blade flashed, the ball sped hither and thither, making the fielding team run and stretch in their baggy costumes. Perspiring madly, they got slower and slower. Butty, by contrast, clapped on full sail and increased his speed across the water. His billowing innings was worth 94 when he was clean-bowled by a yorker.

The whole Gilbert and Sullivan XI converged on him to lift him shoulder-high and carry him from the pitch. Both in costume and performance, he was one of them. In the heady scenes that followed, Butty was unaware of an important statistic. In the race for the Best Batsman Award, he had caught up the incumbent leader.

Pirate King and England captain were dead level.

As soon as he left the hotel, Des Toyovsky knew that he was being followed. When he glanced in the rear-view mirror of his moped, he saw the white saloon car on his tail. Sensing discovery, the car slowed for a mile or so. Des kept driving at the same speed through the northern suburbs of Aragusta. Now that the team were based in the capital, he had the chance to take a much closer look at the living conditions of a substantial number of the citizens of Karistan.

It was depressing. The Presidential palace and the modernistic civic buildings were at the centre of concentric circles of misery and decay. The further out he went, the worse it became. Slum dwellings, poor sanitation, heavy overcrowding and a standard of life that verged on the primitive. Stretch limousines occupied the heart of the city. Its fringes were served by teams of oxen.

When he hit open country, he accelerated slightly and looked for the signal. Tied to a tree, the white rag fluttered in the breeze. Des shot past it at full throttle and tossed the cricket ball into the bushes. Unaware of the message which had just been delivered, the car pursued him as he looped back in a semi-circle and made for the team hotel. To all intents and purposes, Des Toyovsky had simply been for a ride on a moped.

Tiki and Verruka knew otherwise. When they retrieved the ball from the bushes, they removed the piece of paper that was wrapped around it and held in place with an elastic band. Two words brought the rebel leaders great joy.

FINAL TEST.

Barbara Ollerenshaw did not like to be kept in the dark unless Butty was lying beside her in the same bed. The news that he'd been holding something back from her ignited the embers of her combative nature.

'Why didn't you bloody well tell me?' she said.

'I was keeping it as a surprise.'

'So you could pocket the money yourself, you mean.'

'No,' denied Butty. 'I wanted to win the cash for us. As a kind of wedding present.'

'Lady Antonia Titwillow is getting a diamond from the President on her wedding day.'

'She's also getting that useless prick as a husband.'

'What am I getting?'

'Me, love.'

'No sugar to sweeten the pill?'

'I'm *made* of sugar.' Butty kissed her on the cheek. 'Since you found out about those awards, you might as well know that I'm more or less certain of winning the Best Bowler loot. I've taken far more wickets than anyone else. Big Ben needs to take thirteen in the Final Test to overhaul me and he's never bagged that number in a game.'

'Well done, Kevin!' she said, snuggling up to him.

'The Best Batsman Award is between me and Fothers.'

'Only if he selects you.'

'He's got a gun to his head, Barbara.'

'Derek March?'

'Derek, the Colonel and just about everyone else in the team except Penny Coyne. England need to win in order to go home with any pride. That means Kevin Sowerbutts has to be somewhere in the team.'

'Batting his way to £25,000.'

'For you, love.'

She threw her arms around his neck to kiss him. Back from his moped ride, Des Toyovsky saw them in the bar. He walked over to join them.

'Sorry to interrupt an intimate moment,' he said.

'How was your ride?' asked Barbara.

'Interesting.'

'Where did you go?'

'To the real Karistan.'

'Take the President with you next time,' suggested Butty. 'He's never been there. He lives in his old Gilbert and Sullivan fantasy.'

'Could you spare me a few minutes, Kevin?'

'Of course, Des. Sit down.'

'A few minutes in private. If Barbara will excuse us.'

'Take him away,' she said. 'No charge.'

Des gave her a smile of gratitude and led Butty across to the lift. It took them up to the third floor and they strolled along the corridor. Howls of pain brought them to a halt outside a door. A clanging noise was coming from within. It sounded as if someone was having a steel spike hammered into his skull without benefit of anaesthetic.

'It's Dealer's room,' said Butty.

'Who's that yelling?'

'Big Ben. Practising one of his hymns.'

As a fresh yowl came, they banged hard on the door. Dealer opened it to reveal a sight that was at first rather alarming. Wearing nothing but a shirt, shoes and a metal cricket box, Big Ben Jenkins was standing in the middle of the room. Kneeling in front of him with a hammer and administering blows to the box was Snatcher Smart.

'Be careful!' warned Butty. 'You'll castrate him.'

'He wanted it reshaped to fit him,' said Snatcher.

'Well, shape the box to fit his cock and not the other way around. Otherwise Big Ben will end up as Little Dick.'

'I told him to wear a plastic box,' said Dealer. 'I happen to have a few dozen in my suitcase. You can warm them up and mould them to suit your individual taste. But Ben insisted on the Heavy Metal type.'

'It gives me proper protection,' argued Ben.

Butty chuckled. 'Not from Snatcher the Blacksmith.'

Leaving the Welshman to the tender mercies of the hammer, he followed Des along a corridor and into his room. Motioning him to be quiet, Des beckoned Butty into the bathroom and turned on both taps.

'I've already had a bath today,' said Butty.

'The water is just a safety device.'

'Against what?'

'Being overheard.'

'Eh?'

'My room is bugged, Kevin. They're on to me.'

'Are you sure?'

'Yeah. When I went out, they followed me in a car.'

'Then why come up here if they're trying to listen in?'

'To show you how clever they are.'

Des took him into the room and lifted a petal on one of the artificial flowers. A tiny microphone was attached. He then opened the wardrobe to take out the white coat he always wore to cricket matches. Turning back the lapel, he revealed another hidden microphone.

They returned to the bathroom. Water still gushed.

'From now on, I have to be careful what I say, Kevin.'

'So do I when I'm standing next to you.'

'That might work to your advantage.'

'What do you mean?'

'Don't you have a few scores to settle?'

'Yeah,' said Butty. 'First and foremost with Derek March.'

'He's already taken care of,' said Des. 'Who else?'

'Darren Grubb and Penny Coyne.'

'Let's see if we can kill two birds with one stone.'

'How?'

Des smiled quietly. 'I'll think of a way.'

After lengthy and sometimes rancorous deliberations, the selection committee decided on their team for the Third Test. In the interests of winning, both Derek and the Colonel had insisted on choosing Butty. Fothers tried in vain to talk them out of it. Winning the Best Batsman Award was no longer a formality for the England captain.

The team was announced on the eve of the fateful match.

> J. J. Fotheringhay (captain)
> M. D. Mancini
> D. W. C. Elgin
> W. O. Rodger
> H. M. Smart
> E. T. Montgomery
> K. Sowerbutts
> J. J. Cromwell
> R. M. Ryman
> B. V. Jenkins
> W. E. Winslow

Butty's inclusion meant the omission of Penny Coyne. On the coach drive to the Aragusta Cricket Ground, the Lancashireman was still fuming. He sat next to Big Ben.

'They've bloody well left me out, Ben!' he snarled.

'Sorry about that, boyo.'

'I should've been in ahead of Butty.'

'He'd be my first name on the team sheet.'

'They've even selected Wanker Winslow ahead of me! The one-armed bandit. He's the only man who can toss himself off through a cricket box.'

'Don't mention cricket boxes,' pleaded Ben. 'Delicate subject. I've still got the bruises.'

'And how come *you're* playing?' challenged Penny.

'They picked me, mun.'

'Yes, but it's a five-day game. We play on a Sunday. You cried off the first two tests because of that. What's different about this one?'

'He came back from his holiday in Rhyl.'

'Who?'

'My Baptist minister. I rang him in Pontypridd. He gave me permission to play this Sunday. Said I'd be serving the wider purposes of the Baptist Church if I bowled well.'

The coach arrived at the ground to find it crawling with police and soldiers. A helicopter hovered overhead. Sharp-shooters were placed all round the ground. The outfield was mined. There was even a security camera fitted to the back of the wickets themselves.

General Idi Ott was on his way.

Tiki and Verukka mingled with the crowd lining the route to the ground. When the Presidential cavalcade approached, they were pushed back by a cordon of soldiers. All that they saw of General Idi Ott was a glimpse of his Rolls Royce. Strident strains of The Gondoliers emanated from the vehicle.

'This is the time to get him,' said Verukka. 'On his way to the ground.'

'No,' said Tiki. 'Besides, it is too early.'

'Early?'

'The final day of the Final Test will also be his final day,

Verukka. By that time, he will feel more secure. He will think that his defences are impregnable. This is when we will strike on behalf of Karistan.'

'From where?'

'Inside the ground.'

'We'd never get the weapon in.'

'Somebody else might.'

'Who?'

'The American.'

'Can we trust him?'

'He has not let us down yet.'

Overnight rain and overcast conditions made the wicket less appealing to the batsmen. When he won the toss, Fothers put Karistan in and led his team out on to the field. Having delivered the Harfleur speech from *Henry V*, he felt that he had psyched his men up for combat. Since one of the umpires was the nefarious Ravi Rochester-Smith, he warned his team not to quarrel with the officials.

The Karistan openers came out to a tumultuous welcome. Before play began, the umpires, players and spectators turned to bow towards the high concrete tower in which the President sat enthroned behind reinforced plate glass windows. Enjoying his lonely eminence, he waved a lordly hand to the crowd then adjusted the control on his Walkman so that the chorus of Gondoliers would sing up.

Given the new ball, Butty rubbed it to a high sheen on his thigh as he measured out his run-up. Ravi Rochester-Smith gave the signal and the Third Test was in motion. England learned at once what they were up against.

'No ball!' yelled Ravi.

Butty was yards behind the popping crease when he released the first delivery. With superhuman restraint, he said nothing and retraced his steps. Taking a slower run-in this time, he bowled the second ball of the day.

'No ball!'

'What?'

'I give you two no balls.'

'Do that again and you'll have no balls yourself.'

Ravi chuckled. Fothers dived in to prevent another flare-up between bowler and umpire. For once in his life, the captain was astonishingly effective.

'Mr Rochester-Smith,' he said politely, 'we are very grateful that you've been chosen to umpire this match because the England team admires your knowledge of the laws and your total lack of bias. In fact, it was our intention to recommend that you be placed on the international panel of umpires. But,' he continued with a glint, 'if you make one more decision as outrageously partisan as the last two, I will not only take my team off the field, I will use my influence with President Idi Ott and with the international cricketing authorities to have you debarred from the game for the rest of your life.'

Butty was staggered by his captain's forcefulness.

'Well?' said Fothers.

Ravi grinned sheepishly. 'I'm glad we understand each other.'

He did not call another no ball throughout the match.

Unimpeded by aberrant umpiring decisions, the bowlers quickly took the initiative on what turned out to be a good bowling wicket. As before, the Karistan players each contributed something to their score but in smaller amounts. The pace of Butty and Big Ben, allied to the magic fingers of Wanker Winslow, sent a steady stream of players back to the pavilion. When the innings closed late that afternoon, the Karistan total of 215 looked distinctly vulnerable.

It was during the interval that Des Toyovsky saw his chance. Ever alert to discontent in the squad, Darren Grubb was

253

coaxing the embittered Penny Coyne into indiscretions. Des cornered them in the press box, standing between them so that the microphone behind his lapel picked up both their voices clearly. He was also certain that someone somewhere had a pair of binoculars trained on them.

'So what's the final verdict on Karistan?' said Des.

'It's a shit-house!' snarled Penny.

'I rather like it. What about you, Darren?'

'It's an island of barbarians,' sneered the journalist. 'We shouldn't be playing this lot at cricket. We should be throwing nuts at them during feeding time.'

'Don't take that attitude to our hosts,' said Des. 'We've had wonderful hospitality here – thanks to the President. He's done marvels for his country.'

'Idi Ott has only done marvels for Idi Ott,' said Penny. 'He doesn't care a monkey's fuck for anybody but himself and those six weird wives of his.'

'Yes,' agreed Darren, warming to the theme. 'The Presidential prick must be like a six-shooter. I wish he'd stick it to his own thick skull and pull the trigger. What this country needs is a whiff of democracy. Idi Ott makes Joe Stalin look like a soft-hearted social worker. As for all that crap about Gilbert and sodding Sullivan!'

The journalist got no further. Armed stewards materialised out of thin air to overpower both Penny Coyne and Darren Grubb. They were still protesting their innocence as the police van took them away for questioning.

Left alone, Des returned to his seat between Barbara and Lady Antonia Titwillow. Since it was hot, he removed his coat and placed it beneath him, crushing the microphone as he put his full weight on it. Freedom of speech returned.

'What are our chances, ladies?' he asked.

'James will be sublime,' announced Antonia.

'Butty will knock the living daylights out of them,' said Barbara. 'He's already got five wickets. Now he'll help himself to some runs.'

'So will James. He's in a mood for it.'

The mood was fleeting. Fothers started well but the bowlers soon made him batten down the hatches. Frustration made him wave his bat at a delivery verging on a wide and Zaki Meero took the catch. Fothers had gone for 11. It gave the bowlers all the encouragement they needed. On a tricky wicket, England had three more fatalities before close of play. 51 for 4 was a disappointing reply.

But there were compensations. Ravi Rochester-Smith had been muzzled and the pitch would improve as a batting track on the next day. Butty left the ground in high spirits. Des Toyovsky had told him about the arrest of his enemies.

'Penny *and* Darren?' he asked.

'Condemned out of their own mouths.'

'Where are they now?'

'Helping the police with their enquiries.'

The second day's play was like a Greek tragedy. Every known disaster seemed to be heaped upon the House of England. All they needed was incest between a pair of related batting gloves and they'd have reached Sophoclean depths. The invincible Dealer retired hurt after a ball somehow got up to crack his jaw, Wilton Rodger inadvertently went walkabout and got stumped off a spinner and Monty was out LBW. When Butty was caught just inside the boundary for a duck, the whole team seem to collapse inwards. In the light of their misfortunes, a final total of 139 was a small miracle.

With a couple of hours at the crease left, Karistan extended their overall lead to 160 without loss. The advantage had swung decisively in their direction.

On the third day, they pressed it home. Led by the century-making Zaki, they scored fast on a drier and firmer pitch. Wickets were expensive. It took the whole day to bowl them all at a total cost of 331. England were set a target of 406 to win. Nobody gave them a chance.

A night of madness in Barbara's arms revived Butty for the strike that lay ahead. He was lifted by the news that both Penny Coyne and Darren Grubb had been deported from the country in disgrace with their passports confiscated. Butty had two good reasons to cheer. A third was now required.

When they got to the ground, the England team learned that President Idi Ott was already there, so convinced that Karistan would win that he had brought the sword of state in order to knight each member of the team (or behead them if they lost). As he gazed at the huge electronic scoreboard on the opposite side of the ground, he did not realise that two people inside it were studying him through binoculars.

Tiki and Verruka had been smuggled into their place of vantage. While the fate of Karistan cricket lay with the eleven players on the field, the future of the country was now in their hands. Two years of planning during their imprisonment on Shark Island could now bear fruit. The rebels suffered a handicap. They adored cricket. The assassination of their dictator was postponed until their team had achieved its deserved victory.

There was a studied gloom on the tourist balcony.

'We're not selectors,' groaned Derek March. 'We're pallbearers at the funeral of English cricket.'

'We need a Len Hutton out there.'

'And a Peter May.'

'And a Colin Cowdrey.'

'And a Jim Laker.'

'And a Fred Trueman.'

'And a Denis Compton.' The Colonel chuckled. 'Did I

ever tell you about the time I bowled Denis out at the Oval? It was a real feather in my cap.'

The anecdote compounded Derek's misery.

Relief came with astonishing speed. When Fothers and Dealer opened the second innings, they made a firm declaration of intent. England were not going to hang on grimly in the hope of spending two precarious days at the crease in order to secure an ignoble draw. They wanted to snatch victory from the gnashing jaws of General Idi Ott.

Crecy. Poitiers. Agincourt. Could the name of Aragusta be added to the roll-call of English heroism? If it were left to Fothers, it certainly could. His face still bore the vestigial marks of injury but his heart and mind were pulsing with rude health. His eve-of-battle speech to his troops was not enough. He now had to lead by example.

'By Jove!' said the Colonel. 'It *is* Len Hutton.'

'That was more of a Peter May shot,' said Derek.

'James is more in the Tom Graveney mould.'

'With a touch of Trevor Bailey's grit.'

'Don't forget Denis Compton,' said the Colonel.

'I never want to hear his flaming name again!' yelled Derek as the story threatened again. 'Now, watch the game and shut up, you silly old fool!'

The Colonel smiled fondly. 'You sound just like the lady wife. Nostalgia is such sweet sorrow.'

Out on the pitch, the players had no time for nostalgia. They were forging the future. Fothers was setting the pace but Dealer was not far behind him, shedding his reputation as the Cockney Boycott and stepping out from behind his defences to play a series of excellent forcing shots. The first hundred runs needed were up on the board after two hours. 306 seemed more of a Matterhorn than an Everest.

Sherpa Mancini perished on 76 but he'd helped to take the opening stand to 151. By the luncheon interval, it had been pushed on to 203. Halfway up the sheer rock face.

The rope snapped immediately after the restart. Marbles

went for a duck, Wilton Rodger managed only three and a nervous Snatcher Smart suffered the indignity of being stumped off Inta Walliconi by his opposite number for a paltry six runs. 212 for 4 against bowlers who now had their tails up. It was Butty's turn once again.

'Come on, Kevin!' shouted Barbara.

'Show them how two play, James!' counselled Antonia.

'All hopes rest on these guys,' noted Des. 'Not much batting to come once they've gone. Fingers crossed.'

'As long as he doesn't get another duck!' said Barbara to herself. 'Not a pair. Please, please – not a pair.'

The same thought was going through Butty's mind. Facing the deceptive Inta, he started with the utmost caution and sighed with relief when he got an unintended single off an outside edge. After an over to play himself in against Russum at the other end, he was ready to open up.

Even the Jolly Rogering of the Gilbert and Sullivan match could not compare with his performance this time. Butty was twice as strong and three times as fearless. No ball was safe from his heavy bat. Boundaries came in rapid succession and the spinners were soon taken off to prevent further mutilation of their bowling figures. Fothers kept his own score ticking over at the other end but it was Butty who devoured the lion's share of the bowling. When Butty got his century, even General Idi Ott was on his feet to applaud. Cricket of this standard had never been seen in Aragusta before.

When they passed the 350 mark, Fothers began to worry. Delighted that victory was within sight, he had a firm opinion of how it should be achieved. When he looked at the scoreboard, he saw that Butty was slowly overhauling his own total for both innings. Left unchecked, it was the whirring dynamo at the other end of the wicket who would collect the Best Batsman Award. Fothers had promised that to himself.

His attempt to collar the bowling lasted for a mere two

overs. Butty took strike again and despatched the ball with even greater velocity. Having already won the Best Bowler Award for taking the highest number of wickets on tour, he now set his heart on the batting title. The man at the other end of the track had tried to stop him coming on the tour in the first place and had systematically hampered him during the past few weeks. Outplaying him as a batsman would be a triumph to savour.

As 400 runs clicked up on the scoreboard, the spectators watched with disbelief. An unattainable fourth innings total was about to be surpassed. Butty had a personal agenda. He was five runs short of Fothers's aggregate total of runs. Six to win the Test Match and to put an already broken old Harrovian nose even more out of joint. As he faced a new over, Butty was confident of success but he was suddenly afflicted with the jitters. Instead of smashing his way to victory, he became wary and tentative. A match of utter impossibilities threw up yet another one. A maiden over was bowled.

The smiling Fothers now took strike. He could snatch the final moment of glory from his rival but he wanted more than that. When the Test Match was won, he did not want to exchange a handshake with a man whom he loathed and whom the whole crowd clearly loved. Victory was assured. It no longer needed the cavalier brilliance of Kevin Sowerbutts. Fothers would eliminate him as he had eliminated so many before.

The first delivery gave him his chance. Clipped towards mid-wicket, it was a risky single but he was already charging down the pitch towards Butty. A captain's call could not be ignored even though it meant almost certain dismissal.

'Run!' he called. 'Run!'

The ball was retrieved by the agile fielder.

'Run, you bounder!' howled Fothers.

Butty didn't move from his crease.

'I've called a run!'

'Try that game on someone else, mate,' said Butty, leaning on his bat. 'You won't get me to play it.'

Fothers turned in despair and ran back. He was ten yards out when the wicket-keeper took his bails off. It was the most painful walk he'd ever made back to the pavilion. The bat under his arm was a lightning conductor for his flashing thoughts. As he passed the incoming batsman on the pavilion steps, he had one command.

'Score!' he ordered. 'Score a bloody run and stop him!'

But Big Ben Jenkins took his cue from a mightier baton. Butty was waiting for him and his request was simple.

'I've earned this, Big Ben. You know the score.'

'In every sense, boyo. Go for it.'

'Thanks.'

Big Ben blocked the next five balls to leave Butty on strike with six runs to win. Up inside the scoreboard, Tiki was checking his weapon and aiming it at the Presidential tower. Like Butty, he was after the ultimate award. Like Butty, he had salvation in his sights. The two men worked superbly in harness.

When the first delivery came, Butty danced down the pitch and swung murderously, middling the ball and sending it like a bullet towards the concrete tower. Timing was perfect. At the moment when the ball reached the tower, the plate glass was shattered by the incendiary rocket fired by Tiki and General Idi Ott was killed before he could even remember the name of one of his wives.

England had won the Final Test against a country that ceased to exist the moment the last run was secured. It gave a fearful symmetry to the whole event.

Butty gulped as he saw the tower engulfed in flames.

'Fuck me!' he said, looking at his bat. 'Did I do that?'

EPILOGUE

James Henry Fotheringhay left Karistan with feelings of profoundest regret. Every one of his high hopes had nose-dived into the ground. The assassination of General Idi Ott changed everything. Instead of appointing Fothers as Director of Cricket for the elite of Karistan, the new administration had given Zaki Meero a mission that was dear to his heart. He was to cast his net wide and develop the latent cricketing talent in every stratum of society. The budding Butties of the suburbs would be nurtured on the island's cricket pitches and that was a task to which Fothers could bring neither expertise nor enthusiasm. A golden handshake man, he had no common touch.

There was a deeper ache in his soul. As the aircraft left Aragusta and circled the island, he and Lady Antonia Titwillow looked down on the secluded paradise of Jelli. They saw the dot that was to have been their luxury home.

'It was such a super house!' sighed Antonia.

'I'll find another one equally good,' he promised.

'Where, James?'

'Wherever you wish.'

'I fell in love with Jelli.'

'It was rather special.'

'I had visions of raising our family there. You, me and our Jelli babies. We could have opened our own stud.'

'It will come in time.'

Another sigh. 'You always say that.'

He turned his eyes away from the window and shuddered. Expecting to conquer Karistan and remain as its cricketing Governor-general, he was being forced to return to a cold winter in England. As his mind played once more with his book on captaincy, he made a note to include a chapter on Staving Off Suicidal Feelings – if he was able to stave off his own and live to write it.

His melancholy was thrown into sharp relief by the general euphoria all around him. Now that the tour was over, the rest of the tourists decided that they'd enjoyed it immensely. Notwithstanding its many problems, it had been a fun-filled rollercoaster ride that left them with some cherished memories.

Kevin Sowerbutts had more to cherish than most. It is not given to many players to win a Test Match with a soaring six, bring down a corrupt regime and net £50,000 into the bargain. Butty did not, in fact, accept the awards as Best Batsman and Best Bowler. He handed the cheque to Zaki Meero as a donation to the Cricket Fund for Karistan Schools. It was a gesture which gained him the award of Best Friend of the Country and he was invited back in a year to see what progress had been made in the game in the interim.

Barbara supported him to the hilt but she still felt a few pangs when she thought of the money he had won.

'We could have used that cash, Kev,' she said.

'There'll be more to come, love.'

'I know.'

'Fothers wouldn't have ploughed back the profits.'

'It would never have crossed his mind.'

'He'd have spent the money on a new bridle for Antonia,' he said. 'And he'd have bought her a set of blinkers at the same time. She needs to wear those if she's going to marry Fothers. He'll have to get starting stalls fitted in the bedroom for her.'

'The only marriage I'm interested in is ours.'

'Name the day, Barbara.'

'How about April 1st?'

'Perfect.'

They chatted happily for a few hours until Barbara dozed off to sleep. Butty took the opportunity to go to the rear of the plane where Des Toyovsky was reading Dostoevsky. There were still several things Butty didn't understand. He lowered himself down beside the American.

'Hi, Kevin.'

'What are you reading, Des?'

'*The Idiot.*'

'The General's autobiography?'

'Not exactly,' said Des, putting his paperback aside. 'The ex-President's autobiography was written in the faces of his people. All that poverty and suffering. They were terrified of him. Even his own soldiers hated him. As soon as he was killed, his machine crumbled to pieces in a matter of days.'

'With a little help from you.'

'I may have . . . oiled the wheels of rebellion a little.'

'On whose behalf?'

'The cause of freedom.'

'Balls!' Butty leaned in close. 'You were planted on us so that we'd smuggle you into Karistan. But you weren't only there to watch cricket.'

'No,' admitted the other. 'Now that we're hundreds of miles clear of the place, I can tell you this. Posing as a journalist was my deep cover. I really work for a government organisation called the CIA.'

'Clowns in 'ats?'

'Central Intelligence Agency – but we have more than our share of clowns in 'ats. Karistan was bad news for America. Hostile to our values, obstructive to our commercial interests in that part of the world and run by that Gilbert and Sullivan version of Saddam Hussein that we both met on the golf course.'

'Were you supposed to bump him off?'

'Hell, no!' said Des. 'I just gather intelligence. My task was to explore ways to destabilise the Idi Ott regime. By a great stroke of luck, the rebels were ready to do the job for us. I made contact and gave them a helping hand.'

'At least they waited until I'd won that game.'

Des gave a wry smile. 'That's cricket.'

'I owe you a big thank you for getting Darren Grubb and Penny Coyne deported. You really stitched them up.'

'I've been doing some more stitching up as well.'

'Oh?'

'Stay near Derek March at Heathrow.'

'Why?' said Butty.

'Remember those diamonds?'

'How is he going to smuggle them through?'

'I found that out. And tipped off Customs.'

Butty chuckled. 'I've just got to see this!'

The triumphant ending of the tour enabled Derek March to forget some of the fiascos that preceded it and he returned to England with his team manager smile back in place again. Television cameras would be waiting at Heathrow and he would be able to luxuriate in the halo effect created by the star performances of Butty and – to a lesser extent – of Fothers in the Third Test. Once that was done, he could drive home to his wife and family in the East Midlands after first paying a visit to a cottage in Windsor. Annabelle Jansen-Jones would be waiting for him. And for the diamonds.

When the plane landed, Derek could not wait to get through Customs and pushed his trolley ahead of the other players.

'Excuse me, sir,' said a voice.

'Me?' said Derek.

'Anything to declare?'

'Not a sausage, old chap.'

'Perhaps we could look in that bag.'

'It only contains the team's spare kit.'

'Then you won't mind showing it to us, will you?'

There were three of them. Short, officious men in the regulation uniforms. They made him lift the cricket bag up on to the table. Butty and Des were at the front of the knot of curious spectators. When the bag was unstrapped, the Customs Officers picked through it.

'Does all this belong to the England team?' asked their senior man. Derek nodded. 'None of this is yours?' Derek shook his head. 'You didn't buy *anything* in Karistan?'

'Nothing at all.'

'What about those batting gloves?' said the Colonel.

'Shut up!' hissed Derek.

'For his son, he told me. I was in the shop when he bought them.' The old man pointed into the bag. 'Those are the ones.'

The Customs Officer lifted the batting gloves out.

Derek blustered. 'I've never seen them before in my life!'

'Then how come they have your name on them, sir?'

'What!'

'Right here, sir. "Derek March". That is you, isn't it?'

'Who put *that* there!' howled the team manager.

'*You* did, sir.' He took out a small knife. 'Let's see what else you did to these gloves, shall we?'

He cut through the stitching around the edge of one glove and shook it hard. A cluster of uncut diamonds fell on to the table. The three Customs Officers looked at the England team manager. Derek resembled a tomato with guilt problems. He licked his lips and shuffled his feet.

'I wonder how they got there?' he croaked.

'Come and tell us, sir.'

Taking him by the arms, two of the men escorted him away while the third collected the diamonds up. Fothers and Antonia were dumbfounded but Butty led the rest of the team in wild laughter. No revenge could be sweeter for him. Derek March had done his utmost to prevent Butty from leaving the country with the tourists. The team manager was now having difficulty getting back into Britain.

Butty gave Des a congratulatory slap on the back.

'How did you rumble him?' he asked.

'It was when the Colonel told me Derek had bought some batting gloves. Ideal place to hide them. England cricket bags have a kind of diplomatic immunity. They normally get waved through. That's what Derek was counting on.'

'You're a genius!'

'I pinched the gloves from the bag and sewed his name on to them. Just so that they'd know which ones to pick on.'

'You trussed him up like a Christmas turkey.'

'Smuggling diamonds is a serious crime,' said Des with a wink. 'I couldn't condone that, could I? It was my duty to blow Derek's own deep cover.'

'What will he get?'

'That'll be up to the judge.'

Butty cackled. 'I know what he won't get!'

'The chance to give those diamonds to his girlfriend.'

'Bang goes his shag in the back of the Volvo Estate!'

With one arm around Barbara and another around Des, he walked jauntily into the Arrivals Lounge. The media were there to hail him as a national hero. A rebel Yorkshireman had sparked off a rebellion in Karistan. Thanks to Butty's belated presence on the tour, a famous victory had been achieved against all the odds in a foreign land. Fothers was the nominated captain but the whole team knew who their true leader and inspiration was. Butty was beatified.

English cricket would never be quite the same again.

Rogue Female

Nicholas Salaman

A book about living.
Dangerously.

He's shy, retiring and frightened. He's scared he'll be mugged, assaulted or spoken to by a female. Duncan Mackworth is scared of life. So he gets some help. He gets a personal instructor in self-defence. And more.

Duncan Mackworth doesn't know who to expect when he opens the door and he certainly isn't expecting a woman. A woman who will change Duncan Mackworth's life for . . . well, for as long as it lasts.

'Salaman is a crisp, rather droll writer, capable of elegant flourishes at any moment' *Sunday Telegraph*

ISBN 0 00 649029 8

Divorcing Jack

Colin Bateman

'Richly paranoid and very funny' *Sunday Times*

Dan Starkey is a young journalist in Belfast, who shares with his wife Patricia a prodigious appetite for drinking and partying. Then Dan meets Margaret, a beautiful student, and things begin to get out of hand.

Terrifyingly, Margaret is murdered and Patricia kidnapped. Dan has no idea why, but before long he too is a target, running as fast as he can in a race against time to solve the mystery and to save his marriage.

'A joy from start to finish . . . Witty, fast-paced and throbbing with menace, *Divorcing Jack* reads like *The Thirty-Nine Steps* rewritten for the '90s by Roddy Doyle'
Time Out

'Grabs you by the throat . . . a magnificent debut. Unlike any thriller you have ever read before . . . like *The Day of the Jackal* out of the Marx Brothers' *Sunday Press*

'Fresh, funny . . . an Ulster Carl Hiaasen' *Mail on Sunday*

ISBN 0 00 647903 0

The General
Danced at Dawn

George MacDonald Fraser

'It's great fun and rings true: a Highland Fling of a book'
ERIC LINKLATER

'Written in the first person, and reading authentically, it purports to record episodes in the life of a young officer, newly commissioned into a Highland regiment after service in the ranks at the very end of the war . . . Twenty-five years have not dimmed Mr Fraser's recollections of those hectic days of soldiering. One takes leave of his characters with real and grateful regret'
SIR BERNARD FERGUSSON, *Sunday Times*

Private McAuslan, J., the Dirtiest Soldier in the World (alias the Tartan Caliban or the Highland Division's answer to Pekin Man) demonstrates his unfitness for the service in this first volume of stories of life in a Scottish regiment. Unkempt, ungainly and unwashed, civilian readers may regard him with shocked disbelief – but a generation of ex-Servicemen have already hailed him with delight as an old familiar friend.

'It's a while since I enjoyed a book so much, and, indeed, once I'd finished it, I felt like starting it all over again'
Glasgow Evening Times

ISBN 0 00 617681 X

Sharpe's Battle
Bernard Cornwell

When Sharpe orders the execution of two French soldiers for their part in a massacre in a Spanish village, he earns the personal hatred of the dead men's commanding officer, the ruthless Brigadier General Guy Loup. He swears to have his revenge on Sharpe.

Soon after, Loup launches a terrifying night attack on the fort where Sharpe and his men are quartered, and many are killed.

With the army's high command blaming him for the disaster, Sharpe faces the ruin of his career and reputation. His only hope is to redeem himself on the battlefield. To save his honour, Sharpe must lead his men to glory in the narrow streets of Fuentes de Oñoro and once more confront his sworn enemy, Loup.

Chronologically the fourth Sharpe adventure, this thirteenth novel in the popular series takes Richard Sharpe and his company back to the spring of 1811 and one of the fiercest battles of the Peninsular War.

'What makes these books such a successful formula is the blend of action, well-researched historical setting, colourful characterization and a juicy sub-plot'   *The Times*

'More great adventure from one of the most accomplished and stylish storytellers now writing'   *Kirkus Reviews*

ISBN 0 00 647324 5

Dark Rose

Mike Lunnon-Wood

It was a nineteen-year-old civil engineering student who raised the alarm, drew attention to the first invasion in western Europe by outsiders since the Turkish siege of Vienna was broken by a mixed rescue force of Germans, Prussians and Poles in 1592.

Before anyone knew it, Ireland had been taken over, the surprise pawn in a stunning new game of Middle Eastern politics.

But if the invaders thought they would get away with it easily, they were wrong. As the truth dawns, an extraordinary collection of soldiers, farmers, students and expatriates gets together a Celtic resistance force and heads for a titanic confrontation . . .

With a great cast of characters, packed with action, excitement and suspense, *Dark Rose* is a fascinating portrayal of a world event that couldn't happen . . . or could it?

ISBN 0 00 647591 4